Without Justice

What Reviewers Say About Carsen Taite's Work

It Should be a Crime

"Law professor Morgan Bradley and her student Parker Casey are potential love interests, but throw in a high-profile murder trial, and you've got an entertaining book that can be read in one sitting. Taite also practices criminal law and she weaves her insider knowledge of the criminal justice system into the love story seamlessly and with excellent timing. I find romances lacking when the characters change completely upon falling in love, but this was not the case here. I look forward to reading more from Taite."—*Curve Magazine*

"This [*It Should be a Crime*] is just Taite's second novel…but it's as if she has bookshelves full of bestsellers under her belt."—*Gay List Daily*

"Taite, a criminal defense attorney herself, has given her readers a behind the scenes look at what goes on during the days before a trial. Her descriptions of lawyer/client talks, investigations, police procedures, etc. are fascinating. Taite keeps the action moving, her characters clear, and never allows her story to get bogged down in paperwork. *It Should be a Crime* has a fast-moving plot and some extraordinarily hot sex."—*Just About Write*

Do Not Disturb

"Taite's tale of sexual tension is entertaining in itself, but a number of secondary characters…add substantial color to romantic inevitability"—Richard Labonte, *Book Marks*

Nothing but the Truth

"Author Taite is really a Dallas defense attorney herself, and it's obvious her viewpoint adds considerable realism to her story, making it especially riveting as a mystery. I give it four stars out of five." —Bob Lind, *Echo Magazine*

"As a criminal defense attorney in Dallas, Texas, Carsen Taite knows her way around the court house. This ability shows in her writing, as her legal dramas take the reader into backroom negotiations between the opposing lawyers, as well as into meetings with judges. Watching how Carsen Taite brings together all of the loose ends is enjoyable, as is her skillful building of the characters of Ryan and Brett. *Nothing But the Truth* is an enjoyable mystery with some hot romance thrown in."—*Just About Write*

"Taite has written an excellent courtroom drama with two interesting women leading the cast of characters. Taite herself is a practicing defense attorney, and her courtroom scenes are clearly based on real knowledge. This should be another winner for Taite."—*Lambda Literary*

The Best Defense

"Real life defense attorney Carsen Taite polishes her fifth work of lesbian fiction, *The Best Defense*, with the realism she daily encounters in the office and in the courts. And that polish is something that makes *The Best Defense* shine as an excellent read."—*Out & About Newspaper*

Slingshot

"The mean streets of lesbian literature finally have the hard boiled bounty hunter they deserve. It's a slingshot of a ride, bad guys and hot women rolled into one page turning package. I'm looking forward to Luca Bennett's next adventure."—J. M. Redmann, author of the Micky Knight mystery series

Beyond Innocence

"Taite keeps you guessing with delicious delay until the very last minute…Taite's time in the courtroom lends *Beyond Innocence* a terrific verisimilitude someone not in the profession couldn't impart. And damned if she doesn't make practicing law interesting." —*Out in Print*

"As you would expect, sparks and legal writs fly. What I liked about this book were the shades of grey (no, not the smutty Shades of Grey)—both in the relationship as well as the cases."—*C-spot Reviews*

Battle Axe

"This second book is satisfying, substantial, and slick. Plus, it has heart and love coupled with Luca's array of weapons and a badass verbal repertoire… I cannot imagine anyone not having a great time riding shotgun through all of Luca's escapades. I recommend hopping on Luca's band wagon and having a blast."—*Rainbow Book Reviews*

"Taite breathes life into her characters with elemental finesse… A great read, told in the vein of a good old detective-type novel filled with criminal elements, thugs, and mobsters that will entertain and amuse."—*Lambda Literary*

Rush

"A simply beautiful interplay of police procedural magic, murder, FBI presence, misguided protective cover-ups, and a superheated love affair…a Gold Star from me and major encouragement for all readers to dive right in and consume this story with gusto!"—*Rainbow Book Reviews*

Switchblade

"I enjoyed the book and it was a fun read—mystery, action, humor, and a bit of romance. Who could ask for more? If you've read and enjoyed Taite's legal novels, you'll like this. If you've read and enjoyed the two other books in this series, this one will definitely satisfy your Luca fix and I highly recommend picking it up. Highly recommended."—*C-spot Reviews*

"Dallas's intrepid female bounty hunter, Luca Bennett, is back in another adventure. Fantastic! Between her many friends and lovers, her interesting family, her fly by the seat of her pants lifestyle, and a whole host of detractors there is rarely a dull moment."—*Rainbow Book Reviews*

Courtship

"The political drama is just top-notch. The emotional and sexual tensions are intertwined with great timing and flair. I truly adored this book from beginning to end. Fantabulous!" – *Rainbow Book Reviews*

"Taite keeps the stakes high as two beautiful and brilliant women fueled by professional ambitions face daunting emotional choices… As backroom politics, secrets, betrayals, and threats race to be resolved without political damage to the president, the cat-and-mouse relationship game between Addison and Julia has the reader rooting for them. Taite prolongs the fever-pitch tension to the final pages. This pleasant read with intelligent heroines, snappy dialogue, and political suspense will satisfy Taite's devoted fans and new readers alike."—*Publisher's Weekly*

Lay Down the Law

"Recognized for the pithy realism of her characters and settings drawn from a Texas legal milieu, Taite pays homage to the prime-time soap opera Dallas in pairing a cartel-busting U.S. attorney, Peyton Davis, with a charity-minded oil heiress, Lily Gantry."—*Publishers Weekly*

"Suspenseful, intriguingly tense, and with a great developing love story, this book is delightfully solid on all fronts. This gets my A-1 recommendation!"—*Rainbow Book Reviews*

Reasonable Doubt

"I was drawn into the mystery plot line and quickly became enthralled with the book. It was suspenseful without being too intense but there were some great twists to keep me guessing. It's a very good book. I cannot wait to read the next in line that Ms. Taite has to offer." —*Prism Book Alliance*

Above the Law

"…readers who enjoyed the first installment will find this a worthy second act."—*Publishers Weekly*

"Ms Taite delivered and then some, all the while adding more questions, Tease! I like the mystery and intrigue in this story. It has many "sit on the edge of your seat" scenes of excitement and dread (like watch out kind of thing) and drama…well done indeed!" —*Prism Book Alliance*

By the Author

Truelesbianlove.com

It Should be a Crime

Do Not Disturb

Nothing but the Truth

The Best Defense

Beyond Innocence

Rush

Courtship

Reasonable Doubt

Without Justice

The Luca Bennett Mystery Series:

Slingshot

Battle Axe

Switchblade

Bow and Arrow (novella in Girls with Guns)

Lone Star Law Series:

Lay Down the Law

Above the Law

WITHOUT JUSTICE

by

Carsen Taite

2016

WITHOUT JUSTICE

ISBN 13: 978-1-62639-560-2

This Trade Paperback Original Is Published By
Bold Strokes Books, Inc.
P.O. Box 249
Valley Falls, NY 12185

First Edition: December 2016

Credits
Editor: Cindy Cresap
Production Design: Susan Ramundo
Cover Design By Sheri (graphicartist2020@hotmail.com)

Acknowledgments

Thanks to everyone who helped me bring this book to life. Rad for giving my stories a place to thrive. Sandy Lowe for tending to every detail along the way. Cindy Cresap, my editor, for making the editing process more fun than painful. A huge shout out to the entire Bold Strokes team, from PR to proofreading—thanks for everything you do, too!

Ashley Bartlett, Anita Kelly, and VK Powell—the best first readers in the world! Thanks for your honesty and your willingness to deal with my crazy schedule. Barbara Ann Wright, thanks for your generous willingness to brainstorm plot points anytime, anyplace.

A special thanks to the Women with Pride (formerly Jewel) book club in Dallas. I love the fellowship and fun we have each month, talking about our favorite books.

Lainey, thanks for all the sacrifices you make, big and small, to allow me to pursue my dreams. I love you more every day.

To all my readers—thanks for making this journey so worthwhile. I cherish all the emails, notes, and words of encouragement. This story is for you.

Dedication

To Lainey. I can’t imagine a life without you.

Chapter One

August

Cade Deluca stood at the podium and surveyed the grand jurors who were listening in rapt attention to the testimony of Gil Biermann, the moneyman for the Oliveri family. Biermann was the perfect witness, offering an edge-of-your seat tale about finances of all things, without venturing into CPA lingo that could send a layperson scurrying for a nap.

Every few minutes or so, she lobbed him a question just to remind the grand jurors they were in a proceeding instead of watching *Goodfellas*, but while he was talking she ran through a mental checklist of her prosecution of Vincente Oliveri and his hierarchy. The arrest and subsequent flipping of Biermann had been pivotal. His knowledge of the internal workings of the Oliveri family's enterprises was key to taking down the dynasty of illegal business ventures Oliveri had built during his reign as don of one of the most powerful mob families in Chicago. She'd had to make more promises than she preferred to get him to talk, but by enlisting the feds who were also pursuing Oliveri, she'd been able to secure Biermann a spot in witness protection, and her only expense was the promise of continued cooperation with the feds' investigation.

Biermann's testimony lasted the entire day. Cade took the last few minutes to get him to summarize the key points so they'd be fresh in the grand jurors' minds when they returned the next morning to consider indictments for several of the key players in the Oliveri family enterprise. Once she secured those charges, she'd flip the next person, and the next until she had enough to indict Vincente and his oldest son, Mario. She'd work many late nights to make that happen, but the prize would be worth every moment of her abandoned social life.

The grand jurors filed out, and a few minutes later, two suited federal agents appeared to escort Gil from the building. She didn't envy her key witness's role, but he'd put himself in harm's way by hooking up with Oliveri in the first place, which squelched any sympathy she might feel. With a sigh, she packed up her briefcase and strode out into the hallway. A couple of hours of work waited in her office, after which she'd pick up takeout from the deli down the street on the way home.

She was a few steps from her office door when someone called out her name. She recognized the uniformed Chicago cop who'd been working with the federal detail, but she couldn't quite remember his name. Michaels, Morris, something that started with an M. She invited him into her office.

"Actually," he said, "I'm only here to deliver this note from Agent Reilly."

A small prickle of unease crept across her skin, but Cade accepted the folded paper. She barely had it in her grasp before he tipped his hat and walked away. She watched him recede into the shadows of the dark hallway before she opened the paper and read the curt note. *Biermann wants to see you before we take him to the motel. Car out front.*

Pressure built behind her eyes. If Biermann had additional demands, he obviously had no sense of timing. He'd already delivered the goods and, at the end of a very long day, she had no patience with the petty details of his whiny needs. She didn't want to leave the building before she finished her work for the day, but she knew it was probably easier for her to go outside than for the federal agents to re-park their car and drag their posse back inside. Until she had her indictment signed and delivered, she'd humor her star witness.

She pulled out her phone to text Reilly that she'd be right there, but the long day in court meant the battery had died, which was likely why Reilly had sent a note to catch her. She shook out her frustration and made her way to the lobby.

Befitting the hour, only one security guard was on duty, and he barely looked up as she passed by him. She hustled down the courthouse steps and was about halfway down, when she spotted the midnight blue van the feds had used to transport Biermann to and from court idling across the street. She looked both ways before she crossed, but her primary focus was on the vehicle in front of her. Cade assumed a game face, ready to hear whatever Biermann had to say, but prepared to fight to keep him in line.

The closer she got to the van, her shoulders tensed and her annoyance started to morph into a growing feeling of unease. When she was only a couple of feet away, she looked inside the windows. A spark of pure terror shot up her spine.

The driver of the van was slumped over the steering wheel, blood splattered in a chaotic red spray on the window next to him. For a few paralyzed seconds, she just stared, until instinct took over. She ran to the side of the van and tugged on the door handle until it opened, revealing a bloodbath. Agent Reilly and his partner were on the floor of the van in a pile on top of Gil Biermann, identifiable only by the gaudy ring on his left middle finger, the one she'd told him not to wear to court.

Holy shit. "Help! Somebody call an ambula—"

A tall, thin man pointed a gun with a silencer at her. She'd never met him before, but she'd seen his picture plenty of times. Leo Fontana was the top enforcer for the Oliveri family, and she had no doubt he was responsible for the carnage in the van. A second ago, she'd mourned the death of her case, now she was going to die with it, on the street in front of the place that was supposed to deliver justice and protect the public from harm.

But she wasn't going to die without answers. "What do you want?"

His grin was feral. "It doesn't matter what I want. Biermann is a pig. You lie down with the pig. You die with the pig." He jabbed his gun toward her. She didn't have time to think. Instinct propelled her forward. She ducked low and ran toward him, praying it would be harder to hit her if she were in motion.

She was right, but her attempts to dodge the rapid gunfire caused her to stumble. Breathing heavy, she pushed up from the ground and stood to face Fontana who was standing only a few feet away. Sweat poured down her back, and fear rooted her to the ground as she watched the scene play out in slow motion. His grin returned and he raised the gun. Cade flinched in anticipation of the shot, but suddenly Fontana spun around in response to a loud yell.

"What the hell are you doing?"

Cade looked in the direction of the voice and saw a man running toward them. She heard a muffled shot and watched with horror as the man clutched his chest and fell to the ground. Certain she was next, she lunged, determined to take this monster down. Before she could reach him another voice rang out, and another. Fontana looked over his shoulder at more bystanders in the distance headed their way, and then back at her, torn between finishing his work and saving his hide. He fired one last time in her direction and took off running.

A fierce burn tore through her skin, but Cade didn't fully comprehend what had happened until she looked down at the fan of blood blossoming across the front of her suit. She grabbed her side and shouted for help, but her words barely registered. She doubted anyone else could hear. Seconds later, she hit the ground.

Chapter Two

November

"Your new last name is Kelly."

Cade stared at the driver's license Inspector Kennedy Stone had just handed to her. The picture looked like they did on all IDs, slightly off-center. The photographer had captured her mouth slightly open when she started to ask if he was finally ready to take the shot, but the finished product looked as authentic as the rest of the papers she held in her hand: birth certificate, social security card, and the lease for the house in Bodark, a small Texas town she'd never heard of before.

"What about a job? The marshals service in Chicago said you'd have something lined up."

Kennedy shifted. "I'm working on it. I have a couple of good leads and I should have you set up within a couple of weeks. Once we get to Bodark, you can take some time to get settled and I'll be in touch about the job."

Cade had spent time over the past couple of weeks interpreting Kennedy's moods, and she could tell the question about a job had her on edge. Whatever. Kennedy wasn't the one whose entire identity had been ripped apart. From the moment she woke up in the Cook County hospital with a contingent of US Marshals guarding her around the clock, Cade felt the life she'd known slipping away. When she was finally released from the hospital, she'd been taken directly to a safe house where Assistant US Attorney Jodie Waverly offered her a place in the witness protection program in exchange for her testimony against Leo Fontana.

"Good, you caught him." Cade's nights at the hospital had been plagued with dreams of Fontana on the loose, stalking her, and imposing his own special brand of Mafia justice. His capture would give her a large measure of relief while she healed from her gunshot wound. She looked into Waverly's eyes for confirmation the source of her fear was behind bars, but she only saw unease. "What is it? What's wrong?"

Waverly cleared her throat. "We will catch him, but we haven't yet. We need your help."

Cade closed her eyes and took a moment to summon the strength to hear what Waverly had in mind. She listened as the AUSA outlined her plan to have Cade testify before a federal grand jury sometime in the next few weeks, and then assume her new identity, far from Chicago. She'd return to Cook County only when Fontana was in custody and his case was set for trial.

"If it gets to that point," Waverly said. "With any luck, he'll rat out Vincente Oliveri and you'll never have to lay eyes on him again."

"Luck." Cade sighed. "You're going to need more than luck if you think it will be easy to get Fontana to go against omertà," she said, referring to the Mafia's code of silence.

"Let me worry about that. Are you willing to testify?"

There was never any question. Cade's career as a prosecutor had been more than a job—it had been a calling. From the first time she'd witnessed the expression of gratitude on a victim's face during her law school internship with the state's attorney, the siren song of big money from big law held no sway over her.

The month after the shooting had been a blur. Still weak from her injury, she'd spent a portion of her days resting and the balance answering the same questions, over and over, from federal agents about the shooting outside the courthouse. She'd relived the horrific event so many times it played like a movie on a continuous reel in her head, whether she was asleep or awake.

The day after her grand jury testimony wrapped up, two US Marshals had whisked her to the airport. Until they reached the gate and started to board, she hadn't known where she was going, and when the plane touched down in Dallas, they'd handed her off to Kennedy, who was now responsible for keeping her alive.

During the last two weeks, she and Kennedy had remained in Dallas, while the final details of her new identity were put in place. Cade had asked several times about the possibility of opening a new law practice, but Kennedy had dodged all of her requests with a simple "I'm looking into it." Maybes weren't cutting it anymore, and she was determined to push the point. "I'm not going to be practicing law anymore, am I?"

Kennedy pushed a strand of hair away from her face and cleared her throat, but the frown creasing her brow was Cade's answer.

"It's not that easy," Kennedy said. "We don't have the right connections in Texas to get you admitted to their state bar without drawing unwanted attention. Plus, if you continue to practice, no matter where, you'll be more visible, easier to find. The state bar will have your fingerprints on file, and if any of the cases you handle get press, your face'll be in the news. I know it's what you want, but I can't guarantee your safety if you do, and I can't guarantee they'll let you stay in the program."

Cade nodded. She got it, but she didn't have to be happy about it. She'd lost much more than her chosen profession over the past few months. Her family, her friends, her sense of security had all been sucked up into a black hole of chaos. Changing her career shouldn't feel so devastating, but it had become the final straw, sending her once ordered life into a scattered mess of sacrifice and disorder. She'd let go of everything else; it was time to release this as well. "Fine. When do we leave?"

"Thirty minutes. Bodark is a couple of hours away." Kennedy stood up. "Look, I get how hard this is, but—"

"I doubt that." Anger surged through Cade. "You ever have your life turned inside out? No home, no family, no job—all because you were doing the right thing? Get back to me when your life's in total shambles and then we'll compare notes."

"I'm sorry."

A pained expression flashed across Kennedy's face, and for a second, Cade flinched with sympathy, but the sentiment faded quickly. Kennedy might feel bad for her, but that didn't mean she knew what she was feeling, and it didn't mean she cared. Kennedy would find her a new home, a new life, but she wasn't doing these things out of the kindness of her heart.

Cade didn't begrudge Kennedy her mission, but she didn't have to like her or anything about this process. All she had to do, all she could do, was focus on her new life, which meant letting go of the past. "I need to send a letter before we leave," she said. "What's the procedure?"

"Plain paper. Sign with your first name only. Don't put it in an envelope. Give me the address and I'll make sure it's delivered."

Cade made a mental note of the details. How had her life spiraled out of control? She'd never envisioned a time when she'd voluntarily let someone else peruse a personal letter she'd penned, but there was no way around it now. She walked back to her room in the nondescript apartment she and Kennedy had been sharing and found the legal pad AUSA Waverly had given her to keep notes about her memories of the shooting.

She pulled the pad close and fished a pen from her pocket. The pen, a Montblanc 149 her parents had given her the day she graduated from law school, had been nestled in her jacket when she'd been shot, and it was one of the few personal possessions she'd had with her the last two months. Her dad would recognize the pen's fine, smooth lines, and it would make him smile to know that ten years later she was still using the vintage tool even though the words she penned would break his heart.

When they'd heard the news she'd been shot, her parents, who'd retired to Florida to be close to her pregnant younger sister, Chloe, had rushed back to Chicago. Cade loved them both, but a few days of their paternal doting felt like a month's worth of smothering. After a week, she'd pointed out the wonderful care of the doctors, the frequent visits from her friends at the SA's office, the hyper vigilant guard outside her door, and she'd shooed them back to Florida, with the promise she'd be in touch if she needed anything.

In the days since, she'd called them several times—brief conversations, short enough to hide her future plans. Last week, Chloe gave birth to a beautiful baby girl. Cade was immensely happy for her, but happier still her parents would be so distracted by the newest member of the Deluca family, she could slip away, virtually unnoticed. With the pen poised above the paper, she paused to wage a now familiar internal debate about whether she should tell them anything when she couldn't tell them everything. What she had to say would be a dose of cold water on the happiness of the new birth, but if she left without telling them anything, the unknown would be a permanent distraction.

Mom and Dad,

The first thing I need you to know is I love you very much. The second thing is you may never see me again. By the time you read this letter, my life will have changed drastically. For your safety and mine, we can no longer have any contact. You won't see me again and, as hard as that will be for all of us, I'm asking you to accept it as necessary for my survival.

Please know that I love you and if there were any other way, I wouldn't be doing this. You always taught me the importance of sacrifice for a good cause—trust me when I say this decision is worthy. Please give my love to the rest of the family and know always that I love you more than you will ever know.

Cade

❖

Emily shook out of her drenched raincoat and handed it to the bellboy. She took a moment to smooth out the wrinkles of her navy blue suit while she looked out over the ballroom crowd at the Bodark Inn. She'd been here dozens of times over the years for homecoming banquets, prom, and many other election nights like this one, but she didn't remember the room ever being this crowded. Before she could process the why of it, her best friend, Becca Holt, grabbed her by the arm.

"Em, get a look at this crowd. They're all here for you."

Emily shook her head. "Chill. There are a dozen other races on the ticket."

"None of them set to make history." Becca pointed at a reporter and cameraman from the local news network standing across the lobby. "I'm not the only one who thinks so."

Becca was right, but the polls had just closed and it was way too early to call the close race. If things turned out the way she hoped, later tonight she'd be standing at the podium thanking the many donors and volunteers who'd helped her become the first woman elected district attorney of Lawson County, not to mention the youngest. But right now, she would make the rounds of the Democrat watch party and shake a few hands, share a few laughs, before making her way to her room to polish both versions of her speech until the time came to accept or concede.

"Ready?"

She turned at the gravelly voice of her campaign manager, Justin Cutler. Justin was a workhorse, which was why she'd hired him in the first place, and why she'd also grown to hate him during the last months of the campaign. She didn't really hate him, but she had begun to resist his insistence that she be on at all times. For the last six months, she'd lived and breathed the campaign. No fun, no friends, no dating for sure—nothing that could get in the way of the campaign. She'd had to assume she was always being watched, even when she was at private functions with her friends. She found it easier to blow off personal time until the campaign was over than attend social functions and worry that her every move was being posted to social media.

Justin was only doing what she paid him to do, but she couldn't help but resent the intrusion, and tonight their association would be over, no matter what the outcome. Justin would move on to the next election, and she would either assume the rank of the top law enforcement officer in the county or join her family's law practice. Right now, she didn't care which as long as it was over. She took Justin's arm. "I was ready days ago."

The suite was full when they arrived. Damn. She'd hoped for at least a few minutes of semi-solitude to prepare for the long wait ahead, but her father, mother, her two brothers and their wives and kids, along with a few key campaign donors were already indulging in the hors d'oeuvres and tossing back expensive champagne.

Emily understood that her father, Senator Dalton Sinclair, would spare no expense for his only daughter's big night, but the display directly contradicted the scrappy grassroots campaign she'd run, and she gave silent thanks no one from the media was here to see this display of opulence.

"Emily, come over here. Your mother wants some pictures with the family."

Her father's voice boomed, and everyone in the room turned toward her. Before she could take a step toward him, the room erupted in applause. She was averse to premature celebration. As of thirty minutes ago, she was neck and neck with Bradshaw in the polls, and the stormy weather outside meant all those Republican voters who'd voted early might tip the race in his favor. A few seconds in, she raised a hand and the applause faded into the sounds of ice clinking into glasses. "Thanks for coming, everyone," she said. "I appreciate the show of support. Looks like we're in for a long night, so if we run out of shrimp, let's just say I'm glad you already voted."

As the crowd laughed, she made her way over to her father, who pulled her into a crushing embrace. Dalton Sinclair was tall and broad-shouldered, but it was his self-confidence, not his size, that made him seem like the biggest personality in the room. Emily knew him as a generous, loving father, but she was well aware of his reputation as a shrewd lawyer and businessman who would use any advantage to gain a political edge over his opponents.

"I'm so proud of you," he said.

"Thanks, Dad. Couldn't have done it without you."

"Pretty sure that's not true. You put yourself through law school, so I can't even take credit for that."

It was true. She'd always insisted on making her own way, but her family name opened doors that were closed to others, no matter how hard she tried to assert her independence. "Well, thanks for being here tonight." She waved her arm to indicate the entire family. "It means a lot to me that you're all here, no matter what happens."

He pulled her close again. “I have no doubt you’re going to trounce Bradshaw, and I wouldn’t miss it for the world. Relax and enjoy this night. It’s only the beginning of many great things to come.”

She started to reply, but her mother beat her to it. “Dalton, leave the poor girl be. She’s got a ton of people to see tonight, and you don’t need to be monopolizing her with your plans to take over the world.”

Emily smiled as she watched her father raise his hands and assume a who me expression. Senator Sinclair would never be more powerful than the woman who’d worked behind the scenes to get him into the right circles. Megan Sinclair was a model of refinement and good taste and, with her pedigree, she gave her husband entree into circles he’d only dreamed about. In the small town where they lived, they were the first family, but it was her mother’s connections in Dallas that had brought him the funds he needed to win his senate seat three times over. “Thanks, Mom, but a few minutes with family would be nice. Any second now, Justin will show up ready to whisk me away to meet someone else to whom I’m sure I’m deeply indebted.”

“That’s because he’s good at what he does,” her father said. “Thank those people now and then move on. Once you’re the DA, you’ll need a buffer to deal with everyone who wants a one-on-one meeting with you. Have you thought about who you plan to bring on as your first assistant?”

“There’s plenty of time for that,” she said, deflecting the question, but she had given careful thought to her potential staff. Her password-protected files contained a flowchart, listing every attorney currently working in the district attorney’s office along with their new assignment, should she decide to keep them around. The person she ultimately selected as her first assistant would effectively run the day-to-day business of the office, although she’d remain very hands-on.

She’d pretty much decided she would offer the position to her trial partner, Seth London. After trying dozens of cases together, he was in the perfect position to know how she operated, which made him ideally suited to implement her plans for the office. A seamless transition was essential since she’d promised voters the office would see some big changes under her command. But first she had to win.

A few hours later, Emily ditched another barely touched glass of champagne, and joined the crowd gathered around the large screen television. The anchor for the local news had announced before the break they were ready to call the race. For the first time since she'd arrived, the room got quiet and she felt everyone glancing between the screen and her like they wanted to be the first to catch her reaction when the news came down. Fine by her. She schooled her expression into a thoughtful gaze and, as the commercial ended and the show began, she hoped no one could tell she was holding her breath.

Chapter Three

A traffic snarl outside of Dallas delayed Cade and Kennedy's arrival into Bodark. Since they were too late to pick up the keys to Cade's new home, Kennedy found the only hotel in the city limits and drove around the parking lot for ten minutes before she finally found a space.

"Looks pretty busy," Cade said. "You sure they'll have a room?"

Kennedy opened her door. "Only one way to find out."

Cade followed Kennedy into the hotel to stretch her legs and waited off to the side while Kennedy approached the front desk to ask if there were any vacancies. The reception area wasn't crowded, but loud noises billowed from a ballroom a few feet from where Cade was standing, and she stepped closer to take a look. Red, white, and blue balloons formed an arch at the front of the room, and a large sign behind the stage read Sinclair for District Attorney, A New Era.

Election night. Cade had been so consumed with everything happening in her own life, she'd completely forgotten about mid-term elections. Not like she could vote anyway, since the only name she was registered under no longer existed. She looked at her watch. Seven p.m. The polls had just closed, and this hotel was probably about to get a lot busier. She glanced over at Kennedy who was still standing at the front desk, wearing a defeated expression. She was about to join her, until her eyes fixed on a woman entering the hotel, walking toward her. Cade was instantly captivated.

The woman strode closer, her gait confident, her deep brown eyes sweeping the room. Beads of water pooled over the surface of her raincoat, but her lush, auburn hair had been spared a drenching, and it flounced as she walked—jaunty, flirty. The woman stopped and handed her coat to a bellman, discreetly sliding a tip in his hand as he took the dripping coat. She smoothed her hands along the lines of her well tailored, but distinctly feminine suit, and took a deep breath and squared her shoulders. A second later, another woman joined her, and Cade watched their easy conversation and marveled at the way the first woman's expression morphed from slightly hesitant to confident before she plunged into the crowded ballroom. As she disappeared from sight, Cade memorized every detail about this stranger, from her silky, auburn hair, to her well-toned legs, until Kennedy's voice broke her trance.

"They don't have any rooms."

"What?"

"Rooms. They don't have any. We'll have to find someplace else."

Cade was still thinking about the woman from the hotel when they pulled up in front of the tiny motel just outside the city limits. This place looked like something out of a fifties movie, complete with a flashing neon sign and a giant ice machine parked outside of the office. She doubted it had more than ten rooms. Kennedy pulled her Jeep into one of the many empty parking spots and killed the engine.

"How small did you say this town was?"

"You're not in the sticks." Kennedy's tone was a tad defensive.

"Well, it's not Chicago, or even Dallas for that matter."

"It may be small, but it's a pretty progressive place."

"That sounds like code for something."

"It is—liberal. There's a college campus nearby. All those young minds wreak havoc on conservative small town values. Plus, they draw a diverse crowd. They'll probably barely notice your lack of a proper southern accent."

Kennedy grinned as she spoke, and Cade realized it was the first time she'd seen her smile. Kennedy had been intensely focused since the moment they met—a trait Cade considered priceless for someone assigned to keep her alive, but now that she'd seen her smile, she hoped the time had come for them both to relax a bit. "So, you think I'll be safe here?"

"You'll be safe if you follow the rules. No one has ever—"

Cade held up a hand. She'd heard the mantra too many times over the past two months. "I know. You've never lost a witness who followed the rules."

"It's the truth."

Cade nodded. She knew it was true, but she also knew there was a first time for everything. It didn't matter either way, since she wouldn't have changed any of her actions even if the stats weren't in her favor. The testimony she'd given and her continued cooperation amounted to more than duty; they were steps toward fulfilling her personal oath of revenge for the life that had been taken from her, and no price was too great to pay to exact her vengeance. "Tell me the plan."

"We'll check in here for the night, and tomorrow we'll pick up the keys and meet the movers at your new place." Kennedy said. "Once you've moved in, I'll be on my way. I'll know more about the job situation in a few days, but I have a lead on a position at the campus library."

"Doing what exactly?"

"I don't know. Library things." Again with the smile. "I'm kidding. The position is for a reference librarian. You'll help people do research and stuff like that."

Cade sighed. The possibility of practicing law again had been a long shot, but she'd been holding on to hope it might still be possible. With the hope gone, she felt deflated.

She waited in the car while Kennedy checked them in, and she spent the time alternating between glancing around to make sure no one snuck up on her, and plotting her own escape. She could jump out of the car and run toward the woods that lined the back of the motel property. She had a complete set of legal documents all in her new name. She could start fresh, make her own decisions about what to do and where to live, out from under the thumb of government intrusion. Protection be damned.

We've never lost a witness who followed the rules.

The words echoed in her head. She'd walked away from everything. If she died doing it, then the sacrifice meant nothing. She'd spent months dreading this phase, but it was time to embrace this new life and try to make the most of it.

Kennedy rapped on the window, and Cade climbed out of the car and followed her to the unit closest to the office. The room was not at all what she expected. Cozy touches like a quilt on the bed mixed with modern ones like a flat screen TV.

"See, it's not so bad," Kennedy said.

Cade grunted her agreement. "It's actually kinda nice." She gestured to the lone bed in the room, a double. "Where are you sleeping?"

"I have the room next door. They're connected, but don't worry, I'll stay on my side unless you need me." She smiled. "It's the first step in letting go. After tomorrow, you'll be on your own until the agents in Chicago make an arrest, and I need to coordinate your travel for trial."

On her own. Cade wasn't entirely certain what it would be like to go about her life without having an armed guard within a few feet at all times, but she had a feeling she was going to like it. She pushed the comment about returning to Chicago to the back of her mind.

"Of course, after you're settled in with the new job, I'll check on you from time to time, and you'll have my contact information if you need anything."

"I'm sure I'll be fine." She wasn't entirely sure, but she planned to fake it until she was certain. In the meantime, she wanted to get some rest. The drive from Dallas had sucked the life out of her, and tomorrow would be a long day of moving into her new house and getting her bearings in this small town.

Kennedy locked her in and left to go find dinner. Cade flopped onto the bed and flipped through the TV channels, settling on the local news intending to get a feel for her new hometown. The line at the bottom of the screen scrolled election results while the middle-aged, red-haired newscaster promised they would have an exclusive interview with the woman who'd just made history in Lawson County. The newscaster was standing in a hotel ballroom that Cade recognized as the one at the Bodark Inn.

Aside from her near encounter with the intriguing woman in the lobby there, she was relieved to be in this smaller, cozier motel. She actually liked the homey feel of this place over what she imagined the larger, fancier hotel would have to offer. She traced the outline of the pattern on the quilt that served as her bedspread and wondered if the owner of this little motel had made it herself. Or maybe a family member. Part of her warmed to the idea that her hosts would share their heritage with her, but another part said she was romanticizing this entire episode of her life in order to cope with reality. Before she could decide which was more likely, the redhead on TV reappeared with the woman from the hotel by her side. Cade stared at the screen, drinking in every detail. She could tell from the way the woman's eyes lit up as she was introduced that she was excited.

"I'm reporting live from the ballroom at the Bodark Inn, and joining me is Emily Sinclair, the newly-elected district attorney of Lawson County. Congratulations, Ms. Sinclair."

Emily flashed a big smile. "Thanks, Sophie. I'm honored the citizens of Lawson County have put their confidence in me, and I promise I will serve them well."

"You've actually already been doing that as a career prosecutor in the DA's office, but what changes do you envision now that you'll be running the office?"

"Well, I'm going to start by fulfilling the promises I made in this campaign. Number one—I will root out special interest influence in the way cases are prosecuted in this county. By electing me, the voters have made it clear they're inviting in a new era."

"That's true in more ways than one. You're the first woman to be elected to this office. Will that fact influence the work you plan to do?"

"Gender shouldn't play into politics. I don't think I was elected because I'm a woman or in spite of it. With all due respect to my opponent, Mr. Bradshaw, I have more experience as a prosecutor, and I have a solid vision for the future of this office. I'd like to think those are the reasons the voters decided to cast their lot with me. I will make them proud."

"She's good," Cade muttered. District attorney. She assumed the DA was the same thing as a state's attorney, which was what they called the position in Illinois. District attorney was a funny name since the top prosecutor in each county represented the state, not just their district, but she'd be willing to bet different names wouldn't be the only thing peculiar to Texas.

Emily Sinclair looked feisty despite her petite size. Cade imagined she used her short stature to her benefit, luring opposing counsel into thinking she was just a pretty, petite girl so she could knock them out with her legal acumen, while she swayed juries with her charm.

You're letting your imagination run wild. You don't have a clue whether she's smart at all. But if she was, she was probably a force with all the right weapons at her disposal—beauty, brains, and a killer smile. Cade had gone up against lawyers like Emily many times in the past, and she'd won her fair share. While she watched the rest of the interview, her mind wandered, and she wondered if there was much crime in this county worth prosecuting. With a college nearby, they probably had their fair share of drunk and disorderlies, but nothing like the serious cases she'd seen at home.

Home. This was home now, and she would never argue cases in a courtroom again. Emily Sinclair, the gorgeous new DA, would fight whatever crime there was in this small, quiet county, and Cade would probably read an occasional article in the paper or hear a story on the radio about it, but the happenings in that hotel ballroom across town had no bearing on her life. A new era indeed.

Chapter Four

February

"Can we get some help?"

Cade whirled at the sound of the gruff male voice and simultaneously tried to assess the risk and plan an escape route. Two skinny white guys stood in front of her. Both were dressed in worn jeans, one wore a plaid flannel shirt over a well-worn Jordan College T-shirt and the other sported the ubiquitous hoodie. Students. Had to be, but just in case, she made a mental note of the exit door about twenty feet to the left of the circulation desk.

"So, like do you work here or not?" Plaid Flannel asked.

Cade bit back a smartass remark and answered simply, "Yes. What do you need?"

"I need a book about Walt Whitman. Maybe like a biography or something."

Like this, like that. Cade felt like asking him if he like knew how to like type a couple of words into one of the dozen or so computers a few feet away. Instead she punched out her own search on the keyboard in front of her and printed out a list of books. "This should get you started. The biographies are located downstairs and to the right. There should be someone else on staff down there if you have trouble finding any of these titles." She watched them shuffle off, certain they were about to plagiarize the hell out of the books she'd sent them to find, if they found them at all.

She was torn between caring too little and too much. This wasn't the work she would have chosen, but it was her life now. Kennedy had gotten her this gig as one of the staff librarians at the college library, and keeping it was part of her cover. In a small town like Bodark, there weren't a lot of choices, and the transient nature of a college campus caused her to stick out less than she would if she worked at one of the small businesses in town.

She spent the next hour helping several students who actually seemed to care about the research they were doing. One was looking up data for a paper she was writing for her criminal justice class, and Cade had to work hard not to spice up her assistance with personal anecdotes. Everywhere she turned, she had to hide pieces of herself, lying by omission.

When she returned to the circulation desk, Monica Daley, her boss, was waiting. "I thought I'd relieve you while you take a dinner break."

"That's okay. I'm not hungry."

Monica waved her arm toward the front door. "Take a walk, knit a sweater, or heaven forbid read a book, but I'm making the break mandatory. You're making the rest of us look bad."

Monica delivered the words with a smile, but she was probably only half kidding. Since she'd started working at the college library after the winter break, Cade had made a habit of working straight through her shift. Breaks were for people who liked to socialize, share a meal with others, but hanging out with people posed complications she wasn't prepared to address. Better she stayed focused on work while she was at work, and when she wasn't at work…Well, she hadn't figured out what to do with herself in her free time. Between shifts, she generally sat in her Spartan house reading books she'd checked out from the library. She had yet to venture out into the small town where Kennedy had left her to waste away.

She'd managed okay so far. The good thing about small towns was they were kind of a throwback. She'd been able to set up an account at the local grocery, and a kid on a bike delivered a couple of sacks of basics once a week, right to her door. He kept a regular schedule, so she always managed to be waiting at the front door when he arrived. A quick crack of the door, a fistful of money, and a hasty "keep the change" was the only interaction they shared. She'd considered telling the store to have the kid leave the groceries on the front step, but Kennedy had warned her that acting too much like a recluse could be more conspicuous than showing her face all over town. Monica's nagging seemed to indicate Kennedy had a point. "I really want to finish up this research database for Professor Lyon before I leave tonight, but I swear I'll take a real break tomorrow. Maybe I'll even go off campus."

Monica feigned a look of horror followed by a grin. "Now, don't go all crazy on us."

"Any suggestions?"

"There are a few good restaurants on the square. One of them is run by a pretty prominent Dallas chef who decided to give small town living a go. It's called Ambrosia. A little swank, but totally worth it. If you're looking for someplace casual, try The Purple Leaf Cafe—best roast beef sandwich you've ever had. You should try it. Let me know if you want company."

Cade did her best not to flinch at the suggestion. Monica was nice enough, but if she was going to socialize with anyone, it wasn't going to be someone from work. She had a good thing going here. The library job was vastly different from her previous career as a trial attorney, but it provided her with security and solitude. If she started making friends here, they would start asking questions, the kind that seemed normal to most folks. Where did you grow up? Do you have family? Where did you move here from?

She had answers for all of those, but every last one was fiction, and she'd rather not engage than start telling a string of lies. Better to keep work and personal life separate so she wouldn't have to choose between them if the level of deceit became too uncomfortable.

But maybe it was time to start checking out the town that was her new home. She made a mental note of the places Monica mentioned and decided she'd take a walk on the square after work tonight. If this small town was like most others, nothing would be open and she'd be free to explore without fear of running into anyone.

In Chicago, she'd had a fairly large circle of friends. They shared birthdays, anniversaries, dinners, and outings. When she felt like going out, a pal was a phone call or text away. Now the only contact in her phone was a code name with a number for Inspector Kennedy Stone. Her life had changed radically, but nothing surprised her more than how quickly she'd adjusted to the change. Maybe she could make this work.

❖

"Are you joining us for dinner or are you going to work late again?"

Emily looked up at her first assistant, Seth London, who was standing in her office doorway, and shook her head. She'd become used to the question, but the answer never changed. She might be in charge of a small town DA's office, but the level of work that had gone unattended during the previous administration was staggering. Files were in complete disarray, reports due to the county commissioners were months behind, and she had a stack of complaints from local defense attorneys about discovery they'd requested but never received. It appeared that her predecessor had retired just in time, but now she was stuck with his mess.

Seth pulled his cell phone out of his pocket and started dialing while speaking to her. "Okay then, we'll order in."

"No, seriously, you go. There's no reason for both of us to be here. Besides, Vivian will kill me if you don't show up for dinner at least once during my term."

"Vivian knows the deal. She'll understand." He pointed at his cell. "Pepperoni or sausage?"

Not a hard question, but when Emily opened her mouth to answer, she couldn't find the words. She took a long, sweeping glance at the contents of her desk. She and Seth had been working tirelessly with staff to clean up the administrative messes for the last two months and they'd made a lot of progress, but no way would she solve the rest of these problems tonight. She'd been promising Seth she'd join him and his fiancé for dinner, and she'd broken her word every time. If she joined them tonight at least she could cross one thing off her list. She slammed shut the nearest file folder. "Put away your phone. We're going out."

The restaurant, Ambrosia, was only steps away from downtown, but its modern ambience made her feel transported miles away from the stately marble walls of the courthouse. Vivian was already seated at a table for four, apparently confident Emily would be joining them. As she and Seth walked to the table, Emily assessed the woman her friend and first lieutenant had chosen to marry.

Vivian was big-city pretty. Her elegant clothes were probably purchased at Neiman's, and she sported perfectly coiffed hair and an impeccable manicure. She probably had a pedicure too, even though it wouldn't be show your feet weather for at least another month. Emily had met her at the election night party, but she hadn't had a chance to spend more than a few minutes chatting about the news of the day. She'd been looking forward to getting to know the woman Seth had met in Dallas and lured back to their small town. Tonight would be the perfect opportunity.

Her plan was quickly derailed. After they ordered, Vivian launched in with a series of tales about the latest new restaurants, shows, and shopping in Dallas, and left no space between stories for anyone to change the subject. Emily sipped her glass of red wine and let her mind wander. She'd known Seth since they went to law school together. He generally chose his dates by which one looked best on his arm, but most of them had had enough manners not to monopolize the conversation, and definitely not when having dinner with the boss.

Not that she would ever pull rank where Seth was concerned. They'd started their careers together and, although she'd been the one to win the office, she knew his help both during and after the election had been invaluable. She couldn't imagine running the office without him.

"You'll have to try it if you're ever in the city," Vivian gushed. "You do come to Dallas sometimes, don't you?"

Emily smiled at the question while she tried hard not to draw attention to the pained look Seth gave her from across the table. Since she'd zoned out, she had no idea what Vivian was asking about, but she couldn't resist the opportunity to shut her up. "Actually, I have family there. My mother's side of the family lives in Dallas. Well, actually, they live in a smaller town in Dallas County. You've heard of Highland Park?"

She smiled sweetly while she waited for the inevitable blush to rise on Vivian's face. She supposed she should feel bad about baiting her. Highland Park was a wealthy township located smack in the center of the Dallas area, and it was home to the area's elite, including a former president. Her mother had grown up there, and after she returned from college, had planned to stay there until she met Dalton Sinclair. Dalton, Emily's father, whisked the future Mrs. Sinclair away to a small town a few hours away that couldn't have been more different from the wealth and privilege of the place where she'd been raised. Emily enjoyed life in a small town but resented that outsiders often thought they were not as sophisticated or cultured as their big city counterparts.

Vivian must have some other redeeming qualities for Seth to be so smitten, so she changed the subject and hoped they'd find some common ground. "Have you set a date for the wedding?"

Vivian shot Seth a look, and he cleared his throat. "We're still working out the logistics. Vivian has several projects that will keep her in Dallas for a while, so we thought we'd let that play out before we make firm plans."

"Okay." Emily looked between them, certain there was some undercurrent to this topic, but not entirely sure she wanted to probe further. Seth's personal business was his own. She'd been a little bit wary when he'd announced his engagement to a woman from out of town. Vivian didn't seem like the type who would want to live here, and if Seth moved away, it would leave a big hole in her administration, but they seemed to be taking things slow, and she'd settled on a wait and see mode.

The rest of the dinner was painful, but quick. Vivian eschewed all the dessert options as too unhealthy, and Emily was more than happy to cut things short. She declined Seth's offer to walk her back to the office, and said her good nights at the restaurant door.

A full moon hung low in the night sky, and even with a light breeze, the temperature was in the fifties. Emily strolled the downtown square, taking the long way around to the courthouse, enjoying the cool night air and the quiet solitude. The restaurant was the only business still open, and only a few patrons remained inside. The shops that lined the square were shuttered and still. She walked past a plaque, posted to dedicate a large tree to the city from the Sinclair family. The tree had been here for as long as she could remember, and her father had always said it was a symbol of how the family helped the town grow.

Some people thought she'd won the election because of her family name. It probably didn't hurt that she was a Sinclair, but there were some in the town who resented her family's influence. All she'd ever wanted to do was forge her own way, but to be totally independent, she'd have to leave this place she loved, and stake out a new life in a different place. She'd given the idea some thought, especially during long stints when she was off at school, but on her visits back she couldn't deny the pull of the only place she'd ever really considered home. Legacy greeted her at every turn, from her brothers' law firm on the town square to the avenue named after her grandfather that cut through town. She was proud to be a Sinclair, and she planned to show this town and this county they could be proud for electing her to enforce their laws.

As she rounded the corner to the courthouse, she debated whether she should call it a night or go back in and get a couple of case files to take home. It was only nine o'clock. She could curl up on the couch with another glass of wine and get a jumpstart on the next day. She was fishing through her purse for her keys when she smacked into a woman at the foot of the courthouse steps. She looked up into dark brown eyes full of surprise. "I'm sorry. I wasn't watching where I was going."

The woman's surprise faded into an anxious smile. "My fault. There's probably some law against standing in the town square after a certain hour, and I'm for sure violating it."

Emily had to tear her attention away from the women's eyes. So expressive, so revealing. She slowly took in everything about this stranger. She didn't know everyone in town, but she'd met a majority of the people old enough to vote over the last year. The woman's accent signaled she was from somewhere in the Midwest. She'd never seen this woman before. She would've remembered if she had. Tall and lean. She wasn't conventionally beautiful, but with a strong jaw and chiseled features, she was striking nonetheless. Like Vivian, she had a big city vibe, but hers was hip and edgy, complete with a distressed leather jacket, expensive black Frye boots, and low-waisted, slim-fitting jeans. She didn't shop in the small town boutiques that lined the streets of Bodark.

"I'm sure if you were violating any laws, I'd know it," Emily said. She stuck out her hand. "Emily Sinclair."

The stranger's eyes darted around, and she hesitated for a moment before she shook Emily's hand. "Cade. Nice to meet you."

She says that, but it doesn't ring true. And she purposefully left off her last name. Why do I care? "New in town?"

"I haven't been here very long."

"The sights are even better during the day."

"I like to take walks at night. I guess you do too."

Emily pointed at the building. "Actually, I work here. I was just headed back to the office to pick up some files."

A flash of recognition showed in the woman's eyes, but all she said was, "I should let you get to it."

But being let be was suddenly the last thing Emily wanted. She studied the woman's face, but couldn't get a read on her expression. The anxiety had dissipated, but she looked lonely, and a little bit lost. "Do you live close by?"

Emily told herself she was prolonging the contact out of a sense of duty, maybe even a holdover from the campaign where she'd gone out of her way to be nice to everyone, no matter what the circumstances, but the truth was she was drawn to this stranger with her edgy good looks and mysterious mannerisms.

"Not too far." Cade shifted from one foot to the other.

"You're not big on small talk are you?" Emily watched as a smile crept across Cade's face at the remark. Happy she'd been able to dispel whatever had Cade looking forlorn, she pushed a bit. "How about coffee? Do you like coffee?"

Cade looked around. "I love coffee, but unless you know something I don't, there's nowhere around here open and serving."

"Ah the disadvantages to being new in town." Feeling uncharacteristically flirtatious, Emily leaned in and whispered. "I just happen to know secret coffee places that are open at all times of the day and night."

"Is that so?"

"Truth."

"Then I should probably get to know you better."

"What are you doing now?" Immediately after Emily asked the question, she wished she hadn't. The smile faded from Cade's face, and she knew instantly their flirty banter was done.

"Actually, I have to be somewhere. Maybe another time." She took a step and then stopped. "It was nice to meet you, Emily Sinclair."

Cade started walking again before Emily could get another word out. She watched Cade's back until she faded into the dark night. The entire encounter had been surreal, and she'd surprised herself when she'd asked Cade on a date of sorts. She hadn't been on a real date since well before the campaign, and even then the woman she'd been seeing was from Dallas, so they'd only gotten together a couple of times a month. She'd been so busy, she hadn't had time to notice the hole her work had torn in her social life, but the evening with Seth and Vivian had her thinking about what she was missing. That had to be the explanation for why she'd extended an impulsive invitation to a total stranger she'd met on the street.

No, that wasn't it entirely. She'd been drawn to Cade, and it was about more than her appearance. She looked strong, yet vulnerable. Sweet, yet tough. Where did she work? When did she move here and why? Was she lonely? The questions were more than idle curiosity. For the first time in a long while, Emily was intrigued. She'd been ready to see where the feeling led, but Cade obviously had different plans.

Resigned to the fact she was probably making more out of the chance meeting than was actually there, Emily trudged up the steps of the courthouse to her office, wishing the night was ending with something besides a stack of paperwork. "It was nice to meet you too, Cade Whoever-you-are," she muttered to the night air.

Cade didn't breathe again until she was in her car, well on her way home. Emily Sinclair. It had taken a moment, but when Emily had started talking, Cade recognized her as the newly-elected DA who'd been voted into office the night she'd moved to Bodark. Emily was more beautiful than she remembered and that smile…dangerously engaging.

Secret coffee places. Geez, Cade, could you have fallen harder for that line? But it wasn't the line that had her hooked. No, it was the woman who delivered it. Smart, witty, pretty—Emily Sinclair was a perfect package. Sheer force of will had allowed her to walk away, but the once slumbering parts of her longing for human interaction had been shouting for her to stay and take Emily up on her offer.

False hope. Coffee dates were about conversation, and while she had tons in common with Emily Sinclair, the natural topics were off limits. They were both lawyers, both prosecutors, and both women in a field traditionally dominated by men, especially Emily who was the first female elected DA in this county. Their common denominators would only add up to disaster. Figured. The first woman she'd been attracted to in her new life was one she couldn't afford to get involved with.

She pulled into her driveway and stepped out in the cool air. She used the remote to lock the car, although she wasn't at all sure who'd want to steal a Ford Focus, but she supposed there was someone out there that would appreciate four wheels and an engine that worked. She missed her Toyota 4-Runner, but had given in to WITSEC's insistence she drive something completely different than her previous ride, and nothing too flashy, in keeping with her position as an assistant librarian. She had to admit that in the plain-Jane Focus, she completely blended into the traffic around her and the sameness of the car acted as a type of force field.

Her new house, on the other hand, was unique. A smallish 1950s bungalow, it had the look of a garden cottage complete with a sunroom, overlooking scraggly gardens full of potential, but desperately in need of love and attention. She hadn't seen it before Kennedy brought her here on their second day in town, but she'd been instantly taken with it.

Not unlike her instant attraction to Emily Sinclair, except the house would never ask too many questions, never put her in danger. She was much better off having a love affair with this house than she'd ever be with any woman she might meet. She hung her keys on the hook in the kitchen, kicked off her boots, and started a pot of coffee—no secrets involved. She didn't need a woman to satisfy her needs.

Chapter Five

Emily took a sip of coffee and sighed. The taste of the special blend reminded her of her invitation to the elusive Cade. It had been a week, and she had yet to spot the mysterious stranger anywhere in town. And she'd looked plenty. While she enjoyed the smooth brew, she imagined sharing a French press with Cade, followed by a walk under the stars through the streets of downtown Bodark. Silly, maybe, but she let herself give in to the dreamy fantasy for a few moments before deciding her subconscious was merely telling her to get out more, have a social life. She started to pick up the phone to call Becca and suggest a weekend jaunt to Dallas, when she saw the line from her secretary, Janice, light up. She picked up the phone. "What's up?"

"Mr. Jansen is on line three. This is the third time he's called today."

Emily sighed. Ethan Jansen's teenage son had been killed by a hit-and-run driver during the holidays. The sheriff's office had finally made an arrest, and Mr. Jansen had called daily to check the status of the case. Janice had been holding him at bay, insisting he speak to the assistant DA assigned to the case, but he had become increasingly angry with each call, and it was time to set some boundaries. "Put him through." She waited a few seconds until the call was connected. "Mr. Jansen, this is Emily Sinclair. I understand you'd like an update about your son's case."

"How about you start by giving me any information at all. Sheriff Nash said he got the bitch, so all I need to know is when is she going to prison for what she did to my boy?"

Emily silently cursed the overzealous sheriff for tossing this off on her. "I've assigned one of our top prosecutors to handle this case. She's still working with law enforcement to gather evidence, and she'll be presenting the case to the grand jury in the next month. I'm happy to give you her direct line so you can discuss the case with her whenever you like."

A few months ago, she would have been the one getting the shit kicked down to her. She'd thought it would've been easier being on the giving, rather than receiving end, but the truth was she felt bad about foisting Jansen off on her assistants. She'd do it anyway. Ultimately, everything at this office was her responsibility, but part of her responsibility was letting her employees handle their own cases.

"A month? Why so long?"

"Again, I'm happy to put you in touch with Elena to discuss all the details, but it's to our benefit to spend the time up front to do things right if we want the charges to stick. Sometimes that means a delay, and I know that's hard to take."

"Hard to take. You have absolutely no idea what you're asking. My wife has been inconsolable, barely able to leave the house since that mongrel killed our son."

That "mongrel" was a forty-year-old Hispanic single mother with two kids of her own at home. Emily didn't know the whole story, but she figured there was more to it than a woman goes on a drinking binge and plows down a kid in his prime. For her purposes, she didn't care about the defendant's backstory, but there were likely to be mitigating circumstances, and it was best to be prepared up front with a rock solid case rather than rush to trial without all the facts. "I'm deeply sorry for what both you and your wife are going through. Rest assured our office will do everything possible to make sure we get justice for your son."

A couple of seconds of silence passed before the sharp crack of the phone being slammed down reverberated through the line. She stared at the handset and then replaced it gently on the base. Before she had time to process the conversation, Janice appeared at her door.

"Sorry, boss."

"Not your fault. He'll probably keep calling until the trial. Maybe after, if it doesn't go well."

"Do you want me to get Elena on the line?"

Leave it to Janice to anticipate her needs. She should talk to Elena to give her a heads-up that Jansen was on the warpath, but her mind was already whirring its way to another solution. "Let's wait on that. Is Seth around this morning?"

"He had a hearing in Judge Latham's court, but I bet he's back by now. You want me to have him come by?"

Emily stood up. "No, I need to stretch my legs. I'll wander by his office." She wasn't used to all the desk time her new position required. As an ADA, she'd moved around a helluva lot more, meeting with witnesses, complainants, police, and going back and forth to court proceedings. If she didn't start making a point to get out from behind her desk, she was going to age exponentially before she finished serving out her term, and God knows she'd age enough from calls like Jansen's.

Seth's door was cracked. She peeked in and saw he was on the phone, but he waved her into the room. She sat in one of the chairs in front of his desk and looked around the room while he finished up his call.

"I know, I know," Seth said into the phone. "I promise I'll be there in time for dinner. Yes, black suit. I can pick out my own tie. Okay, okay. Got it." He hung up the phone and sighed. "Is it just me or is it always painful meeting the parents?"

"You haven't met her parents?" Emily was genuinely surprised.

"They've been on one of those round the world trips, planes, trains, cruise ships, since we got serious. Now they're back, and it's like I have to start all over again."

"I get it. You already got the girl, so you've gotten all relaxed. Don't worry. You'll wow them even if you wear the wrong tie." The look on Seth's face signaled her assurances weren't having much affect. "When's the meeting?"

"Friday night. At the Petroleum Club. I'm sorry I'm going to miss your thing."

Emily waved him off. She was scheduled to be part of a panel at the local college, discussing the topic of law enforcement in the future. She'd learned pretty quickly after taking office her duties extended way beyond regular courthouse activity. Town hall meetings, panels, dinners, lunches, and breakfasts now consumed much of her time. "Don't be sorry. I'd skip out if I could, even to have dinner with potential in-laws. But you can do me a favor—do you have a minute to talk about Ethan Jansen?"

Seth scowled. "Is he still calling you?"

"Just got off the phone with him. Pretty sure I'm on his blacklist now."

"Join the club."

"Talk to me about what's going on. We have a solid case?"

"Actually, I was going over the file with Elena yesterday, and I asked her to leave it here. She wanted some advice before the grand jury presentation." Seth reached behind his desk, pulled out a folder, and started thumbing through the pages. "Okay, here are the facts. We have two witnesses who can ID a car that matches the description of the defendant's leaving the scene of the accident. The next day, the defendant tells one of her friends she's feeling guilty about something. She takes her kids to her mother's and leaves them there, but she goes about her daily business for a whole week. After one of the sheriff's deputies leaves a card on her door, she turns herself in and makes a full confession." He closed the file. "That about sums in it up. Her car was parked behind her house, and the damage is consistent with the description of the incident."

"The confession is solid?"

"Yes. She signed the acknowledgment of rights before she wrote out her statement."

"I thought we were going to start getting video statements."

"The sheriff's office said they didn't get the budget allocation they were promised."

Emily nodded, but she made a mental note to check further. She knew the sheriff's office had received plenty of funding at the start of the new year, but she imagined most of the money had gone into the new SUVs she'd seen the deputies driving around town.

One of her campaign platforms had been to provide a more transparent process, and recorded statements were one way to achieve that promise, but she had to rely on law enforcement to do their part. Unfortunately, Sheriff Nash had supported her opponent in the primary, and had only grudgingly offered his support when she became his party's candidate. She hoped they could find a way to work together, but in the meantime she might have to find some funds in her own budget if she wanted to keep her campaign promises. For now, she'd have to make do with what they had on this case. "Any mitigating circumstances we need to be aware of?"

Seth shook his head. "She's got two young kids, but for all we know they were with her that night which only aggravates her culpability in my book. I imagine if she gets a decent lawyer, whoever it is will argue she panicked at the scene and was scared that if she was arrested, there would be no one to take care of her kids. She ultimately confessed, but we'll be quick to point out she didn't come clean until the sheriff's office had already shown up at her door. Once we get the forensics back from the lab, we'll have an indictment in no time."

Seth had the case well in hand, and Emily only hoped Mr. Jansen could find the resolve to wait through the process without burning up their phone lines. Emily stood. "Thanks for filling me in. We should have our new grand jury packet procedures ironed out before this case is presented. Can you get something to me this week?"

She watched while Seth looked at his calendar and frowned. She suspected his expression had more to do with his disagreement with her new policy than it did about his schedule. She'd promised the local defense bar that part of her move to transparency would include the right to present a packet of information to the grand jury to try to convince them not to indict a case. The DA's office would still have veto power if the packet contained information more likely to inflame than inform, but the new process would allow defendants to try to convince grand jurors the charges should be tossed before the case was held over for trial.

She saw the procedure as a win-win. If the grand jury decided to no-bill, or to not indict the defendant, then the people had spoken. If they decided to true-bill, or indict, in spite of whatever pitch the defense made, that only made her case stronger going forward. But some prosecutors, Seth included, saw the move as ceding sacred ground. The grand jury had always been the secret sanctuary, dominated by the prosecution. They acted like letting the defense in, in any capacity, was the end of the world.

"It can be really simple, but I want the new policy in place before this case is heard. Okay?"

"Okay," Seth said with a resigned tone. "I'll get it done before I head to Dallas Thursday night."

"They'll love you, you know."

"What?"

"Vivian's parents. I know parents can be intimidating, hell, look at mine, but you're smart, handsome, and you have a great job."

"They might be a little more impressed if I was you."

"A woman?"

"No, the district attorney."

Seth's smile was laced with a tinge of regret, but Emily couldn't tell if he regretted he'd said the words or regretted he'd said them out loud. "Oh please. You're one of the best trial lawyers I know. They'd be lucky to have you as a son-in-law. You can tell them I said so."

Seth laughed, for real. "I might just do that. Now, go boss someone else around so I can get some work done." He shooed her out the door.

On the way back to her office, she paused at the top of the stairs and looked out one of the tall windows. In the middle of the day, the square was bustling with activity. It was almost lunchtime, and many of the people who worked downtown were walking to their favorite lunch spots. It was a vastly different atmosphere from the night she'd run into Cade in the dark, cold, and silent night. She closed her eyes for a few seconds and conjured up the image of Cade, standing at the foot of the courthouse steps, dashing and handsome.

She'd looked for Cade in the week since, scouting every face she saw, looking for a smile of recognition, but she'd come up empty. She contemplated asking one of the investigators at her disposal to assist, and then laughed at herself. No way was she going to raise questions about her ethics by using county resources to find a woman who she only knew by her first name, but who had occupied her thoughts since the moment they'd met.

Emily sighed. Time to get back to the work that defined her life. She'd take a few more months to get settled into her new role, and then she'd find a woman to fall in love with, get married, and raise a family. But right now she had duties to fulfill, and chasing strangers with eyes she could drown in wasn't one of them.

❖

Cade hung her coat on the back of the office door and put her bagged lunch—leftover white bean and chicken chili that would taste even better today than it had last night—in the mini refrigerator by her desk. Making her own lunch was only one of the many ways her life had changed. Lately, she'd spent her nights watching cooking shows and jotting down recipes. If she wasn't careful, she was going to start packing on extra pounds, which would require buying new clothes, which meant shopping. When had she started to measure her life by the various ways she could figure out how not to leave the house?

"Hey Cade, there's a woman out front who asked for you."

Cade turned to see Harry Spader standing in the doorway. Harry was a student, working his way through his degree by putting in hours at the library. She studied his face for signs of something, anything to tell her whoever was asking about her wasn't nefarious, but she couldn't get a read and she didn't want to ask. "Did she say who she was?"

"Kennedy. That's all she said. You want me to tell her you're busy?"

Kennedy. This was the first time she'd shown up at her work, and that put Cade on alert. Was something wrong? Was she in danger? She looked around the office she shared with two other librarians. It was private right now, but any moment someone else could come in. Better she talk to Kennedy about whatever it was far from here. "No, tell her I'll be right there."

She took a moment to steady herself, forcing calm breaths and fixing her face into a neutral expression, and then strode out to the circulation desk. Kennedy was standing off to the side. She probably thought she was being discreet, but Cade would have made her as a cop within seconds even if she didn't already know. The familiar bulge in her jacket, the way she feigned nonchalance while standing at full alert—all signs she was on the job. Cade watched Kennedy's eyes track her as she approached, but she didn't call out a greeting, instead she waited until they were right next to each other before saying, "Not here."

She led the way with Kennedy on her heels. The student union was two buildings down, and, although they covered the distance in about five minutes, by the time they got there, Cade was freezing because she'd left her coat back at the library office. She walked straight to the snack bar and ordered a coffee from the young woman behind the counter.

"Hi, Miss Kelly. Good to see you."

Cade frowned. Did she know this girl?

The girl took her reaction in stride and shot out a hand. "Darcy Winters, future microbiologist. You helped me find some reference texts from another school a few weeks ago. Saved my butt and my paper. I never forget a life saver."

Ah. She remembered now. Darcy had been desperate when she learned the campus library didn't have one of the source materials she was relying on, and she didn't have funds to order the expensive texts online. Cade had made a few calls and managed to borrow what Darcy needed from another library, making special arrangements for a quick delivery. Like most of her interactions with strangers, Cade had kept her head down and her focus on the details of the transaction. For the first time, it occurred to her this method of hiding out also meant she didn't have an opportunity to notice details about the people around her, which was equally as dangerous as being recognized for her past life.

"Sorry, I didn't recognize you. Must have been the apron." She smiled. "Can I get a coffee and whatever my friend here wants?" She pointed at Kennedy who shot her a curious look before ordering a coffee, black.

A few minutes later, Cade led the way to a table in the back of the room, far from any other activity in the union building. She didn't waste any time getting to the point. "What are you doing here?"

"I wanted to talk to you."

"And you couldn't just call?"

"I wanted to check on you, see how you are doing."

"Showing up at my work isn't a good idea."

"It's a college campus," Kennedy said. "There are tons of people here. Showing up at your house is a helluva lot more conspicuous than dropping by the library. Besides, maybe folks will start thinking you actually have some friends."

"What's that supposed to mean?"

"Hiding out in your house all the time will draw more attention than having some semblance of a social life. Every neighborhood has a Gladys Kravitz, and I'm betting yours is already gossiping about the recluse who moved in last November, has everything delivered, and only leaves her house to go to work."

Kennedy's words stung, but she had a point. Cade thought back over the past couple of months. The first few weeks, she'd ventured out after work only to gather necessities. She'd practically starved as her first few attempts at home cooking went horribly awry, but a simple pizza delivery seemed too risky. Now that she was fairly confident in the kitchen, her forays into town had tapered off and she was becoming more and more of a hermit. Except for last week when she'd been compelled to check out downtown Bodark, and ran into Emily Sinclair.

A flush of warmth coursed through her at the memory of Emily standing in front of the courthouse. Her survival skills should have directed her to walk away from Emily the moment she saw her, but she'd stayed put, unable and unwilling to deny the attraction between them. What would the neighborhood nosey think if she had a ringside seat to the fantasies Cade had harbored since running into Emily?

Kennedy stared at her with a curious expression, and Cade shook her head to clear away the crazy, hazy fantasy. "Sorry, you're right, of course. Every time I go out I feel exposed. I'll feel a lot better when Fontana's in custody. Any updates on that front?"

Kennedy shook her head. "The FBI in Chicago had what they thought was a good lead but it didn't pan out." She grimaced. "They'll find him, and I promise you'll be one of the first to know when it happens."

Cade didn't necessarily believe her. The longer Fontana eluded law enforcement, the more likely it was they'd never bring him to justice. If they did catch him, and he didn't rat out any of his associates, there would be a trial. She'd have to testify, which meant sitting across the room from the man who'd tried to kill her. She shifted in her chair. The prospect of seeing Fontana again even if he was wearing an orange jumpsuit instead of wielding a gun filled her with dread so deep she couldn't bring herself to examine it. Desperate to change the subject, she feigned nonchalance. "So, checking up on me—that's really the only reason you're here?"

"Pretty much. It's my job. Is there anything you need?"

Cade laughed. "That's a leading question. Let's just say nothing. I don't need anything you or your marshal pals can get for me."

"Cade, you should live your life. I'm not saying don't be careful, but…"

"But this is my life now and I should get used to it."

"That's pretty blunt, but yes. I've been doing this a while and I know it can't be easy, but it can be more than what you're making it. Make some friends, leave your house for something besides work. Besides having the benefit of making you less conspicuous, you might actually have a better quality of life."

Build relationships based on lies. That's essentially what Kennedy was telling her to do. What kind of relationships could she have under these circumstances? Her mind flashed to Emily Sinclair. In another time, under different circumstances, they would be peers. Now, if her fantasy came true and they did have a date, would the conversation be strained because she couldn't share too much for fear of being discovered? Would Emily think less of her because her conversational skills were limited?

Before all of this, she'd been totally and completely dedicated to her job. Her friends were fellow prosecutors and cops. They did everything together—played softball, drank beer—and all they ever talked about was the job. Without it, she was a shadow of her former self. Her topics of conversation, once colorful and bold, were now gray and boring. Circulation desk anecdotes didn't hold a candle to courtroom war stories. She wondered if Emily was the same way—married to the job, defined by it. Hell, she was the elected DA. If anything, Emily was probably more immersed in her work than Cade had ever been.

Emily Sinclair was out of reach for the person she'd become, but maybe Kennedy was right. She needed to have some sort of social life or she would go crazy. Maybe she would start by striking up a conversation with one of the professors who did research in the library. One in particular, a cute blonde who taught art history, was always hanging around, and Cade had picked up on the fact she wasn't there just for the books. She'd ignored her attempts to flirt so far, but she resolved that next time, she would talk to her about something other than the Dewey Decimal System.

After Kennedy left, Cade walked back to the library. For the first time in a long time, she felt empowered, ready to try something new. When her boss asked if she'd mind working a little late to be on hand for a panel discussion that evening, she volunteered to stick around. Maybe she'd have the opportunity to try out her newfound resolutions.

CHAPTER SIX

Emily saw the time on her computer screen and realized she should've left ten minutes ago to allow enough time to get to the library for the panel discussion. She shoved the file on her desk into a drawer, grabbed her coat, and headed toward the door of her office, but before she could cross the threshold, Janice appeared out of nowhere.

"Do you have your notes?"

"Yes, ma'am," Emily said.

"Don't ma'am me. It's my job to make sure you have what you need."

"What if I need you to find someone to stand in for me tonight?"

"Not a chance. Everyone will be there to see the new DA. Bet you get most of the questions from the audience."

"I bet no one shows up. It's a Friday night on a college campus. Unless there's a bar at the library I don't know about, it's going to be me, Sheriff Nash, Professor Radley, and a herd of stodgy librarians. I'll be lucky if I don't fall asleep on stage."

"Then I suggest you take some coffee along. Want me to get you a cup to go?"

Emily shook her head. "I'm good. And late. Mostly late. Go home. Enjoy your weekend."

"You do the same. You know, as soon as your date with the stodgy librarians is done." Janice's smile morphed into a semi-stern expression. "Seriously, take the rest of the weekend off. The world won't end if you do, and you might be in better shape for it come Monday."

On the drive to the campus, Emily considered Janice's advice. She hadn't had a day off since she'd taken office, but she always expected having the top job would be hard work. What she hadn't expected was the tedium associated with trudging through all the administrative duties of the office. Budget planning, meeting with community leaders, appearing before the county commissioners, and speaking engagements. She couldn't remember the last time she'd seen the inside of a courtroom, and as for litigation? At this pace, she couldn't begin to conceive of actually trying a case.

One of her campaign promises had been that she would personally take the lead in the prosecution of any major case that went to trial during her term. It was a good thing major cases were few and far between in Lawson County, because she couldn't imagine having time to fulfill her promise without letting her other duties fall behind.

The college was a short twenty-minute drive away, and Emily made it in fifteen. She pulled into the parking lot in front of the library, shut off the engine, and engaged in a familiar routine. She closed her eyes and pictured the main courtroom at the Lawson County Courthouse. She loved the space with its gallery seating and ornate marble and wood—it reminded her of the courtroom in the movie *To Kill a Mockingbird*. She'd cut her teeth in that courtroom, and before she'd started her campaign for DA, she'd tried dozens of cases, from basic shoplifting charges to one of the few murder cases the county had ever seen. The courtroom was both her boxing ring and her sanctuary. Imagining the place and the way she felt in it, in charge and full of purpose, simultaneously relaxed and rejuvenated her, and within moments she was ready to deal with tonight's panel.

When she reached the library doors, she spotted her picture on a poster advertising the event. She suppressed a smile that her photo was almost twice as large as Sheriff Nash's. His head had probably exploded when he'd seen it. She pushed through the doors and looked around for a sign inside that would direct her to the event.

"Miss Sinclair?"

Emily turned to face a young man dressed in jeans, Converse, and a Drake T-shirt. She pegged him for a student. "Yes. Can you tell me where the Sable Room is?"

"I can do you one better." He stuck out a hand. "I'm Harry. Ms. Kelly asked me to watch for you and show you the way." He crooked his arm in an adorable show of gallantry. She paused for a second, slid her arm through his, and walked beside him past the circulation desk, through the stacks to a set of double doors near the back of the first floor. While they walked, Emily tried to remember if Ms. Kelly was the librarian who'd contacted her about the panel. Before she had time to figure it out, Harry opened one of the doors with a flourish and she got her first glimpse of the panel audience.

She gasped. The room was packed. There had to be over a hundred people seated in the rows lining the auditorium. Sheriff Nash was already seated on stage alongside criminal justice Professor Radley, and she recognized at least two reporters from local news outlets. The clock on the wall told her she'd arrived about two minutes before the panel was scheduled to begin, but the size of the crowd caught her by surprise and she felt like she was way behind. She searched her mind for the calming image of the courtroom again, and had just settled on it when she heard Harry's voice in her ear. "I'll turn you over to Ms. Kelly now. She'll be introducing everyone on the panel."

Emily nodded and turned to greet the librarian who had organized the event, and her heart stopped. Instead of a fussy, gray-haired librarian, she was face to face with Cade, the striking stranger from the courthouse steps. If she wasn't thrown enough by the size of the crowd, now her expectations were completely off base.

Cade Kelly. Librarian. Not stodgy at all. She knew exponentially more about her now than she had before, but she wanted to know even more. How long had she worked here? Where had she come from? Was she single?

"Miss Sinclair, nice to see you again. Would you like to take your seat? I'm about to start the introductions."

Cade didn't make eye contact with her greeting, but her voice held the same husky, low tone she remembered, and Emily couldn't wait to hear more. But not here. Somewhere they could be alone. Cade had already turned away to answer a question from Harry, but Emily vowed to talk to her as soon as they were done. The panel was supposed to last ninety minutes. It would be the longest hour and a half of her life.

❖

Cade stood behind the podium and looked out over the crowded room, steeling her nerves and hoping she didn't look as disconcerted as she felt. She'd known since late this afternoon she'd see Emily tonight, but nothing had prepared her for the actual event.

Emily looked like she'd stepped off the pages of a fashion magazine. She was dressed in tall, chocolate brown suede boots, a plaid wool skirt, and a jacket that hid no curves. She'd looked surprised, but glad to see her, and Cade wished they'd had a moment to talk before they plunged into tonight's event. At the very least, she wanted time to recover from the nervous way she'd greeted her at the door.

She looked down at her notes and shut out thoughts of her undeniable attraction to Emily Sinclair. She delivered the introductions and thanked everyone for attending before handing the panel over to the moderator, and taking her seat next to Harry in the front row in the audience. As she sat down, Harry leaned over and whispered, "Do you know Miss Sinclair? She seemed to be locked on you the whole time you were talking."

Cade shook her head and focused on the discussion. Professor Radley served as the moderator and he was well prepared and a bit ruthless in his biting questions about the state of the criminal justice system. She watched as the panelists tackled issues related to race, gun control, and mental health. She might be biased, but in her opinion Emily held her own despite the showmanship demonstrated by Sheriff Nash and the defense attorney on the panel.

"Where do you draw the line between protecting a community and justice for everyone, including the accused?" Radley asked. "Miss Sinclair?"

"That's a pretty broad question, Professor."

"Fair enough. Let's use an example. Should bonds be restrictive or just high enough to make sure a defendant shows up for court?"

Cade watched Emily cock her head, and she could tell by the slightly raised eyebrows, Emily was surprised by the example. She was too. Bonds weren't the juiciest of subjects, and she wouldn't have expected them to be one of the topics in front of a lay audience.

"Bonds serve the dual purpose of making sure the defendant is accountable, and protecting the public, but Texas law clearly states they can't be so restrictive they keep people in jail when no specific danger has been articulated. We don't want to be in the position where only rich people are out on bond pending trial, but if the defendant poses a current danger, we will take appropriate steps to make sure they are either in custody or under some other restrictions pending trial." Emily delivered the reasoned response, but as the last words fell from her lips, Sheriff Nash was already speaking into the mic.

"Well, isn't that a sweet answer that says a lot of nothing. If we go to the trouble of investigating and then arresting someone, you darn sure better bet they deserve to be locked up. I hope the DA's office will continue to support us as they have in the past."

His words were delivered with a heavy dose of sarcasm, and Cade watched to see how Emily would respond. She wasn't the only one. Every eye in the audience was glued on Emily, likely anticipating how she would respond to the sheriff's challenge.

Radley took up the baton. "Miss Sinclair, do you wish to address the sheriff's remarks?"

Emily turned in her chair and faced Nash. "Billy, we've known each other a long time and if there's only one thing you know about me dead certain it's that, like you, I'm completely dedicated to upholding the laws of this great state. You will find no greater law enforcement allies than me and the attorneys who work in my office. You have my word."

The room broke into applause, and Cade grinned at the flummoxed expression on the sheriff's face. No doubt he wanted to point out that Emily's words were more fluff than substance, but to do so again after her impassioned response would only make him look like a bigger jerk.

The rest of the panel was fairly tame with each of the panelists answering questions about how to pursue a career in their various professions, which Cade figured was why so many students had attended this evening. She had to restrain herself from mouthing Emily's responses right along with her, and she wondered if she would always feel like she was trapped outside of herself and the life she used to have.

When the panel was done, the audience rose to their feet and Harry turned to her, practically frothing at the mouth. "That was awesome. I mean I only came to help out, but I'm thinking I might be interested in law school now. Do you think Miss Sinclair would talk to me about it?"

Cade opened her mouth to say she didn't know her well enough to answer, but someone from behind her spoke first.

"I'd be happy to." Emily pulled a card out of her purse and handed it to the star struck Harry. "Give my secretary a call and set up an appointment."

Harry stared at the card for a moment, like he couldn't believe his good fortune. "Would you like me to walk you to your car?"

Cade shooed him away. "Go help break the room down. I got this." She waited until he was across the room before facing Emily. "That was very sweet. I think he has a mild crush on you."

"Mild, huh? I must be losing my edge."

"Oh, college boys are your thing? Well, you should hang out here more. There're plenty to go around."

Emily laughed, a smooth and silky sound. Cade wanted to wrap up in it. "Not hardly. I'm more interested in the over thirty female set. You don't happen to know anyone who fits that description, do you?"

"I might, but I have a feeling she won't be interested unless you reveal the location of your late night coffee spot."

"I'll have to show her the place personally. It's kind of a well-kept secret. You can keep a secret, can't you?"

Cade froze for a second, but forced a quick recovery. Emily was kidding around, and there was absolutely nothing about her tone or visage to suggest her reference to secrets was related to anything besides coffee. She'd need to learn to be less jumpy if she was going to fit in. "Of course. When would you like to meet her?"

Emily looked at her watch. "How about now?"

Cade took a deep breath. She was about to jump off a cliff, but maybe this was exactly what Kennedy had been talking about. Act normal, she'd said. What was more normal than being attracted to a beautiful woman? Telling herself it was only coffee, she took the plunge. "Now is perfect."

Chapter Seven

Emily stood at the entrance to the Bodark Inn and tugged her scarf tighter against the blistery cold that had snuck up after a week with temperatures in the sixties. She wasn't used to the weather, but she didn't want to risk missing Cade who was clearing up things at the library before leaving for the night.

Fifteen minutes later, she was about ready to bail. Asking Cade for coffee had been impulsive at best. She didn't know a thing about her. Okay, she knew two things: her full name and she worked at the library. And she liked coffee, so three things. Still, Cade was virtually a stranger, and she'd never dated a complete stranger.

Date. The fact Cade was a stranger made it impossible to deny this was, in fact, a date and not simply catching up over coffee. Emily felt a grin coming on. She didn't want to deny it. She couldn't remember the last time she'd been on a date she'd actually enjoyed, and she had a good feeling about this one. Well, she'd had a good feeling, but it looked like Cade had decided not to show.

"You must love the cold."

Emily whirled at the familiar sound of Cade's voice and sucked in a breath at the sight of her. Cade was bundled up in a black pea coat, her face ruddy from the chilly night air. "And you must be invisible. I didn't see you drive in."

Cade waved her hand vaguely behind her. "I parked back there." She rubbed her hands together. "Are we going inside?"

Emily pulled her gaze from Cade's long, tapered fingers. "Yes, and soon before no amount of coffee will warm us up." She motioned for Cade to follow, and she pushed through the doors of the hotel, nodding to the bell captain who doubled as the concierge.

"Good evening, Miss Sinclair."

"Good evening, Ralph. I called Miss Holt and let her know I'd be coming by this evening."

"She's expecting you. And your acquaintance." Ralph gave Cade an appraising glance. "You can head on back."

Tongues would wag for sure. Emily trusted Becca implicitly, but Ralph, dear as he was, was a talker. She imagined tomorrow she'd be hearing rumors about how that young girl DA was running around town with a perfect stranger, but right now all she cared about was delivering on her promise. She glanced back at Cade who was looking between her and Ralph, her expression full of questions. "This way."

Cade followed her down the hall, past the restaurant, around the corner to an unmarked door. Emily rapped on the door with three quick knocks. She waited a few beats and repeated the sequence. She'd barely finished the last knock when the door flew open and Becca pulled her into a tight hug.

"'Bout time you came by," Becca said. "I figured now that you're a big deal, you don't have time for me anymore." She released her grip and turned her focus to Cade. "Becca Holt, pleased to meet you."

Cade stuck out a hand, and Emily watched her best friend and this woman she barely knew exchange introductions. The Bodark Inn was a Holt family business, and Becca had been running the restaurant since her mom and dad retired several years before. The food was great, but Emily's favorite thing about the place was the semi-secret coffee shop in the back. When Becca had taken over management, she'd insisted on upgrading the java offerings at the restaurant. She'd purchased a fancy commercial espresso machine and a coffee roaster, and added a number of fancy coffee drinks to the menu. For her special friends, she'd created a counter and small lounge just off the kitchen where folks in the know could order her special blend even when the restaurant had closed for the night.

"So you're the secret coffee mistress?" Cade said as she shook Becca's hand.

"Guilty as charged. I won't tell you how many times a day Emily visits my humble establishment, but let's just say she bought the better part of my new boat."

Emily playfully punched Becca's shoulder. "Don't be a goof. I may drink a lot of coffee, but someone had to pay for that fancy roaster in the back."

"You roast your own coffee beans?" Cade asked, her tone incredulous.

Becca grinned. "Is there any other way?"

"I guess I just didn't expect…I mean…"

"Let me guess. You're not used to living in the sticks, and you assumed we all brew whatever's been sitting in a can on a grocery store shelf. Am I right?"

It was Cade's turn to grin. "Something like that."

"Then I have a treat for you. Why don't you two settle in and I'll be right back."

Becca didn't wait for an answer before she shot through the double doors to the kitchen, leaving them standing in her wake. Emily turned to Cade. "She's a pistol."

"I like her."

Emily scoured Cade's face for anything resembling infatuation. She'd known Becca since high school and they had a habit of attracting the same type. She hoped she hadn't brought Cade here only to have her fall head over heels for her best friend. "I'm sure she'll put you on the list if you ask. Ralph keeps a close watch on the doors so you've got to be a friend of Becca's to get back here."

Cade stepped close. "Are you trying to pawn me off on your friend?"

"Not even."

"How about this? If I want good coffee in the future, I'll call you. Does that work?"

"Perfectly."

Cade raised her hand and slid a finger along the lapel of Emily's coat. "Are you warm enough now?"

"What?" Emily heard the stutter in her voice. Warm enough? Hell, she was on fire.

"Can I take your coat?"

Emily felt the slow burn of a blush along her neck and face. Of course, her coat. Cade was being sweet, and all she could think about was Cade's hands, close, but not quite close enough. She shrugged out of her coat and handed it to Cade who hung it along with hers on the coat tree in the corner. Cade motioned to the couch. "So, what's the protocol here? Do we just wait for Becca to come back or will she ring a bell or something?"

"It varies. Sometimes, she has someone else from the kitchen deliver the drinks, but I have a feeling she's going to do the honors all on her own tonight." Emily chided herself for the tinge of jealousy she harbored and quickly changed the subject. "So, you're a librarian?"

A beat passed and Emily could swear she saw a slight jerk from Cade, but then she set her jaw and answered simply. "Yes. Yes, I am."

"That seems interesting."

"Said no one ever." Cade flashed a brilliant smile. "Sorry, occupational hazard—making fun of the job before anyone else can."

"I can beat you at that game. I know all the best lawyer jokes. Steals everyone's thunder, but it's more fun to give than receive," Emily said. "I was actually serious when I said your job must be interesting." She leaned in close and whispered. "All those books. Dreamy." She placed the back of her hand to her forehead and mock swooned until a sharp clap practically had her jumping out of her seat. "What the hell?" She turned to see Becca standing in front of them with an amused smiled on her face.

"You okay, sweetie?" Becca asked, her tone syrupy sweet. "You look ill."

"I will be when you hand over the steaming cups of heaven on that tray."

Becca handed them each a cup along with a small pitcher of cream and a bowl of raw sugar. Emily watched as Cade ignored the condiments and raised the mug to her lips, ignoring the heat to take a healthy sip.

"Oh my God, I haven't had coffee like this since…" Cade's words trailed off into another sip and she veered in a different direction. "Guatemalan?" she asked. Becca nodded, her face bursting with pride, and Cade raised her mug in a toast. "It's amazing. Subtle spice with a touch of cocoa on the finish. Perfection."

Becca punched Emily on the shoulder. "See, this is a true java connoisseur. Where have you been hiding her?"

Emily noticed Cade's eyes narrow at the question, and she wondered what Cade had been about to say a moment ago. If Becca weren't there, she'd simply ask, but she wasn't ready to share the mystery of Cade Kelly with anyone else yet.

Like a mind reader, Becca announced she had a pressing matter to attend to in the kitchen. "I'll leave the press. Help yourselves to more." She gave Cade's shoulder a squeeze. "Come back anytime." Emily caught her sly smile as she left the room. Luckily, she knew Becca had a wonderful woman waiting at home, or she would have called her out for flirting with her date.

"She's nice," Cade said.

"She's an incorrigible flirt. Using her mad barista skills to woo women everywhere."

"Did you just say 'woo'?"

"I did. Would you like a definition?"

"Oh, I know the word. I'm just not sure I've heard it used in casual conversation. Or any conversation for that matter."

"You've been conversing with the wrong folks is all I have to say on the subject."

"That may be true. I'll have to remedy that."

"She's married."

"Wow. First you're using fancy throwback vocabulary. Now, you're queen of the non sequitur. What's next?"

"Sorry. I just didn't want you to get the wrong idea about Becca. She comes on strong with the coffee, but it's all steam and no substance."

"I'm not interested in Becca." Cade winced. "I mean, I'm sure she's wonderful, even above and beyond her coffee magic, but I came here because you asked me."

Emily took a sip of coffee to hide her grin, but she couldn't help savoring the sweet satisfaction of knowing Cade was interested in her and not her gorgeous, culinary magic friend. Happy with this newfound fact, she settled back into the couch and relaxed. "So, now that I've shared with you my favorite secret place in all of Bodark, it's your turn to tell me something about you."

Cade hesitated for a moment, her face barely betraying a slight frown, and Emily resisted the urge to fill the uncomfortable silence with her own words. Then Cade cleared her throat and offered one of her brilliant smiles. "Well, I love coffee, but I guess that secret's already out of the bag."

"Seriously."

"Oh, now we're being serious. Okay, well, I'm developing a growing fondness for small towns."

"Is that so?"

"It is indeed."

"And why is that?"

"I suppose it's because of all the secret gems they have, waiting to be found."

"The coffee."

"Not just the coffee."

Cade met her gaze and Emily saw genuine interest, but she sensed there was something more. Cade had secrets and she was adept at skirting over anything that got too personal, which made Emily all the more interested in digging deeper. Before she could consider how far she wanted to go this time, her phone buzzed. "Sorry, always on call." She glanced at the screen and read the text from Seth.

Sheriff called. Shooting in Rymer. Needs us to draft a warrant. Can you call him?

Damn. Of course, the one night she'd decided not to work since she'd taken office and there's a shooting. Emily instantly regretted the thought. Whoever had gotten shot was having a way worse night than she was. She looked up at Cade who was watching her intently like she could sense something was up, and she realized that for the first time in a long time, Emily didn't want work to come first. At least not tonight.

She could call one of the other attorneys in the office, but a shooting wasn't an everyday event in their small county. She'd just as soon handle it herself. Besides, it would be a good opportunity to show Sheriff Nash she had the chops for the top job.

The expression on her face must have given her away because Cade said, "Let me guess. You have to go."

"I do."

"Work or pleasure?"

"Excuse me?"

Cade held up the French press. "If you're leaving because you have to work, then you might need to take the rest of this coffee with you. If you're leaving to meet your second date of the evening, then I think I'll just keep it for myself."

"You're pretty funny."

"Don't meet many funny people in your line of work, do you?"

"Funny peculiar, but not funny ha ha." Emily violated her no PDA on the first date rule and reached for Cade's hand, pleased at the strong grip from her smooth fingers. "How about a rain check for the remainder of this evening?"

"Sure." Cade pushed up from the sofa and Emily watched, reluctantly as their hands slipped apart.

"Do you think Becca has to-go cups back there?" Cade asked, already headed toward the kitchen.

Was it her imagination or had the atmosphere shifted from intensely personal to super casual in the span of a few minutes? Emily shook away the regret. She'd made the right decision about leaving, and she wasn't going to rehash her choice. As handsome and mysterious as Cade might be, she was a passing fantasy. Fun for the evening, but she'd likely never see her again. Unlike her work, which occupied her every waking moment.

She stood. Time to pay attention to the mistress she'd chosen for at least the next four years.

❖

Cade pulled into her driveway and slammed on the brakes, narrowly missing the form standing in front of the rising garage door. She jammed the car into park and jumped out to confront the intruder. "What the hell?"

"I'm sorry," the woman said. "I rang the doorbell, but no one answered, and then I heard your car coming down the street so I decided to wait here. I live across the street. Mavis. Mavis Percy. I didn't mean to startle you."

Cade looked down at the woman, who looked thoroughly shaken at her nosy neighbor routine gone awry. Mavis was holding a medium-sized box in one hand and what appeared to be a bread pan in the other. Despite the cool weather, she wasn't wearing a coat, and her out of style housedress made her look completely harmless. Cade decided to take pity on her if only to get this encounter over with as quickly as possible. "Sorry, I didn't mean to nearly run you over. Did you need something?"

"What? Oh, yes." Mavis thrust the bread pan toward her. "I knocked on your door to deliver some of my fresh baked banana bread." Next came the box. "And I found this on your doorstep, and I didn't want anyone to steal it."

Cade stood holding the banana bread, but she only stared at the box. It was brown with no visible markings other than her handwritten address. She hadn't ordered anything she could remember, and she had alerts set up on her phone to tell her if a package from UPS or FedEx landed at her door. "I don't think that's mine," was all she could think of to say.

Mavis laughed. "Of course it's yours. Why else would it be on your front porch?"

Cade watched her set the box on the hood of her car. All she could think about was how she could get Mavis to scram so she could call Kennedy and report the suspicious package, but Mavis wasn't going so easily.

"The banana bread is best heated. About ten seconds in the microwave, and then top it with a touch of butter. Not margarine. Use the real stuff. It's better for you, more natural…"

Cade snapped out of her trance. She'd heard enough. She could be neighborly later when she wasn't preoccupied with the crazy, but possibly real threat the mysterious box imposed. "Ten seconds, butter, got it." She picked up the box and held it at an arm's length, like a spider she planned to evict from her home.

"Maybe we can talk another time," Cade said. "I'm really tired, and I'm going to call it a night. Thanks so much." She didn't wait for an answer before walking into the garage and hitting the button to activate the door. She'd pull her car in later when the street was clear of prying eyes. As the front door lowered, she caught a glimpse of Mavis standing in the driveway, empty-handed and seemingly bewildered about her encounter with her new neighbor.

Inside the house, Cade set the box on the kitchen table and walked a few paces away, the banana bread still in her other hand. She wanted to open the package, but if it was a threat of some kind, she didn't want to risk compromising evidence. She hated to call Kennedy, but she didn't know what else to do short of calling the local cops, which would involve cooking up some story to explain her suspicions.

Kennedy answered on the first ring and said she'd be there in fifteen minutes. The first five felt like hours, so Cade settled in with two fingers of a new brand of whisky one of the hipsters at the library had told her about. The amber liquid bit at first taste, but burned its way into a smooth finish, calming her jangled nerves.

What a crazy night. She'd never imagined when she agreed to work the event she'd wind up in a kind of coffee speakeasy with the hot new DA. The moment the panel had started, Emily Sinclair had captured her attention, from the way she held her own with the egos on the rest of the panel to her fun, impulsive side. When Emily got the late night work call, Cade had wanted to tell her that she understood. That she'd gotten lots of similar calls over the years. That she'd had to leave many dates in the lurch for the demands of the job. But she couldn't say anything like that because she was a librarian, not a lawyer. Reference desk emergencies would certainly never merit interrupting a Friday night date.

Emily's abrupt departure with no certain plan for when they would see each other again was for the best. Their chemistry was off the charts, but Cade knew it would never amount to anything since there was way too much she couldn't share. Fontana had robbed her of so many things. The only way she could keep him from continuing to take was to stop wanting, stop needing, and be content with the solitary life she'd carved out for herself. She could accept an occasional neighborly gesture, but anything else was too much risk.

A sharp knock at the door pulled Cade out of her funk, and she rose to let Kennedy in.

"Show me the package."

"No, hey, nice to see you? I mean it's been since this morning."

"I figured you were worried about this or you wouldn't have called me late on a Friday night. Where is it?"

Cade led her to the kitchen and pointed. While Kennedy studied the box, Cade considered how little she knew about the woman assigned to keep her safe. Did she have a husband, a wife? Where did she live—in town or out in the country? She'd gotten here quickly. Was it because she was driving nearby or did she live only a few blocks away?

Hell, she was as bad as Mavis, but she couldn't help but be curious. If she couldn't have a life of her own, she'd have to settle for living vicariously. Definitely not through the lives of the students who came through the library. She felt old just listening to their tales of all-nighters and last-minute term papers. She barely knew her coworkers.

Did Emily have a life?

The question crept up on her, but she followed its trail. Emily wasn't married, she knew that much from the TV coverage of her election, and she would've been disappointed to find out otherwise considering their date this evening. But she knew virtually nothing else about her. Making a mental note to spend some time with Google after Kennedy left, she turned her attention back to the ominous box in time to see Kennedy holding the box with a gloved hand while using her other hand to slice through the packing tape with a pocketknife.

"What are you doing?"

Kennedy didn't look up. "Finding out what's inside."

"Well, I could have done that. I guess I thought you might have something a little more sophisticated in mind."

"Closest place to get a look inside is Dallas. I'm thinking this is something innocuous, but if it isn't, I imagine I'll know here in a sec, and then I can hop in the car and start the drive." She bent back the cardboard and peered inside. "Pears."

"What?"

"Fruit." Kennedy pulled a piece of paper out of the box, and Cade watched her read the scrawled lines before handing it over.

Mark, I remember how much you liked these last year. I'm sorry I missed you on this trip, but I'll be back around Thanksgiving and maybe we can catch up then. Call me sometime. Nancy.

"Well, these obviously weren't for me."

Kennedy rubbed one of the pears on her shirtsleeve and took a bite. "Too bad. They're pretty tasty."

Cade grabbed the box. "They're not for you either."

"The guy who used to live here got transferred to Cairo. Pretty sure these pears aren't going to last much longer. You may as well enjoy them."

Cade studied the note, wondering who Nancy was to the man who used to live in this house. An old girlfriend? A business associate? Whoever she was, she didn't rate notice from Mark that he was leaving the country. The thought bubbled up memories of all the people she'd left behind with no notice, no explanation, and she released her grip on the paper in her hand and let it drift onto the tabletop. "Sorry for the false alarm."

"You did the right thing." Kennedy sat down at the table, her eyes on the remaining pears. "So, you just got home?"

Cade joined her at the table and pushed the box her way. "Take them all. Unlike you and Nancy's friend who moved to Cairo, I'm not a big fan."

"Are you avoiding my question?"

"Maybe. Do I have to tell you everything about where I go and who I'm with?"

Kennedy shrugged. "No, but if you've finally started venturing out into the world beyond this house and work, it might be a good idea for me to run a quick check on whoever you're spending time with just for peace of mind."

Cade sighed. She could try to forget it all she wanted, but until Fontana was arrested and tried, Kennedy's overbearing ways, while annoying, were a necessity she'd have to accept. "I stayed late to help out with a panel on criminal justice. They needed someone to introduce the moderator and make sure things stayed on track."

"The criminal justice thing? I saw a sign for that this morning." Kennedy looked at her watch. "Thought it wrapped up a while ago."

"I went out for coffee with some people after."

"People from work?"

Cade hesitated, unsure why she was reticent to share that she'd spent the rest of the evening with Emily Sinclair. She had no doubt Emily would meet Kennedy's criteria for persons deemed safe to be with, but a nagging feeling cautioned her not to share, so she lied to Kennedy for the first time since they'd met. "Yes. See, I'm still the same old boring person you've come to know."

Kennedy studied her face for a moment, and she did her best to maintain steady eye contact, willing her not to push for more detail. She'd barely had time to process her own feelings about her cut-short-too-soon, quasi-date with Emily, and the last thing she wanted was to have Kennedy pick it apart.

CHAPTER EIGHT

Emily burst through the doors of the county jail and walked to the deputy at the night desk. “Hi, Randall, is the sheriff back from the scene yet?”

Randall Jacoby hastily minimized the game of Tetris on his computer and moved papers around on his desk in a poor attempt at appearing busy. Emily knew better. She and Randall had attended high school together, and she’d never seen him work hard at anything in his life, which was why he was stuck here at the station instead of out doing actual police work. “No, Em. I mean, he’s on his way back, but he’s not here yet.”

“I’m here to pick up the information for the warrant. He said he was sending someone back with a preliminary report. Do you have it?”

“Uh, well…” Randall’s ears blushed red and he wasn’t making eye contact as he fidgeted around for something to say.

“I know you were expecting Seth, but he’s not here. I am.” Emily had grown accustomed to the deputies deferring to any man over her, but it was time they got used to having a woman in charge. She held out her hand. “So, let’s have the report.” She watched the torn emotions play out across his face for a few seconds before he finally reached into the desk, pulled out an envelope, and handed it over. “They emailed some info and I printed it out.”

She pulled open the envelope and looked at the contents. The information was pretty darn thorough for being done on the fly. It detailed what the responding officer had found at the crime scene. An older man, dead outside his home, and a neighbor who’d seen a guy he recognized from one of the dilapidated housing units on the outskirts of town running from the house. The sheriff wanted an arrest warrant for the guy, and a search warrant for his apartment, but he hadn't quite included enough information for her to convince a judge.

"Do you know if someone has gone to the apartment complex to try to talk to this guy?" she asked.

Randall shrugged. "Doubt it would do any good. He was running off, after all. Doubt he went running to where someone would find him."

"I need a name, an apartment number, something before I can convince Judge Latham to issue a warrant." Emily used her best authoritative voice, but she knew that wasn't quite true. Latham, the judge on call, would issue a warrant with only a couple of vague allegations written on the back of a gum wrapper, but his helpfulness up front never paid off. He'd been overturned on appeal too many times to count, and she'd rather have an arrest and conviction that held up for the long haul than a quick arrest that led nowhere. She stared Randall down, hoping he had more information than what he'd shared so far, but his gaze was fixed on something behind her shoulder. She looked back to see Sheriff Nash walking in the door with a crowd of other folks, one of whom was in handcuffs.

"Hey, counselor," he called out. "Sorry to bother you. We've already got most of what we need. You can go back to your Friday night fun, and we'll take it from here."

She strode over and assessed the situation, certain the ragged-looking, handcuffed man in the center of the huddle was the murder suspect. "I think I'll stay. I don't have anything more important to do than serve the citizens of Lawson County."

"Suit yourself." He turned to his deputies. "Take him back and I'll see you in a minute." He waited until they'd shuffled the suspect out of the room, and then motioned her to follow him to his office.

Emily crossed the threshold and surveyed his kingdom. The wall behind his desk was a collage of photos featuring Nash glad-handing with notable figures in the county from businessmen to legislators. It only took a few seconds to find the photo-op with her father.

He tracked her gaze and said, "He was a big supporter of my campaign. The man knows his business."

"Well, he was a big supporter of my campaign too, so I guess that's right."

He chuckled. "Fair enough." He leaned back in his chair. "I'm sure you'll do a great job once this case gets handed over to you, but we've got this tonight. You can go on home and get some rest."

Emily resisted the urge to snap at his patronizing tone. "What about the warrant?"

"Don't need it anymore. The suspect consented to a search."

She pictured the man they'd just brought in. Bloody and disheveled. Had he looked that way when they found him, or had he wound up that way after the sheriff had extracted his consent? "Are you booking him?"

"We are. Murder. It's a clean case. He confessed in the car, and we're about to get it on tape so you can tie this case up with a pretty bow." He pushed back from his desk and stood as if the matter was closed.

It wasn't. "Who's the victim?"

"Some guy who works at the college. Found his work ID along with his driver's license. Guy was killed in his own driveway."

"So, this wasn't a robbery gone bad?"

"Excuse me?"

"It sounds like you found his wallet. Was it on him or somewhere else?"

He fixed her with a cold stare, but she didn't back down. The silence was a tug-of-war, but she won when he finally spoke. "Found it nearby, but no cash. Perp probably ditched it when he realized he'd been caught." He took a step toward the door. "I'll send you a final report after we've finished questioning him."

"I think I'll stay and watch if it's all the same to you."

"Your call, counselor."

Despite his words, his expression told her he wasn't happy, which made her all the more convinced her decision to stick around was the right one. She followed him out of his office and through a back hallway that led to the jail. She'd been back here plenty of times in the past, interviewing witnesses, hashing out deals with defendants, but it felt different this time since she would be in charge of every aspect of this case. "I read the preliminary report you sent over. How did you manage to locate your suspect?"

He shot a hooded glance over his shoulder, and she could almost hear his brain clicking out a devised response. "I have a good team. I'm sure you know our closed case rate is the highest in the state."

She didn't bother stating the obvious. How hard could it be to close cases when most of the crime was petty stuff that didn't involve a ton of mystery? He pressed on, apparently presuming his answer was good enough, but she wasn't about to be mollified. "I'm well acquainted with the good work your team does, but I'm going to need something a little more specific to present to the grand jury when the time comes. The report I read said the murder suspect took off. Where did he turn up?"

"Everyone eventually comes home, and this guy did too. It was easy really. We nabbed him the minute he walked in the door." He stopped in front of a large metal door. "You okay watching through the glass?"

"Yes." Emily followed him into the room that was split into two sections: one for observation and one for interrogation. She could see the suspect through the glass. He was ragged and unkempt, but he seemed fairly docile for someone who'd just been arrested for murder.

"Let Randall know if you need anything," Nash said as he walked into the room where the guy sat waiting. Emily watched him take the cuffs off of the prisoner and ask him if he wanted something to eat or drink. She knew the acts weren't out of kindness. No one confessed on an empty stomach. Suspects were much more malleable if they were comfortable. The man asked for a Sprite and a hamburger, and the Sheriff barked the order to one of his deputies while Emily idly wondered how far he was going to have to drive to find a hamburger this late at night. There was a Dairy Queen out on the highway, but they generally only stayed open late during football season.

The next few minutes were spent with Nash tossing the suspect softball questions. What was his full name? Kevin Miller. How long had he lived in Rymer? A while. What did he do for a living? Between jobs. Nash's tone was friendly and engaging, and like the food that would come later, was designed to soften up the suspect and keep him from delivering well-prepared answers to the harder questions that were to come.

Randall walked in with a can of Sprite and walked past her to deliver it into the interrogation room. She listened as he explained they were working on the hamburger. Miller drank deeply from the can and wiped his lips with the back of his hand.

"That taste good?" Nash asked.

"Did the trick."

"Glad to hear it." Sheriff drummed on the table with his fingers. "You know why you're here, right?"

"Not hardly. Your guys chased me through the creek behind the old Johnson place. I wasn't doing anything."

"Pretty late to be mucking around in a swamp."

"Best time of night to get bait. I sell it down at Barney's. He pays two bucks for a dozen shiners. Good money, if you can get it."

"You hard up for money?"

"Hard times, man."

"What did you do with the money you took from Sam Wade's wallet?"

The man shifted in his seat, his eyes darting around the room. "I don't know who that is."

Emily made a note he didn't address the money issue. Strike one.

For the next hour, Nash conducted a traditional soft interrogation, leading the suspect through a series of questions, tiptoeing around the issue, going back and forth over the same ground, as he locked him into the details of his story. It didn't take long for Emily to grow bored with the repetition, and she wished she had another cup of Becca's coffee.

The thought conjured up an image of Cade relaxing on the sofa in Becca's lounge. What was she doing right now? Was she asleep or was she up late too? Was she a bookworm or a late night TV watcher? Emily cursed her phone and Seth for choosing tonight to meet his in-laws. If he'd gotten the call, who knows where her date might have led.

Emily shook away the fantasy. Even if Seth had been in town she would've wanted to be part of this investigation from the beginning, including all the boring parts. She remembered only two other murder cases in Lawson County in all the years she'd worked at the DA's office. Crime-free neighborhoods had been one of the tenets of her campaign, but she couldn't deny the surge of adrenaline at the prospect of a juicy trial. If Miller elected to go to trial, it would be the perfect showcase to let her constituents know she was the right person for the job, which meant her job had to be her main priority. Any designs she had on Cade Kelly would have to wait.

❖

Cade sipped coffee from the mug she'd purchased at the university bookstore and frowned at the bitter brew. She'd have to get her hands on some of Becca's special roast now that she was too spoiled for the community pot in the staff lunchroom.

The very act of drinking coffee reminded her of the night before. Emily had surprised her. Yes, Bodark was a small town, but she hadn't expected the elected DA to be so down to earth, so approachable. Emily was completely at ease with the power of her position, unlike Sheriff Nash who swung his badge around like a sword, and was a lot like the state's attorney in Cook County. Her former boss, Dunkirk, had been an absolute dick when the feds stepped in to take the Oliveri case away from him, despite the fact that her being shot meant the entire office had a conflict of interest in pursuing the case.

She wondered what Dunkirk would think if he knew she was in witness protection. The marshals service hadn't wanted her to have contact with anyone at her old office on the off chance someone there might have been involved in leaking Biermann's arrangements for getting to and from the courthouse during his grand jury appearances. At their request, she'd drafted a brief letter of resignation, stating simply that she was pursuing other interests, and the marshals had arranged for it to be delivered on her behalf. If Dunkirk knew the truth, he'd probably be pissed off he hadn't been kept in the loop. If she ever had to go back and testify, one of the conditions she'd set with the feds had been to make sure she didn't have to deal with him.

"I didn't expect to see you here today."

Cade looked up to see her boss, Monica, standing in the doorway. "If I said I came in for the free coffee, would you believe me?"

"Not a chance."

"Fair enough. I came in to catch up on a project for Professor Sorenson. She's in a rush to finish her paper, and I promised I'd locate a few source materials she needs for the final section."

Monica cocked her head, like she only half believed the story, and Cade had to credit her instincts. Sorenson did need the source materials, but Cade had come in to work mostly to avoid the lonely void of her house. The time spent in Emily's company last night seemed to have ruined her usual love of solitude and, for the first time since she'd left Chicago, she was happy to be surrounded by other bodies, other voices.

"How did the panel go?"

Adding mind reader to the list of Monica's many qualities, Cade answered, "Fine. There was a pretty good sized crowd and a vigorous debate."

"I guess it was a pretty long night for Ms. Sinclair and the sheriff."

Cade's face must have shown her puzzlement, because Monica asked, "Didn't you see the morning paper?"

"No, why?" She'd read the news for the first few weeks after she moved here, but found it to be a glorified list of county gossip, and she'd abandoned it for an online subscription to the *Dallas Morning News*.

"The sheriff arrested a guy last night for a murder over in Rymer. The paper didn't have a ton of information, but they did confirm it was a shooting. They haven't released the name of the victim yet, because his family hasn't been notified."

"That's horrible." The mention of a shooting was enough to spike the anxiety she'd been keeping at bay. She drummed her fingers on the table debating whether more detail would be comforting or disconcerting. So that was the reason for Emily's sudden departure last night. If she were to call Emily and ask for details, would she share? Probably not, but she could call to say she'd heard about the shooting and let Emily know if she wanted to talk, she was available.

No. That kind of offer seemed too personal, especially considering they barely knew each other. If she wanted to see Emily, she'd have to be direct. In her old life, she never would've hesitated to go after what she wanted. She would've picked up the phone, called Emily, and said, "I enjoyed the time we spent together, but it wasn't enough. When can I see you again?"

But now she worried more about the reception than the delivery. Would overconfidence chase Emily away? Did it matter either way since overconfidence seemed to have left the building?

If Emily was interested, she'd call, and if she wasn't, then Cade was probably better off on her own. The trick was defining what *on her own* meant. She'd enjoyed the friendly banter with Emily and Becca last night, and even if she wasn't ready to tackle dating, it felt funny to go back to hermit status. Maybe she was ready to wade, slowly, into the waters of a social life. She could start with something simple, see how it went.

"Hey, Monica," she said, "What do people do around here for fun?"

Chapter Nine

Emily slapped her nightstand with the palm of her hand several times to no avail before she realized it was a ringing phone, not her alarm clock interrupting her hard-fought sleep. Through half-lidded eyes, she recognized her brother's number on the screen and answered the call. "You better have a really good reason for calling so early on a Sunday morning."

"Why? Am I ruining your beauty sleep? Besides, your clock must be broken if you think it's early."

Emily glanced at the clock. It was eight thirty. She must've forgotten to set her alarm. If she didn't hustle, she'd be late for the ten o'clock services at the First United Methodist Church, an unforgivable offense, at least as far as her father and many of her constituents were concerned. She jumped out of bed and padded her way to the kitchen. "I'm getting ready now," she lied. "What do you need?"

"Sierra wanted to know if she could snag a few minutes with you before lunch today."

"And she couldn't ask me herself?" Emily shifted the phone to her other ear and pinned it between her chin and shoulder while she put a pot of water on to boil for the coffee she desperately needed. She and her sister-in-law had a good relationship despite the fact they had virtually nothing in common. Sierra likely hadn't worked a day in her life, choosing to leverage her upbringing in a prominent family for positions on charitable boards instead of career advancement.

"She's getting the kids ready for church, so I said I'd call." His voice dropped to a whisper. "Don't tell her I told you, but she plans to ask you to help out a woman she met through the church food pantry. Something about a shoplifting arrest that's keeping her from getting work. All I know is Sierra doesn't want to discuss it in front of the Committee."

Emily laughed at the reference. Since high school, she and Travis had referred to their parents and much older brother and his wife as the Committee. The Committee approved all big family decisions, monitored social mores, and generally served as the gatekeeper for anything associated with the Sinclair name. Although Travis aspired to Committee status, she'd never really cared for the baggage that came along with it, and she'd learned plenty of tricks to avoid their scrutiny. "Sure. Tell Sierra to catch a ride with me after church and we can talk in the car. If anyone asks, tell them she's trying to talk me into speaking at a luncheon or something."

"Good plan. Don't be late for church."

He hung up before she could respond, which was just as well because if she didn't get a move on she'd be late for sure. She set her phone on the counter and poured hot water into her French press over some of Becca's special brew. She'd need a double dose this morning. She'd spent her entire Saturday trying to clear her desk in preparation for the new murder case that had landed in her lap, including a long meeting with Seth to bring him up to speed. Seth had apologized profusely for not being around on Friday, but she'd waved off his apology. She'd actually started to embrace the fact she was going to make good on her campaign promise within the first quarter of her time in office. As soon as she did the obligatory church and then family brunch at the club, she'd head back to the office to start preparing the case.

The coffee was perfect, but it reminded her of Cade. Was she enjoying a leisurely Sunday morning, or was she up and getting ready to satisfy family obligations? Did she work on the weekends? Emily allowed herself a few moments to muse. Maybe she could concoct a reason to make a trip to the library later today.

She shook away the thought. She barely had time for Sunday rituals with her family, let alone time to chase a woman she barely knew. Besides, if Cade was working, she had no business disturbing her. Out of the corner of her eye, she caught sight of her laptop, sitting on the table near her bed. A few simple strokes would likely reveal Cade's home address and some relevant background. She took a couple of steps toward the computer before stopping herself.

No. She wasn't going to use the resources of her office to dig up information on potential dates. Doing so seemed seedy. And useless. Cade Kelly might have a perfect pedigree and live in the best part of town, but it didn't matter right now. She needed to focus on the job, and later, when things settled down, she could meet someone to date. If Cade Kelly was around then, she'd give it a go, but pursuing her now was disingenuous, at best.

She downed her now cool coffee and zoomed through a shower. A midnight blue sweater dress hugged her form, but not too much for the church-going crowd, and she raced out the door. When she arrived at church, her family was already seated in the front two rows, and she joined them just as the organist started playing the opening chords to the processional. Ignoring her mother's pointed look, she rose with the crowd and buried her head in a hymnal. One day she would show up here with a woman on her arm, merging her new family with the traditions of her current one, but for now, this was her life and she would make the most of it.

❖

Cade sorted through the clothes in her closet, but it didn't take long to determine she had nothing appropriate to wear to play tennis at a country club, even if said club was located out here in the sticks. When she'd received Monica's message last night inviting her to fill in for a foursome at the local country club, her new resolution to be more social prompted her to say yes, but her survey of the closet left her skeptical.

The marshals who had smuggled her out of the hospital in Chicago had been tasked with arranging for her personal belongings to be moved to Texas. Figuring she'd start fresh, she'd made a list of essentials and directed the rest to be donated to charity. Tennis whites hadn't made the cut, and she finally settled on Nikes, a pair of khakis, and a vintage track jacket she'd found on one of her forays to the Goodwill near the college.

She surveyed her image in the mirror. Dressed like this, she was more likely to be mistaken for someone who worked at the country club than a member, but she didn't look bad. Apparently, Monica wasn't a member either, but their opponents were, and Monica said she joined them as a guest to play there often.

Funny. Monica didn't know a thing about her other than the half-truths in her personnel file, but on her first invitation outside of work she'd landed on one of Cade's favorite pastimes. From her past life, anyway. When she was growing up, her parents' Winnetka country club had been like a second home, and she'd played games of tennis on clay courts the way some kids played pickup ball on dirt lots, even earning a scholarship to play as an undergrad. She hadn't played in a while since her salary as a state's attorney hadn't afforded her the luxury of membership, and the long hours meant she had to find less time-consuming ways to burn energy, but she was excited to revisit the sport.

The drive over was short, and she was pleasantly surprised to find a fairly large brick building with a valet. Monica had kept her promise, and she was waiting outside the front door, holding two racquets and a duffel bag.

"I'd about decided you were going to bail on us," Monica said.

"No chance." Cade waved at her attire. "I was searching through my closet for the closest thing to tennis whites I could find." She grinned. "I might have come up a little short, so if I'm not suitably dressed for this place, tell me now."

"Hell, I don't care. I doubt anyone else will either. It's not like it's the Ritz or anything."

"Is the pro shop open?"

"Save your money. Everything in there costs double what you'd pay in the real world. You look fine. Besides, I'm sure everyone will go easy on you since it's your first time."

Cade bit back a smart remark. The temptation to relax and enjoy herself was great, but she would do well to be careful. An assistant librarian didn't buy clothes at the country club pro shop. Little mistakes built up to bigger ones. "Where's everyone else?"

"Inside. Come on."

Monica led the way through the doors of the club, and Cade followed her down a long hallway lined with trophy cases. Tennis, golf, skeet shooting—all the privileged sports were represented. When they reached the end of the hallway, they were standing at the opening of a large dining room. Monica waved to a woman across the room, dressed for tennis, who smiled and waved back. Cade watched as the woman turned, and she realized it was Becca, the coffee savior from Friday night.

Cade waved and Becca waved back, but then she shook the shoulder of a woman seated at the table, and motioned for her to look across the room. Emily Sinclair turned in her seat and their eyes locked.

Small freaking world. She'd gone two months living here without running into Emily Sinclair, and now she seemed destined to see her at every turn. Of course she was at a country club. From everything Cade had managed to find out through the wonders of Google, the Sinclairs were the first family of Bodark. Her father was a US Senator. A quick glance at the rest of the members of the table told her that was probably him, engaged in lively conversation with his socialite wife to his left. Emily's brothers and their families rounded out the bunch. Suddenly, she cared very much that she didn't fit in here, and she wished she could melt into the parquet floor.

She didn't melt, but she was paralyzed in place as she watched Emily stand up and walk toward her. The rest of the room fell away, and only Emily filled her vision. A midnight blue sweater dress and tall black suede boots showcased her fantastic figure. Her auburn hair flipped in sexy waves around her face and her full lips were fixed in a bright smile. But as she drew closer, Cade noticed her eyes reflected exhaustion and stress. Something was troubling her. She only had a few seconds to wonder what it might be before Emily was standing directly in front of her. She cast about for what to say, but Emily beat her to the punch.

"Cade Kelly," she said, her voice smooth like silk. "So you're the mysterious stranger who's rounding out the tennis set. I have to warn you, Becca's a sore loser. Beat her and you risk being frozen out of the underground coffee supply."

"I love a challenge."

"You must."

Emily punctuated her remark with a gentle brush of her hand against her arm. Cade wanted to lean into the touch, to offer a witty retort, anything to continue the gentle flirtation, but the sound of a clearing throat reminded her they weren't alone. She turned to see Becca and Monica. Becca wore an indulgent smile, but Monica looked puzzled.

"You two know each other?" she asked.

"We met at the panel Friday night," Cade explained.

"Actually, we met before then." Emily corrected her. "A few weeks ago, I found Cade here wandering the streets looking for coffee, but I wasn't entirely certain she was worthy of our underground supply until Friday."

Cade looked at Monica. "So, you knew about Becca's coffee bar, but you didn't tell me?"

"Sorry, pal, but it looks like you had all the help you needed."

Cade followed her glance. Emily's hand was no longer on her arm, but she was standing close. In your personal space close. Close enough for Cade to drink in the scent of lavender from her hair, and for a brief moment, she imagined those lovely waves fanned out on her chest. Holy shit. She needed to get a handle on her emotions right now or she was going to make a fool of herself. She turned to Becca. "Who's the fourth?"

"My sister, Laura. She's in the locker room, changing. Come on, I'll show you the way."

Cade started to say she hadn't brought anything else to wear, but Monica saved her. "Cade came ready to play. She says she doesn't need tennis whites to whip your butt on the court, and that's why she's my partner today." She stuck out her tongue at Becca, and Cade shot her a thank you smile.

"Big talk," Becca said as she grabbed Monica's arm and pointed to a door at the west side of the room. "Cade, we're headed over there. Meet us in five minutes or lose by forfeit."

Cade watched them walk away, acutely conscious of the fact Becca had set things up to give her a few minutes alone with Emily and not entirely sure how Emily felt about the maneuver.

"I guess I should get back to the table," Emily said, but her questioning tone told Cade she wasn't convinced that's what she wanted to do. On impulse, Cade said, "Join us."

Emily's glance flicked back to her table and Cade followed her eyes. The handsome man with gray hair she'd pegged as Senator Sinclair, was regaling the table with a story, and everyone was listening with rapt attention except the woman seated next to him, who she imagined was his wife. Mrs. Sinclair was looking in their direction, barely hiding the fact she was staring straight at them, her expression at once curious and annoyed. She watched as Emily offered her mother a tacit nod. "I need to get back, but…"

"Yes?"

"But I'd like to see you again."

"Me too, you."

"I don't know if you saw the papers, but the weekend got a little crazy after I left you Friday night. I can't really get into it right now, but I'm going to be tied up for a while."

"I may have heard about that. But you eat, right?"

"What?"

"Meals, nutrition, sustenance. Even busy prosecutors have to fuel up for the fight, right?"

The smile again and this time it reached Emily's eyes. "I suppose. What do you have in mind?"

"Well, I could bring a peanut butter and jelly sandwich to your office and chat while you munched on it. I'd even bring chips too, good ones, but I'm thinking you're not exactly a peanut butter, jelly, and chips kind of girl."

"Oh, you think that huh?"

Cade made a show of glancing around the ornately decorated room. "Uh, yeah, I do."

"I like sandwiches."

"Those little finger ones they serve with tea, right?"

Emily hung her head. "Guilty as charged. But I do love a good chip."

"Then how about I take you to dinner? You choose the place and time. Whenever's convenient for you." Cade pulled her phone out of her pocket. "Tell me your number."

"What?"

"Your number? You know, I call you and then you have my number on your phone. No pressure. Call me when you can. I promise I won't bother you until you're ready."

"And when I'm ready?"

"Well, then we'll have to see about that."

Cade punched in the numbers and looked up to find Emily staring at her with a curious expression. She put the phone to her ear and her hand up, palm out. "Hold on, I'm on a call. Hey, Emily," she said into the phone. "It was great seeing you at the club today. I was thinking we might meet up for tiny little finger sandwiches. What say you? Give me a buzz." She clicked off the line and saw Emily shaking her head. "What?"

"Nothing. It's just you're very different from the women I'm used to meeting."

"I'm hoping that's a good thing."

"It's a great thing." She pressed her palm against Cade's chest. "I have to go. I'll talk to you later. Go kick Becca's butt."

Cade watched Emily walk back to join her table while she relished the slow burn of her touch. She'd be lucky to win a single game of tennis as distracted as she was at the prospect of a real date with Emily. Excited yes, but also terrified. It was one thing to give vague responses to coworkers about where she was from, what her family was like, but fending off a date's questions was another matter entirely. She should never have pushed the point, never given Emily her number, but she hadn't been able to resist.

She was almost to the door that led out to the tennis courts when her phone vibrated in her pocket. She fished it out, glanced at the screen, and answered, "I thought you'd never call." She didn't even try to hide the grin in her voice, but she did turn around and lock eyes with Emily who was standing where she'd left her with her phone to her ear.

"Well, I had to give it a lot of careful thought."

Cade laughed into the phone. "And your conclusion?"

"I think we should make a plan. Just know that if I wind up having to reschedule, it's—"

Cade cut in. "I know, it's not me, it's the job, right?"

"Right."

"Got it. So, how does dinner sound? You name the date."

"How about Friday? That'll give me time to get through whatever this week holds."

"Perfect," Cade lied. Perfect would have been dinner tonight, tomorrow at the latest. Now that she'd made the leap, she was ready to dive full in. A week of second-guessing her decision was not her preference, but she'd have to make do with the prospect of a perfect Friday night. "I'll call you on Thursday with the details. Now, go eat your tiny sandwiches."

She hung up and shoved her phone back in her pocket. When she looked back up, Emily was still standing across the room, phone in hand, returning her grin. She had a date with Emily Sinclair and she couldn't wait.

❖

"Who's the girl?"

"Girl?" Emily slid into her seat at the family table, wishing she could ignore her brother's remark, but it was no use. She'd caught everyone's eyes on her while she was talking, make that flirting, with Cade, and her family was an inquisitive bunch.

"Sorry, woman," Travis said. "Who's the woman? I don't recall seeing her around here before."

Emily looked around the table, noting the expectant looks and knowing they, her mother in particular, would want more than the few simple details she had to offer. Megan Sinclair had carefully screened both of Emily's brother's wives before they became official members of the family, and they'd passed with flying colors. She didn't know much about Cade, but she sensed that no matter how worthy she was, she might not meet her mother's criteria: high social standing and a deep pedigree.

She hadn't given her mother's criteria much thought in the past since she hadn't been remotely interested in settling down until she had her career goals achieved, but now that she had accomplished her major goal, the desire for a wife and family was edging its way into her thoughts. She confessed to daydreaming what it would be like to come home to someone every night, share a meal, share a bed. Children, family vacations, growing old together. She wanted all of these things, but the timing might not be quite right, especially since a murder case had landed in her lap within her first quarter in office.

She might not be ready to settle down and Cade might not be the one, but she was seriously attracted to her and she wanted to explore her feelings. The first step was acknowledging them. "Her name is Cade Kelly and she works at Jordan College."

"Professor?" Her mother's expression was neutral as she asked the question.

"Librarian."

"She doesn't look like any librarian I've ever met," Sierra remarked.

Emily bristled at the catcall tone in Sierra's voice. "Well, I doubt you see many librarians at the club getting ready for a tennis match."

"True. Are you dating?"

Emily hesitated, certain the moment she answered in the affirmative, there would be a free-for-all of questions. She looked from Sierra to her mother, but she saw only kind curiosity reflected back at her, and she decided to take the plunge. "We just made our first date."

She was relieved to see Sierra and Travis smile in response to her declaration, but it was her mother who surprised her by saying, "I'm glad you're starting to have a personal life."

"Thanks, Mom, me too. This past year has been a little crazy work-wise."

Megan sighed. "The life of a politician. It's hard, but fulfilling. If you're really interested in dating, Beth Farber is single and very accomplished. I'm sure she'll be at the next Junior League meeting."

Emily watched her mother closely, but she couldn't quite get a read. It was certainly the first time her mother had ever mentioned setting her up on a date, but no one was more attuned to the travails of politics than she. Megan Sinclair had tirelessly worked side-by-side with her husband for the last twenty years while he worked his way up from representative in the state legislature to lieutenant governor to his current seat in the United States Senate. The power payoff was grand, but the climb had taken its toll on their entire family. During election years, Emily rarely saw either parent, except for when the cameras called for the candidates to trot out their families. The woman who managed their house and personal affairs, Clara, had filled in at teacher conferences and pretty much anywhere else a parent was needed.

In a little more than two years from now, maybe longer if she didn't draw a challenger in the primary, she'd have to start running for office again. She'd vowed that as much as she wanted to keep the office, she wouldn't let her career interfere with achieving her next goal, which was a wife and family. With any luck, by the next election, she'd be happily married. She allowed herself to fantasize about walking down the aisle toward a woman waiting at the altar. She couldn't make out the woman's face, but that made sense since she hadn't dated anyone since well before she'd made the decision to run for district attorney. For a brief second, she pictured Cade standing in the front of the church, smiling as she approached, but just as quickly as it came, the image vanished. It was ridiculous really since they'd just met. Emily shook her head. This was why fantasies were a waste of time.

She'd reach the goals she'd set not by having crazy daydreams, but with deliberate action. Step one, start dating. Step two, narrow down the choices. Step three, commit. There was a proper order to things, and she wasn't going to let anything, not even the searing attraction she felt whenever Cade looked her way, get her off track.

Chapter Ten

Monday morning, Cade showed up for work and went about her usual routine, but when she went to put her lunch in the break room fridge, she spotted Monica chatting with one of their coworkers, and she tried to duck by without being spotted.

"Cade, is that you?"

Damn. Oh well, it wasn't like she was going to be able to avoid Monica all day, but she'd hoped to make it until lunch before enduring more questions about whatever she had going with Emily Sinclair. Plans thwarted, she stepped into the break room. "Hey, Monica."

"Good morning. I was just telling Luke here you've been holding out on us."

Cade's heart froze. "Excuse me?"

"We have a tennis pro in our midst. I'm not sure what you're doing working in a library when you could be out on the circuit."

"Give me a break." Cade ducked the praise, relieved that Monica was only kidding around with her big reveal.

"Seriously, Luke. Star quality, this one. Makes me wonder what other surprises she has in store."

Cade cleared her throat while she tried to think of another topic, anything to change the subject. She was pretty sure Monica was only teasing, but the subject of secrets cut a little too close to home. "I doubt Luke cares about my future as the next Martina. Luke, how was your weekend?"

"It was okay until I heard about Sam Wade."

Cade searched her memory, but she couldn't place the name. She shot a help me look at Monica.

"Sam worked in administration," Monica said. "He was killed by some homeless guy on his way home from work Friday night. Remember the shooting I was telling you about?"

"That's horrible. Did you both know him?"

"I'd met him a couple of times," Monica said. "But he and Luke were good friends."

Luke shifted in his chair. "We went to college together. He got me this job when my last place laid me off."

Cade sank into a chair. "I'm so sorry." She was, but she couldn't help her brain from kicking into prosecutor mode. "Did the police make an arrest? Do they know anything about motive?"

"I heard they arrested some guy who lives in some shady apartments nearby. Not exactly homeless, but only a rung above. I think their theory is it started as a robbery. Such a waste." Luke drained the last of his coffee and pushed back from his chair. "Really made me think about what's important in life, and how I shouldn't wait to do the things I dreamed about. Monica, if it's all right with you, I'm going to take some of that vacation time I've been storing up."

"Of course." Monica pointed at Cade. "Besides, now that we have Cade on board, we can spare you."

Cade nodded, but her mind was still on the murder, ticking through all the questions she'd have if the case had landed in her lap. She glanced at her watch. It was time to get to work, but she vowed to check out the news on her first break to see if there were any updates. She wasn't quite sure why she was so interested. Maybe it was because Emily was involved. Maybe it was because she missed the work she'd spent her whole life preparing for. Whatever the reason, she figured she would satisfy her curiosity and be done with it. Besides, she had a date to plan, and right now she couldn't think of anything more she wanted to do.

❖

"Are you sure you don't want me to handle the hearing?"

Emily shook off her haze. Seth was seated across from her desk, and judging by the look on his face, she'd zoned out again. No small wonder. She'd barely gotten any sleep all week, and she was completely preoccupied with the prospect of tonight's date with Cade. "No, I've got it. I want you there of course, but I need to take the lead on this one. We can split the witnesses, but I'll argue."

"Okay."

She caught the uncertainty in his tone. "Don't think I'm up to it?"

"Give me a break. No, it's just I know Nash can be a pain in the ass, and I'm happy to handle his direct, if you want."

"Nash doesn't like to be questioned by a woman, especially not one young enough to be his daughter, but that's his problem, not mine. If he wants his arrest to stick, he'll play ball. Trust me, I got this."

"No problem. I can take the crime scene tech." Seth thumbed through the files on her desk. "Should be pretty quick. I don't think there's any major issues with the evidence."

"To be honest, most of it's circumstantial." Emily shoved the file toward Seth. "If Miller hadn't confessed to being at the scene, I'm not sure I'd push this."

"You watched the interrogation. It was clean, right?"

Emily yawned at the memory. The interrogation had gone late into the night, and Miller had consumed two sandwiches, a bag of donuts, and three Sprites before he finally gave up enough detail to convince her Nash had arrested the right guy. She'd seen longer, more drawn out questioning, and Nash, while employing the usual tricks of the trade, hadn't crossed any legal lines in order to secure the confession. But she had to admit seeing the interrogation in real time was a whole lot different from the video she usually saw after the fact. She had a new appreciation for how wearing the process could be for all parties involved. Tempers flared, and exhaustion certainly factored into the result. Still, when it came down to it, jurors didn't believe someone would confess to a crime they didn't do, so the defendant's statement was golden.

"It was clean," she said. "But I'd like some more physical evidence, and I'd definitely like something that shows a motive. Did Miller know Wade? If he robbed him, can we prove any of the cash came from his wallet? Finding the gun would be nice, and a bonus if Miller's fingerprints are on it."

"We have time," Seth said as he paged through the file. "For now, we have enough to indict and we definitely have enough for a bond high enough to keep Miller behind bars until trial." He set the file down. "I heard Judge Nichols's grandson got appointed to this one."

"You're kidding. I thought he was doing estate planning, family law, that type of thing."

"I guess he decided to branch out. He's been handling a few criminal cases here and there, but nothing like this."

"Nobody around here handles much of this." It was true, yet she couldn't help but wonder why Judge Burson had appointed one of the greener members of the criminal defense bar for what was likely to be such a high profile case. She figured it was some form of deference to Judge Nichols who had retired several years ago, but he certainly wasn't doing the defendant any favors and, if they wound up going to trial, having a novice as opposing counsel usually meant lots of delays while he found his footing.

Whatever. She had a stellar record at trial, and she'd win whether it was fast and clean or long and dirty. If they went to trial. The likelihood was once the defendant figured out he wasn't getting out on bond and a guilty verdict at trial was going to result in life in prison, they were likely to get him to plead guilty to an agreed sentence. She was torn between the excitement of litigation and the desire to have more time to implement the changes she'd promised during her campaign. Whichever way it went, within a year, she'd be able to have some semblance of a personal life.

As if on cue, her cell phone rang and she saw Cade's name flash across the screen. "Seth, I need to get this. How about I meet you downstairs in just a minute?"

"Sure."

He scooped up the file and ducked out of the office, and the moment he cleared the door she punched the button to answer her phone. "I thought you'd never call."

"And here I thought I was giving you space."

"Space? Is that a type of food? I don't think I've eaten a full meal since brunch on Sunday. I hope you're planning to feed me tonight."

"I did ask you for dinner. I don't know about you, but in my world, that involves eating."

Emily started to make a smart remark about the double entendre of the word eating, but stopped before the words tumbled out. What was it about Cade that made conversation so easy and, more importantly, why did she feel compelled to resist?

She decided to skip the innuendo, but stick to their plans. "Dinner, complete with lots of food, would be wonderful. I've had kind of a crazy week, and I'm really looking forward to tonight."

"Excellent. I assume the crazy has to do with the case in the news?"

"That's the one. We have a bond hearing this morning, and we're presenting to the grand jury this afternoon. I have to warn you I'm not sure exactly what time I'll break free."

"So, should I make a late reservation or just play the timing by ear?"

"There's only one restaurant in town, besides the club, that even takes reservations, Ambrosia."

"Trust me, I've already scoped that out. Memorized the menu and everything. I was thinking dinner at eight?"

Emily opened her mouth to say yes, but another idea edged its way in, and before she could consider the implications, she blurted it out. "How about you get dinner to go and bring it to my place? It doesn't have to be anything fancy, doesn't even have to be from Ambrosia."

"Actually, I was counting on fancy, but I'm happy to bring the fancy to you instead of the other way around."

"Perfect. Order me whatever you're having. Don't let them skip the breadsticks—they're divine."

"Text me your address when you're ready for delivery and I'll be there within thirty minutes. I have to warn you, I'll be expecting a big tip."

Emily hung up in a much better mood, and she refused to question her impulsive decision to invite Cade over. It was just a dinner date, nothing more. It didn't matter where they ate. She repeated the mantra several times, but the repetition did nothing to quell her growing excitement that when this hell of a day was done, she had something to look forward to.

❖

Judge Burson drummed his fingers on the bench as he considered defense counsel's objection. Emily stood in front of Sheriff Nash, waiting patiently for the inevitable result. The only reason the judge was even giving the objection a second thought was because he had no idea what Brody Nichols was talking about. She'd already chimed in with her response and then clammed up. When she was a young, green attorney like Brody, she would've gone on and on to try to reinforce her argument, as if by continuing to hold the stage, she was somehow winning the argument, but she'd learned to use the power of confident silence to her advantage.

"I'm going to overrule the objection," Burson said. "Counsel, you may proceed."

"Thank you, Your Honor." Emily watched Brody deflate and slide back into his seat again. Once more, she wondered why he'd been appointed to this case. She didn't blame him for taking it on. When she was new, she'd taken everything she could get, never once admitting lack of experience. Born litigators always did, but based on what she'd seen so far, she wasn't convinced Brody had trial work in his blood.

"Sheriff Nash, please describe what you found when you entered the defendant's apartment."

Nash directed his answer to the judge. "The place was a mess. Newspapers everywhere and trash all over the floor."

Emily bit back an objection of her own at Nash's irrelevant commentary. "What steps did you take to secure potential evidence implicating the defendant in the death of Mr. Wade?"

"I posted a deputy at the door, and we contacted the crime scene unit. Once they arrived and took photographs, we put on gloves and began to search the room, item by item."

"Tell the court what you found to support your theory the defendant was involved in the death of Mr. Wade."

"I suppose the most important things we found were two knives and three crisp twenty-dollar bills."

"Tell us the relevance of those items."

"Well, in addition to being shot, Mr. Wade had his throat slit." Nash looked over at the judge and demonstrated by drawing a finger under his chin, from ear to ear. "And the money, well, we think that was stolen from Mr. Wade."

Brody sprang out of his seat. "Objection, your honor, no foundation."

Burton waved for him to sit back down. "Hold on, son. I bet they're getting there."

Emily smiled at the judge and asked Nash to explain the relevance of the money.

"We found an ATM receipt in Mr. Wade's front pants pocket. He withdrew one hundred dollars in cash that afternoon from the Wells Fargo machine on campus."

Emily looked over and saw Brody scribbling furiously on a notepad. She figured she knew what he was thinking so she beat him to the punch. "You say he withdrew a hundred dollars, but you only found sixty dollars in the defendant's apartment?"

"That's right, but we also found a grocery store receipt in the amount of thirty-five fifty in Mr. Wade's pocket, so I'm thinking he spent some of the money before Mr. Miller robbed him."

Brody kept scribbling, but he didn't object this time. Maybe he was learning he'd do better to save his energy for when they were in front of a jury. This hearing had one purpose only and that was to determine if the evidence the sheriff's office had gathered so far was enough to support the high bond. Brody had likely requested the hearing to get a sneak peek at the state's case, but Emily was only going to reveal enough at this point to make sure Miller stayed in jail. Later this afternoon, when she presented the case to the grand jury, Brody and his objections wouldn't be allowed in the room, and she might be inclined to show a bit more to seal a true bill from the grand jurors.

Emily finished presenting her case and then took notes while Seth put the crime scene investigator on the stand. Footprints found near the victim's body were a likely match to the defendant's boots.

Evidence of blood on one of the knives seized from the defendant's apartment. A series of little things, on their own not conclusive, but taken together, the pieces all lined up to point to the defendant's guilt. Since all they needed was to show they had a fairly strong case, Emily was confident Miller wouldn't be going anywhere.

When the evidence concluded, Burson asked, "Ms. Sinclair, it's my understanding you are presenting this case to the grand jury today?"

She half stood. "That's correct, Judge. It's likely they will report out on Monday."

"Excellent. Then I'm going to hold this hearing over until then, and I will announce my decision at that time." He looked down his glasses at Brody. "If there's no indictment, then your client will be free to go." Without waiting for a response, he stood and waved at the gallery and said, "Have a nice weekend, everyone," before disappearing through the door behind the bench that led to his chambers.

Emily looked over at Brody who appeared stunned to learn all his hard work hadn't netted some kind of decision about the fate of his client. She waited until the bailiff took his client into the holdover before saying, "Don't feel bad. Judge Burson isn't big on making decisions if he doesn't have to, but come Monday, he'll make a ruling, because I have no doubt your client will be indicted."

"I guess we'll see, won't we," Brody said. Emily watched him gather his things and leave the room without another word. She almost felt sorry for him. She hadn't been bragging with her remark about the indictment, but she had wanted to give him a realistic expectation of what would go down. She shook her head.

"He'll learn," Seth said.

"I know, but it kind of sucks for his client that he's learning on a murder case."

"Not our problem. You want to grab some lunch? It's going to be a long afternoon."

Seth gathered the file and swept it into his briefcase, not at all disturbed about dominating a weaker adversary. He was right, of course. It wasn't their problem, but she couldn't help but wish Miller had a better lawyer. Brody hadn't even asked if he could make a presentation at this afternoon's grand jury hearing. Granted, her predecessor had never allowed defense presentations, but she'd promised the defense bar she'd do things different. Apparently, Brody hadn't gotten the memo or, more likely, he didn't even know where to begin.

It probably didn't matter either way. Despite the fact the evidence was circumstantial, they had enough to indict, but she couldn't help but acknowledge she'd feel a lot better about kicking the ass of a more formidable opponent. And with no opposition, she'd be home in plenty of time for dinner with Cade.

CHAPTER ELEVEN

Cade pulled up to the address Emily had texted her and did a double take at the giant, three-story Victorian a couple of blocks from the center of town. She checked the address again, but she was at the right place. Granted, Emily was a top county official, but the county was small, and this place made the residence of the Cook County state's attorney look like a dollhouse. There was plenty of room in the spacious drive, but she parked on the street on the off chance she'd written down the wrong address.

The door opened before she could ring the bell, but the woman standing on the threshold was about twenty years older than Emily and wearing an apron.

"Ms. Kelly?"

Someday the surname would feel familiar, but it took Cade a second to respond. "Yes?"

"Come in, please. Ms. Sinclair will be right down. Would you like me to take those for you?"

Cade glanced down at the bags in her hand that contained a four-course meal from Ambrosia, along with the most expensive bottle of wine she could find at the only decent liquor store in the county. The stranger's request was reasonable, but for some reason, she was reluctant to relinquish control. "That's okay, I've got it."

"Very well, I'll show you to the kitchen."

Cade followed the stranger through the entryway, past a sitting room and an enormous library, into a vast kitchen. The kitchen was outfitted with high dollar modern appliances while still retaining its antique charm.

"Does anything need to be kept warm? I have the stove on just in case."

"Uh, no, everything should be fine." She stared at the woman, trying not to be rude, but unable to figure out the relationship. She'd seen Emily's mother at the club, so she knew it wasn't her. Another relative, an aunt, perhaps? "I didn't get your name."

"This is Clara." Emily breezed into the kitchen. "And Clara was just leaving, right, Clara?"

"Of course, Miss Emily. I was just making sure you have everything you need." Cade watched as Clara picked up an oversized handbag from the kitchen counter and pulled on an overcoat. "It was a pleasure to meet you, Miss Kelly."

Cade waited until Clara was out the door before she blurted out. "Okay, so you live in a mansion and you have a maid. Wow."

Emily laughed. "It's not exactly a mansion, and Clara isn't exactly a maid."

"This requires more explanation, but over dinner. I bet you're starving."

"I am and whatever you have in that bag smells delicious."

"The guy at the restaurant said it was your favorite."

"Gerry?" Emily winced a little as she asked the question.

"He's the one. I'm thinking you must eat there a lot."

"Guilty. It's easy to stop by after work and grab a meal on the way home. Plus it's great networking. I think all the donations for my primary campaign came from my fellow diners." Emily pointed at the bottle in her hand. "Do you want to open the wine while I get us some plates?"

Cade took the fancy wine bottle opener from Emily's hand, lingering for just a moment as their fingers touched. She'd been eagerly anticipating this date all week and now that she was here she was uber conscious about not messing up. As she twisted the opener into the cork, she silently repeated the mantra she'd adopted for this evening. *Keep the conversation light. Be casual. Do first date things.*

First date. The very idea had her nerves on edge. She hadn't been on one in forever, but her recollection was that first dates were usually share all the background stuff kind of events. She'd prepared by spending the afternoon doing a self-quiz on the details in her dossier, but other than a few random questions at work, she hadn't had to regurgitate the lies the feds had dreamed up for her in any significant way, let alone to someone she was intensely attracted to.

The prospect was both scary and exciting. In a way it meant she had a blank slate. Women had always assumed things about her because she was a lawyer. Wealthy, argumentative, cutthroat: she was none of those things. Well, except maybe argumentative. And she did have a decent nest egg, thanks to an inheritance from her grandparents, but her regular salary as a state's attorney had been fairly modest. She'd never met anyone she cared enough about to dispel those misconceptions.

But Emily was different. She wanted to get to know her, and that meant she'd have to do some sharing of her own. She'd have to find a way to deal with the fact the details she would share were mostly lies.

"I bet you're starving too," Emily said, breaking into her thoughts. Cade looked down at the wine bottle in her hand and wondered how long she'd been standing there, fiddling with the opener. "Sorry," she said. "Must be low blood sugar. Let's eat."

"Bring the bottle and those glasses over there and follow me."

Cade watched as Emily lifted a serving tray loaded with their plates and a basket of bread, and led the way to the back of the house. She deftly handled the tray with one hand and opened the back door that led out onto an expansive cedar deck.

"I turned the heater on when I got home, but if you think it's too cold we can go back inside," Emily said as she set the tray down on a slate table for four.

Cade took a moment to soak in the contrast of the fresh, cool night air against the gentle warmth from the propane patio heater that stood to the side of the table. "No, it's perfect."

Emily sighed. "Thanks. I spend so many hours cooped up inside, I like being able to adjourn to this little oasis when I get home."

Cade took a moment to glance around the backyard, and she could see exactly what Emily meant. The entire space was filled with special garden features from an ivy covered arch to a sweet birdbath surrounded by irises. "You have a beautiful garden."

"Thanks. It's one of my passions." She pointed to the left. "Those are my grandmother's champion roses. I'm pretty sure our mutual love of gardening is why they left me this house. It's in the town historical register, so I couldn't bear to sell it, which is why this single gal lives in the largest house in Bodark proper."

"I see."

"I could tell you wanted to know." She reached for a breadstick. "And Clara is not my maid. She was my grandparents' right-hand person. Managed the house and most of their personal affairs for as long as I can remember. She was pretty lost when they died, so she comes around and does little things for me now and again even though she should be enjoying her retirement. I don't have the heart to tell her no." She chewed on the breadstick for a moment. "Is it all a little too much?"

Cade was surprised to hear the hesitancy in Emily's voice. She'd been so concerned with her own first date jitters, she hadn't considered Emily might be nervous too, although for completely different reasons, and she found it endearing. "Fancy country club, Victorian mansion, personal assistant? No, it's pretty much what I expect from all of my dates." She watched expectantly as Emily's face slowly relaxed into a smile.

"Got it. Trappings of wealth fall into the plus column." She pointed at her plate. "Just so you know, you've met all of my expectations by bringing me food. Good food," she patted her heart, "is the path to my soul."

"Duly noted." Cade picked up a fork and dug into her rich pasta dish, letting the delicious combination of earthy mushrooms and buttery sauce comfort her palate. "This is amazing."

"I know, right? I have to confess, I go there so much, the chef makes a few off the menu meals for me."

"So you have your own secret coffee shop and your own secret menu at the fanciest restaurant in town. Someone's popular with the in crowd."

"Comes from spending life in a town founded by your ancestors."

"Seems like you're doing all right, making a name for yourself."

"I do my best. There are folks who say I wouldn't have been elected if I wasn't a Sinclair." Emily's tone was more resigned than defensive. "They have no idea how hard I worked in the trenches as a prosecutor to get where I am. If I wanted to trade on my family's good name, I could have simply become a partner at the family firm, or taken any number of positions in Dallas with reputable firms."

"That answers my next question."

"Which was?"

"What inspired you to go into law? Sounds like it's in your blood."

"I suppose. Maybe I just like to argue." Emily smiled and took a sip from her glass of wine. "This is delicious, by the way."

"Glad you like it."

"There aren't a lot of places around here to get a good bottle of wine."

"True."

"When we first met, you said you were new in town. What inspires a handsome librarian who appreciates excellent wine to move to a tiny town far from normal civilization?"

Cade anticipated the question before Emily could finish asking it, and she'd prepared by shoving an enormous bite of food into her mouth. Despite this prescient planning, she couldn't seem to find the words or the will to deliver the well-practiced lies that formed her false background. Her throat tightened, and the resultant fight for breath caused her to choke. She could feel her face redden and she saw Emily's look of concern. Not at all how she expected this night to go, but she should've known better than to think she could get away with avoiding talking about anything personal. She reached for her wine, desperate to appear as if nothing was wrong, but before she could bring it to her lips, she doubled over in an uncontrollable coughing fit.

Emily grabbed the glass from Cade's hand and reached around to rub her back. "Hold up a hand if you can breathe."

Cade held up a few fingers, and after a moment, her coughing eased. Cade started to talk, but Emily rubbed her back some more and urged her to stay quiet. "Give it a minute." She eased away. "If you think you'll be okay, I'm going to go get you a glass of water." Cade nodded, and then Emily gently extracted herself and went inside to the kitchen.

Emily pulled a couple of bottles of cold water from the fridge and took a moment to consider what had just happened. She believed Cade had really choked on her food, but something about her expression right before it happened—fear, distress—made her think something else was going on. She'd asked her why she'd moved to town, and she wasn't exactly sure what would be so scary about answering that.

Maybe she was shy and first date personal questions weren't her thing. Maybe she moved to get away from a bad situation like abuse or family troubles.

Maybe you're making too much of the fact she choked on a piece of food. Emily shook her head, resigned to the probability that making too much of things was merely an occupational hazard. Despite being occupied with the hearing, she'd spent the day eagerly anticipating this date. The last thing she needed to do was let her work creep into these few hours of personal time.

Personal time. She'd barely known what it was before she'd made the decision to run for office, and now that she was DA, nothing about her life was her own. When she wasn't at the office working, she was either doing paperwork in front of the TV or off at some speaking engagement. Becca had already started to complain that her weekly trip to pick up a pound of coffee was the only quality time they spent together anymore. She desperately wanted this night, this date, to be different, which was the reason she'd asked Cade here instead of going out where one of her constituents was likely to buttonhole her about whatever issue was bugging them at the moment.

But dining here came with different distractions, all having to do with her desire to know more about this illusive woman. Added to the mix was the snug fit of Cade's low-slung jeans and the crisp cut of her black collared shirt with its teasing row of tiny buttons. All through dinner, she'd been consumed with want, plotting how to get in those jeans and how to tear through those buttons, but she'd been dissuaded by the notion of what would happen next. Once she started, she was pretty sure she couldn't stop. Resolving to control her libido and concentrate on the non-physical getting-to-know-you part of this date, she walked back outside.

Cade leaned back in her chair, looking like absolutely nothing was wrong. She took one of the water bottles and chugged it halfway down. "Sorry about that," Cade said with a grin. "I usually chew my food before I swallow it."

"I'm just glad you're okay. I can hear it now: DA murders librarian with pasta on the patio in small town tragedy. News at ten."

"Yes, it would be a tragedy to kill the librarian before she shows you the dessert she brought."

Cade seemed relaxed and casual, but Emily still felt a hum of tension beneath the surface. Was she imagining that her earlier question had provoked Cade's nervous response? Only one way to find out. "So, before your near-death experience, I think you were going to tell me how you came to live in our little town."

"Yes, I was. Not a big story, actually. I used to work for a university up north, but due to some funding issues, they had to let go a portion of the staff. I took a nice severance package, and a friend let me know about the position at Jordan."

"And how are you liking it so far?"

"It's growing on me."

Cade reached over and put her hand on top of Emily's, reinforcing the subtext of her declaration. Despite the sweet gesture, Emily couldn't help but notice a slight tension in Cade's shoulders. She wanted to know more. "And your family? Where do they live?"

"Just me, I'm afraid." Cade took a deep drink from her wineglass. "Only child and my parents are both dead."

Cade's curt summary seemed to preclude exploring the subject further. Emily curled her fingers into Cade's open palm, enjoying the gentle stroke of skin against skin. "I'm so sorry. You'll have to forgive me. I ask questions for a living, and I have a bad habit of letting it pour over into my personal life."

"You're just apologizing so you can have dessert."

Cade delivered the words with a smile, and Emily took note of the way her left eye winked slightly when she smiled, almost as if she didn't know she was doing it. Did she realize how irresistible she was? How kissable?

"What are you thinking right now?" Cade asked.

"I shouldn't tell you."

"What if I guess?"

"Go for it."

Cade pushed back her chair and stood. Emily watched her move closer, and her breath hitched as Cade closed the distance between them and leaned forward. She knew what was coming and she wanted it. She wanted it bad. Cade's lips were soft, but their touch was strong and claiming, pulling her in. She parted her lips and moaned softly as Cade ran her tongue lightly around the edge of her mouth, tasting, teasing. She hadn't had enough wine to be heady from the alcohol, but the contact made her swoon. She placed a hand against Cade's chest and pulled back for a second to say a single word, "Inside?"

Cade answered by holding out her hand. Emily grasped it and allowed Cade to lead her through the French doors into the house. The sensation of having someone else take charge in her own home, or anywhere for that matter, was at once thrilling and completely foreign, and she shivered with anticipation when Cade pulled her into the velvet cushions of her oversized couch.

"You smell so good," Cade said as she kissed her way up Emily's neck.

"It's Fracas. I have it bad for good perfume."

"It's making me crazy."

"You're making me crazy." Emily reached a hand around Cade's neck and tugged her close until their foreheads touched. "You are the most amazing kisser. Ever." She sighed. "It's always the quiet ones."

"You think I'm quiet, huh?"

"Assumption. Sorry. You know, librarian."

Emily watched Cade's puzzled look quickly fade, and she nodded. "Got it. Right." She leaned closer and whispered in her ear. "I have a secret."

Cade's breath against her skin was pushing the boundaries of her arousal. "You do?"

"I'm not always quiet."

Cade proved the point with a light groan as she ran her hand over Emily's sweater and under the curve of her breast. Emily arched into her touch, heady with want, and Cade stoked her arousal with a rhythm of slow and steady strokes. Surrendering control, Emily closed her eyes, and while her body simmered with passion at every pass of Cade's hands, she let her own explore Cade's body. Lean, firm muscles. Luscious, gentle curves. Tight, soft skin.

Skin. Emily's eyes fluttered open and her practical side set off alarms that cut through her aching need. She forced air through her lungs, and managed to say, "That feels amazing and I don't want to stop."

Cade eased away and looked at her with hooded eyes. "I'm sensing a but."

"Not a 'but' really. More like an 'and.'"

"And?"

Emily took a deep breath, torn between wanting to stay on the couch and ride this fantasy for all it was worth and slowing things down to a more manageable pace. If she didn't slow things down, there was a high likelihood Cade's car would be parked in her driveway the rest of the night—an error that would lead to a lot of gossip from the neighbors about the new DA and her loose morals. Not exactly the reputation she wanted to cultivate. Besides, she was looking for a long-term relationship, not a first date lay. She took a breath. "And I'd like to have dessert now, the one you brought."

"Okay."

Emily watched Cade take a deep breath, but she couldn't quite read her expression. "Not what you had in mind?"

"What? I'm always in the mood for something sweet."

Cade's slow smile drowned out the internal voices shouting for her to take Cade to bed now, to hell with the consequences. Before she could change her mind, Emily stood and held out her hand, resisting the urge to fall into Cade's arms when she grasped it. She could do this. They would have dessert, talk some more, and exchange good night kisses. Just not on the couch. Or anywhere where she wasn't standing upright.

A few minutes later, they were standing in the kitchen tucking into enormous slices of chocolate caramel cake. "This is amazing," Emily said. "I may fall into a coma any moment."

"Oh great. Local librarian drugs DA with cake. I can see it now. I'll probably get the death penalty."

"Oh, I doubt that."

"I'm not so sure. From what I hear you're pretty well liked around here."

"Why, Ms. Kelly, have you been asking around?"

"Didn't have to ask. People talk. Everyone at the college thinks you're great. You taught as an adjunct?"

"A couple of semesters. Once the election cycle started, I had to give it up. Too many rubber chicken dinners and town hall meetings to fit much else in." She took another bite of cake.

"Glad I didn't meet you then."

"I might've been distracted."

"My timing is perfect. I arrived in town the day you won the election. Saw you on TV that night."

"That whole night was a blur. I don't remember anything I or anyone else said after the network called it." Emily closed her eyes for a second as she relived the monumental moment. Did Cade think she was silly? Lawson might be a small county, but her victory was a huge event in her life. Of course, Cade might have moved here from a small place herself, which spurred her to ask, "Where did you move from?"

"What?"

Emily wondered if perhaps Cade was suffering food coma herself, or maybe she'd just switched topics too quickly, something Becca was constantly ribbing her about. "You said you moved here the night of the election. Where from?"

Cade blinked. "Uh, Wisconsin. Outside of Milwaukee."

"Hence the slight accent. University of Wisconsin?"

"Pardon?"

"Was that the university you worked for before transferring here?"

"Yes, that's the one."

Emily detected a hint of uncertainty, but she wrote it off to the food coma and Cade's persistent shyness when it came to discussing anything personal. "I've heard stories about the governor up there and the university layoffs. Bet you were glad to get out of that system."

"Yes, and how about you? Did you always want to be a prosecutor?"

Emily pretended not to notice the poor segue. Cade seemed determined to avoid all things personal, but maybe she had a good reason. They'd only just met after all, or maybe Cade was shy. The memory of Cade, on the patio, striding toward her to make the first move rushed her thoughts, and she wrote off putting Cade and shy in the same sentence again. No, something else was the cause of the barrier. If they were going to go any further with whatever was happening between them, she was going to find out what it was, but right now she had no desire to spoil the easygoing mood of this evening.

A loud buzzing cut into her thoughts, and Emily instinctively reached for her cell phone that was sitting on the kitchen counter. She turned it over, but nothing showed up on the screen, yet the buzzing persisted. "Weird."

"It's me."

She looked over at Cade who was frowning at her phone. "Do you need to get that?"

"Sorry, I do." Cade raised the phone to her ear and started walking toward the patio. Before she made it out the door, Emily heard her say. "I'm in the middle of something."

Well, that was one way to describe a date. Whoever it was must've been important for Cade to have even answered, and whatever they wanted was enough to merit a private conversation. She watched through the big bay windows as Cade paced the outdoor deck, but she couldn't hear any other portions of the conversation. In less than five minutes, Cade was back at her side.

"I had a great time tonight."

Emily heard the unspoken good-bye, but she had to ask. "Are you leaving? Is something wrong?"

Cade smiled, but it didn't reach her eyes. "Nothing's wrong, but I have to go. Can I see you again? Are you busy this weekend?"

Emily paused. She could let herself be distracted by the promise of seeing Cade again soon, or she could let tiny seeds of doubt cloud the anticipation. Who had called? What had they said that caused Cade to abort their date? Why didn't Cade just tell her why she was leaving?

Funny, less than an hour ago, she'd been worried about what the neighbors would say if Cade stayed too late, and now she was second-guessing Cade's decision to leave. Her reaction might not make sense, but she was certain there was more to Cade's sudden departure than she was letting on, and her certainty led her to say, "I'm pretty busy this weekend. We're finishing up our presentation to the grand jury on the Miller case on Monday, and I've got lots of prep work to do."

"Well, damn." Cade frowned. Either she was an excellent actor or she was legitimately disappointed. Emily wasn't sure which, but her instincts told her it might be a little of both. Despite not knowing, she couldn't resist making an overture. "We should be done Monday night. I'll call you."

"Perfect," Cade said as she leaned in for a kiss.

Emily hesitated for a second, but arousal beat out caution. She touched Cade under the chin and drew her closer until their lips met in a soft and lingering kiss. She had no clue exactly how long they'd been standing there when a voice inside her said, "Don't get used to this." The voice broke the spell. She raised her head and took a step back, determined to put distance between them, certain it was the only thing that would keep her sane. "Good night."

Chapter Twelve

As Cade turned onto her street, she spotted Kennedy's Jeep sitting in front of her house. Damn. She'd figured she'd have a little time to regroup from her date with Emily before she'd have to deal with whatever Kennedy wanted, but it looked like she was ready to plunge right in.

All Kennedy would tell her was that they needed to meet tonight and she was headed to Cade's house. Cade had no idea what would merit an impromptu meeting on a Friday night, but she didn't think it could be anything good. If Kennedy had interrupted her date with Emily for nothing, Cade was going to be really pissed.

Cade pulled into the garage, entered the house through the side door, and strode toward the front certain Kennedy would be waiting on the other side, but as she walked by the living room, a voice called out, causing her to nearly jump out of her skin.

"I'm in here."

She flicked the switch on the wall. "Holy shit, Kennedy. You ever heard of knocking?"

"You took long enough to get here. Where were you?"

"Normal people don't break and enter." Cade walked over to the window and peered through the blind. "I bet Mavis called the cops the minute she saw you."

"Mavis?"

"Nosy neighbor. She sees everything that happens in this neighborhood. You probably should've checked that out before you moved me in here, especially if you were planning to bust in at all hours."

"I didn't bust in. I used a key. We've got some work to do. Can I get something to drink?"

Cade shook her head, knowing she didn't have a choice. She'd been happy to agree to assist in the prosecution of anyone involved in the shooting of Biermann and his guards in exchange for protection. Hell, she'd spent her life trying to put bad guys away so this was just more of the same.

Except it wasn't. Heading up a prosecution was vastly different from being the witness, and she was quickly developing empathy for the witnesses she'd worked with over the years. She'd always assumed their willingness to help gave her carte blanche to make demands on their time, ask intrusive questions about their personal life, and risk their safety for the greater good. In the scheme of things, having her date interrupted was a small thing, but after she'd given up her home, her friends, her family and, above all, her identity, to help strangers prosecute a man she didn't know who had killed a man she barely knew, tonight felt like a massive intrusion.

"You want a drink, make it yourself—you know, since you're making yourself at home and all. What's so important you had to come over on a Friday night?"

"The FBI arrested Officer Martel."

Cade sank onto the couch. Martel was the guy who'd lured her out to the van where Fontana had been waiting. "When?"

"Earlier today. He was hiding out near Bloomington."

"Okay." Cade's mind whirred with the information. If Martel was in custody, the feds were one step closer to finding Fontana. All they had to do was get him to talk, and they were well on their way to closing this case. If Martel did flip, then it was more likely Fontana wouldn't force them to go to trial, which meant her involvement would end. She'd remain under protection because the possibility always existed the Oliveris would come for her out of revenge, but it was more likely they would wash their hands of the enforcer who'd almost put them out of business by leaving a witness behind. "What do you need me to do?"

"Waverly wants to go over your grand jury testimony before she meets with Martel and his lawyer. She's flying out in the morning and she'll meet us in Dallas. I think it would be better for us to leave tonight. We'll be there for a couple of days."

Kennedy didn't need to say more. Cade got it. Kennedy must have some reason to believe there might be some danger if she was spotted leaving for the weekend. She wanted to know more, but knew Kennedy well enough to know that it wasn't worth arguing about. She left the room to pack a bag, figuring she could get her answer during the road trip. Good thing Emily hadn't taken her up on her request for another date this weekend. It would be hard enough explaining why she'd cut tonight short, but she had no clue what excuse she'd offer for leaving town without any notice. It was probably best. A woman like Emily would ask too many questions, and lies were a pretty sorry foundation for any kind of relationship, even a casual one. Time to hole back up and keep to herself.

❖

Emily looked up at the knock on her door to find Seth filling the frame. "I'm on my way." She'd been finishing up a list of questions for the medical examiner who they were about to prep for his testimony. He would be their last witness before the grand jurors when they resumed hearing testimony tomorrow morning.

"You look tired."

"You are the master of the obvious." She yawned and stretched her arms. She'd come directly to the office after church, skipping the family brunch to get back to work on the Miller case. "First big case. I just want to make sure we get it right."

Seth walked in and took a seat. "We will. To tell you the truth, I think it's going to be a slam dunk. Brody doesn't know what the hell he's doing, and Miller seems good for it."

Emily practically growled. "Dammit, Seth. Take it back. Light some candles, do something to erase the bad mojo you just stirred up. We don't take anything for granted. If Miller's good for it, I want to lock this up tight and get him to plead guilty. No sense dragging Wade's family through a trial." She pushed back from her seat. "Let's go talk to Dr. Narey. We'll put him on in the morning, and then get our indictment. I don't want Miller getting out on bond tomorrow afternoon. With any luck, we can get him to take a plea by the end of the week."

She led the way to the conference room down the hall from her office where the ME was waiting. As she walked, she did a bit of mental math. It was three o'clock and they'd probably spend an hour or two, three tops, prepping Narey. She was as ready as she could be for tomorrow, so she'd head home, have an early dinner, and try to get a good night's sleep. When she thought about relaxing, one name came to mind. She'd told Cade she would be too busy to see her this weekend, but the closer she got to being done working on the case for the weekend, seeing Cade again was all she could think about. The memory of Cade's abrupt exit had faded, and now she wondered if she was being overly sensitive. Seeing Cade again, looking into those deep brown eyes would tell her all she needed to know. She was going to eat dinner anyway. Why not with someone she'd enjoy spending time with?

She stepped aside and motioned for Seth to go on into the conference room. "I'll be right there." She waited until he crossed the threshold and pulled out her phone, pausing before taking the plunge. *Wrapping up early. Dinner tonight?* She pressed send before she could second-guess the overture. Determined not to stare at the phone, waiting for an answer, she reached to tuck it into her briefcase. Before she released it, the phone buzzed to signal a new text.

Can't make it tonight. Sorry.

Emily stared at the screen for a few seconds, trying to read between the lines. Can't make it because I have other plans? Can't make it because I don't want to? Sorry on a personal level or sorry because it seemed like the right thing to say?

As the questions raced through her mind, she grew more and more annoyed with her reaction. She can't make it. It's as simple as that. Quit overanalyzing. She tossed the phone into her bag without replying. They'd had the one date. On a scale of one to ten, the attraction level had been off the charts, but now she wasn't convinced Cade was really interested, and she wasn't sure she wanted to risk her own heart discovering the truth. She faced the door to the conference room. She had a job to do, and it was time to focus on that. When this case was over, she'd refocus on her personal goals, without Cade Kelly, but until then she was all business.

❖

Cade shoved her phone back in her pocket and stared at the women seated across from her.

"If you need to take a break to make a phone call," Kennedy said, "That's okay."

"No, I'm fine." She wasn't fine, but the sooner they got through this, the better off she'd be. She tensed, waiting for a buzz in her pocket to tell her Emily had responded to her text, but it didn't come. What did she expect? She'd dashed out of Emily's house on Friday night without explanation, and now when Emily reached out in spite of it, she was blowing her off. No doubt Emily had nothing left to say to her.

She'd spent the better part of the last two days answering the same questions over and over again. AUSA Waverly had described how they'd found former Chicago police officer Mike Martel hiding out near Bloomington, a couple of hours south of Chicago. He'd been running a deli. In the mob's own version of witness protection, they'd set him up with a new life, and if a fellow officer hadn't been visiting relatives in Bloomington, there was no telling how long he would have remained undetected.

So far he wasn't talking, but Waverly was confident an indictment would loosen his tongue. Cade had listened to her bluster over the past couple of days while she was forced to repeat her story over and over again. She wondered if Waverly remembered she was talking to a fellow prosecutor, and not just any other potential witness. "I don't know that it will be as easy as you think."

"Pardon me?"

"If Martel talks, he dies, unless you're going to offer him protection, and even then it's probably going to be a hard sell. Whatever the Oliveris gave him or threatened him with to get him to give up his badge and his retirement was probably more persuasive than anything you have to offer."

Waverly shook her head. "I can't talk about the specifics of his case."

"I get it. Look, I don't care what you do as long as you catch Fontana and make him pay for what he did." She watched as Waverly exchanged glances with Kennedy. Something was at play here, but she wasn't sure what. Whatever it was, apparently, they didn't plan to share it with her, which pissed her off after the last two days of endless repetition. "Are we done? I have a fake life to get back to."

The first hour of the car ride back to Bodark felt like six, most likely because of the silence. Kennedy pointed out a giant billboard advertising one of those megaplex travel centers. "You want to stop and stretch your legs?"

"I'd rather keep driving if it's all the same to you."

"I need a Coke. You can wait in the car if you want."

"Fine."

"Look, I know you're mad, but catching these guys is a slow process. They'll eventually get Fontana, and whether Waverly said it or not, your help is invaluable."

"If she really wanted my help, she might ask my opinion. She's either got to threaten Martel with something worse than the mob could do to him, or convince him she can keep him safe."

"I think she knows that, but I also think she has her sights set on bigger fish."

Cade took a moment to process what Kennedy was saying before she realized the implication. "Wait a minute. It's Fontana she's going to protect, isn't it?"

"I don't know for sure, but that's my bet. If she can get Martel to flip on him, then she can use him to get to the family."

"He'll never turn on Vincente Oliveri. The man practically raised him. I spent years working on these cases. I should know."

"You might be right, but I'm sure you know she has to try."

Kennedy's words lingered after she left the car. After watching her fade into the crowd of people entering the building, Cade closed her eyes and played back the gruesome crime scene outside of the Cook County courthouse. Blood spray, bullet holes, tangled bodies. She shuddered at the memory of the red-hot pain of Fontana's bullet searing through her skin. The idea he might get a new name, a new identity, and be permitted to live out his days under the protection of the federal government was inconceivable. She wanted justice. Real justice.

Kennedy returned to the car and they drove in silence for a while. Cade nearly fell asleep with the slow and steady rhythm of the ride.

"So, where were you Friday night?"

"Excuse me?"

"Well, you weren't at home and you weren't at work. I'm curious, that's all."

Cade opened her mouth to say she'd been at Emily's, but she clamped it shut before the words came out, uncertain about the reason behind her reluctance to share anything personal with Kennedy once again.

"You don't have to tell me, but if you're making new friends, it would be a good idea for me to check them out."

"You can't possibly check out everyone I come into contact with."

"Not everyone, true, but we do a pretty good job of vetting the people you spend any significant amount of time with. We did a pretty deep background on everyone who works at the library, and, frankly, you don't hang out with anyone you don't work with, so you're fairly low maintenance."

"Okay."

"So, were you with someone from the library?"

"I could've been at the grocery store."

"Then you probably would've had groceries when you came home."

Cade sighed. "I was with someone, but I don't think you need to check this one out."

"Oh, so now you're the expert. Why don't you stick to your job and I'll stick to mine?"

"Right. I'll stick to my fake job as a librarian and you can help Waverly put a criminal back on the street in exchange for her pie in the sky dreams of taking down the Oliveri family." Cade was tired and frustrated, and she didn't bother to hide her anger. "You want to know who I was with? I was with the district attorney, Emily Sinclair."

Kennedy's face scrunched into a frown. "What were you doing with her?"

"Not that it's any of your business, but we were on a date. You've been after me to acclimate? Well, I tried, but it's kind of hard to fit in when you get mysterious phone calls in the middle of a date and you can't offer a reasonable explanation to the person you're with."

"Slow down for a sec." Kennedy pulled over into a cutout by the side of the highway. She left the car running but turned in her seat to face Cade. "You're dating Emily Sinclair? The DA? Senator Sinclair's daughter?"

"Yes," Cade said. "I mean, we had one date. I'm not sure I'll get a chance at another."

"Yeah, well, that's a good thing."

Cade felt the slow burn of anger course through her veins. "What's that supposed to mean?"

"When I said you should socialize, make some friends, I meant you should do it to fit in. Chumming up to the most powerful family in the county will make you stick out like a sore thumb."

"Give me a break. I think you might be blowing this out of proportion."

"Seriously, Cade. The Sinclairs are very well connected. How did you even meet Emily?"

Cade started to say she'd met her at the library. That wasn't accurate, but she didn't want to share anything about the instant, mutual attraction on the courthouse steps with Kennedy. Every encounter since had only served to reinforce her initial reaction. Emily Sinclair was someone she wanted to get to know, inside and out. Kennedy's warning only made her less inclined to share the details of how she'd met Emily, let alone describe any specifics about their date Friday night, but it definitely piqued her interest in seeing Emily again. She settled on a vague answer. "We ran into each other around town."

She glanced at the clock on the dash. Too late to take back her no response to Emily's invitation for dinner tonight, but she had a renewed desire to fight for what she wanted, and right now, all she wanted was Emily.

Chapter Thirteen

Emily stood at the tabletop podium in the conference room and took a moment to assess the eighteen grand jurors. The medical examiner, Dr. Narey, had spent the last hour describing the condition of Wade's body at the crime scene, and his testimony and the accompanying photos were pretty gruesome stuff. This was the perfect time to take a vote, but she wanted to make sure none of the jurors had any lingering questions.

"Do any of you have anything you'd like to ask?"

She looked around while she waited for them to answer. Most of them were shaking their heads, and she'd about decided they were done, when Josh Howard tentatively raised his hand. Emily knew Josh and his family well. They owned a couple of drugstores in town—local places that had managed to stick around despite the invasion of the bigger chains. Josh's family, like many in town, had contributed to her campaign, and she figured she could count on him to return the indictment she was requesting based on the fact that he'd backed her reputation in the past. "Mr. Howard, what's your question?"

"Has there been any progress on finding the gun?"

"No, but the sheriff's deputies are still looking for it and will do everything they can to locate it before the defendant goes to trial." She cleared her throat. "Your task today is to determine whether or not there is probable cause to believe that a crime occurred, and whether it is likely that the defendant committed that crime. Basically, you are ratifying the decision Sheriff Nash made when he chose to arrest the defendant."

She knew many of the grand jurors respected Nash and would uphold his decision under any circumstance. "It is not your job to decide if the defendant is guilty, so you need not concern yourself with whether or not that's been proven here." She paused, hoping she'd delivered just the right balance of practical and authoritative. It wasn't that she didn't want them to ask questions, but she'd seen grand juries run amok in the past, getting bogged down with issues that didn't have anything to do with the legality of their task. Even if they decided to start running down rabbit holes, she'd presented them with enough evidence to indict, and she wanted to have that indictment when she walked into Judge Burson's court this afternoon. "Are you ready to take a vote?"

A few minutes later, she had her true bill, signed by Josh. She thanked the group for their service on this case and turned the grand jury room over to one of her assistants to carry on the rest of the day's docket while she made her way to Burson's courtroom, stopping to make a couple of copies of the indictment on her way. Seth rushed her the minute she pushed through the courtroom doors.

"Judge is about to take the bench. I was beginning to wonder if they'd gone rogue on you."

"Nipped that in the bud." She handed him a copy of the indictment. "Not a chance in hell Miller's getting out on bond. That one's for Brody. I'll let you deliver the bad news."

Emily settled in at counsel table while Seth walked over to Brody and handed him the indictment. To his credit, Brody didn't look surprised. He glanced at the paper in Seth's hand, and then waved it away as if it was a pesky insect. More likely than not, he was resigned to the fact his client was going to be spending the next however long in jail. She planned to approach him after the hearing to make the first volley in the inevitable plea negotiations. A quick and clean end to this case would be the best result for everyone involved.

A loud knock shook her out of her thoughts, and she looked up to see the bailiff rap his knuckles on the hard wood door that led back to judge's chambers. He commanded everyone to rise as Judge Burson pushed through the door. When Burson took the bench, he motioned for them all to sit down, and then he spent a moment sorting through the file in front of him before calling their case. "Counselor," he said to Emily, "where were we?"

She stood. "Good afternoon, Judge. It was my understanding you continued the bond hearing to determine if an indictment would be returned against Mr. Miller. I can report the grand jury true-billed Mr. Miller's case today, and a copy of the indictment has been provided to defense counsel and one has been filed with the court clerk."

Burson spent a minute flipping through the papers on the bench. While he did so, Emily looked around the courtroom. Seth had mentioned the victim's family might be on hand for the bond hearing, and she wanted to be able to point them out for the judge if they'd shown up. Indictment or not, the judge would keep Miller in custody, but it wouldn't hurt to have the sympathy factor in evidence to seal the deal.

She recognized the only two folks in the courtroom. A reporter from the local paper and a student blogger from the Jordan College campus newspaper. She'd almost decided the family hadn't been able to bear to hear more about the death of their loved one when the courtroom doors opened and a lone figure walked through the doors. A welcome face for sure, but not one she'd expected to see here, today or any other day.

Cade took a deep breath as she walked into the courtroom, memories of her own time as a prosecutor flooding her memory, but this room, with its ornate wood benches and soaring balcony, was nothing like the modern, more sterile environment of the courtrooms in Cook County.

The room was eerily quiet, and she noticed right away court was already in session. Emily was standing in the well of the courtroom a few feet from the judge who was thumbing through some papers. She looked over at the defense table and saw a young man, probably late twenties, dressed in a suit, sitting next to an older guy wearing an orange jumpsuit and handcuffs.

She probably shouldn't have shown up like this, but she'd spent the morning waffling about whether she should see Emily again until she could no longer resist the urge. She told Monica she needed some personal time and left work after lunch. When she'd shown up at Emily's office, she'd been thrown when her secretary said she was in court, and she almost abandoned her impromptu plan, but curiosity combined with attraction, and she'd wandered down to the courtroom, hoping for a glimpse of Emily in action.

As Cade started to slide into the nearest seat, Emily turned and their eyes locked. Knees bent, she remained transfixed for a moment, trying to get a read on Emily's expression. Was she glad to see her? Annoyed she'd shown up while she was working? Before she could process the look in Emily's eyes, she heard the judge say, "I'm ready to make my decision," and the spell was broken. Emily turned back to the bench, and Cade sat down, certain she'd caught a hint of a smile on Emily's face before she turned away.

The rest of the proceeding was like a mismatched tennis game.

"Based on the evidence presented last week about the defendant's history, and his lack of ties to the community, and the grand jury indictment today, I'm setting the bond at one million dollars. Please see my coordinator about an announcement setting, and we'll check in then to see where you are on the case."

Cade had done some reading on Texas court procedures and knew that an announcement setting was basically a check-in with the court to see where things stood, primarily regarding plea negotiations. Apparently, it was customary to have several of the settings to give the defendant time to review the evidence and consider any pleas before he or she made a decision about whether or not to go to trial. Considering this, she was shocked when the kid at defense counsel table stood up and addressed the judge.

"Your honor, Mr. Miller would like to exercise his right to a speedy trial. Provided the prosecution produces discovery, we can be ready to go in a month. May we go ahead and get a date while we're on the record?"

The judge looked down at the kid, a surly frown on his face. "You sure about that, Mr. Nichols?"

"Yes, sir, I am. Absolutely."

The judge shook his head and looked over at Emily, who didn't bother trying to hide the look of surprise on her face. "Ms. Sinclair?"

Before she could answer, the kid piped in. "Judge, I'm not sure the DA's office should be consulted about this. My client's right to a speedy trial is not something they get a say in."

"Maybe so, Mr. Nichols, but I still want to hear their position, and since we're in my courtroom, I think we'll do this one thing my way, if that's okay with you?"

"Yes, sir."

Emily seemed to be watching the exchange with a touch of amusement, her lips turned up in the tiniest trace of a smile. "Judge, we have no problem granting the defendant's wish." She reached down and grabbed a binder from the table. "I have my calendar and I'm happy to set a date right now."

Cade watched as they worked out a trial date a mere thirty days away. Without knowing much about the case, other than it was a murder trial, she was stunned. In all her years as a prosecutor, she'd never seen a defendant rush to trial on such serious charges, and she wondered if the kid in the suit knew what the hell he was doing. Obviously, the state didn't have a problem with the quick date, so they were either confident in their own evidence, or certain the kid didn't have the skills to mount a proper defense.

Before she could give what she'd just seen more thought, the judge smacked his gavel and the proceeding was over. She rose as he left the bench and stood at the back of the courtroom while Emily packed up her things, trying not to bore holes in her as her own anxiety grew. She hadn't planned this part. How would she explain her abrupt departure the other night and her curt decline of last night's dinner invitation?

"Are you here for the defendant?"

Cade looked over her left shoulder to see a young woman standing beside her dressed in a hooded sweatshirt, low-slung skinny jeans, and Chuck Taylors. She looked vaguely familiar. "No, I'm not."

"Damn. I was hoping maybe someone was here for him that I could talk to and get a personal angle." She cocked her head. "Don't I know you?"

Cade edged away, "I don't think so."

"Wait a minute. You work at Jordan College, don't you? In the library?"

Relief. "Yes, that's me. Are you a student there?"

"Yep." She stuck out her hand. "Asher Risley. You've probably heard of my campus blog *The Risley Report*."

Cade nodded, a small lie. She hadn't heard of the blog, and she didn't read the campus paper, although now she wondered why she hadn't. If she was going to really fit in with this community, she should really take some time to try to get to know it. "Let me guess, journalism major? Are you reporting on this case?"

"You bet I am. Do you know the last time there was a murder case in this county?"

"Matter of fact, I don't."

"It was three years ago, and then it was some dude whacking his wife's boyfriend. Nothing like this where a guy murders somebody for no reason. Well, other than to steal his money. Crazy, right?"

"Crazy."

"Anyway, I'm hanging out, hoping I can get a quote from Ms. Sinclair. Maybe get her to explain what just happened."

Cade opened her mouth to offer her own explanation, and then shut it again. She could explain plenty, but she wouldn't be able to explain how she knew so much about what had just transpired, and the best route would be to keep her mouth shut. Luckily, Emily appeared at her side and saved her from comment.

"Asher, nice to see you again."

Cade looked between them. "You two know each other?"

"Asher covered my entire campaign," Emily said. "For a while there I thought she was collecting one of every bumper sticker, but then I realized she was really lying in wait with tough questions. Right, Asher?"

"You know it. I've got some questions about this case if you've got time now."

Cade sighed. She'd hoped she could catch Emily for a few minutes at least. See if they could pick up where they'd left off, before Kennedy had yanked her back into her past, but she'd been silly to think coming here, where Emily worked, was a good idea. Of course, she probably had things to do, and talking to a reporter, even a kid like Asher, would take precedence. She started to tell Emily she'd see her later, but Emily surprised her.

"Asher, I'm happy to talk to you, but I've got to be somewhere right now." She scrawled a note on a piece of paper and handed it to the young reporter. "Call Janice, she's my secretary, and let her know I want to schedule a meeting with you tomorrow. Does that work?"

"Absolutely, thanks!"

Cade watched Asher head over to the defendant's side of the courtroom. Kevin Miller had already been taken back into the holdover, but the young attorney was gathering up his things. Asher approached him and he waved her off, a scowl on his face. She had no doubt whatever Asher wrote about this case, it was going to end up one-sided if he declined to talk to her.

"You interested? She's cute, but a little young."

Cade swung back around to face Emily. "You're funny. She's a student at the college, but I guess you already know that since you seem to be pals."

"Hardly. She dogged me worse than anyone in the professional press. She's a tiger, that one."

"Uh-huh." Cade was tired of talking about anything other than the reason she'd shown up here. "You have to work tonight?"

"Matter of fact I don't."

"You have plans?"

"I might now."

"Is that so?"

"I was thinking I might make dinner for a certain librarian I know."

"Sounds great." The whole exchange was going way better than Cade could've hoped. "Should I bring anything?"

"Just you." Emily paused, and her expression became serious. "There is one thing, though. Kind of a deal breaker."

"Uh-oh." Cade hoped she was kidding around, but she braced for whatever Emily was about to say. "Spill."

"This time I need you to check your cell phone at the door."

Emily leaned in close as she delivered the whispered demand, and Cade couldn't help but read the promise of something more than dinner into her words. If the memory of Emily's lips on hers was enough to leave her breathless, the anticipation of more was almost paralyzing. Almost. "Can't wait."

Chapter Fourteen

Emily opened the oven and peered one last time at the lasagna bubbling in the stoneware baking dish. Satisfied the lasagna was done, she switched the setting on the oven to keep it warm. Cade wouldn't believe she'd whipped it up after work, but at least it wasn't a Lean Cuisine from the freezer, which, aside from the salad on the counter, was the only other food in the house. In a panic, she'd called Clara from work and asked her to save the day. Clara had commandeered a portion of the food her parents' chef was preparing for dinner, placed it in a smaller dish, and now she had a mini lasagna—perfect for two. She sniffed the air, drinking in the rich aroma and stifling her guilt. She was going to serve Cade a homemade meal, even if it wasn't made in her home.

But food was really the last thing on her mind. Her invitation to Cade had been a swift and sudden reaction to seeing her tall, sleek self standing in the back of the courtroom. For all her doubts after Cade's abrupt departure the other night and her curt decline of Sunday's dinner invitation, the fact that she'd shown up this afternoon brought back, full force, the rush of arousal she'd experienced the first time they'd met. All she wanted to do tonight was explore those sensations and see if the reality was anything like the fantasies she'd played out in her head.

The sound of the doorbell signaled Cade's arrival. Emily glanced around the kitchen in a last-minute check to make sure everything was just right. Bottle of Chianti decanting, salad ready to be dressed. Clara had even added a beautiful vase of lilies to the mix. Perfect.

She swung open the front door and faced a smiling Cade holding a bouquet of Gerbera daisies. "Hi." She pointed at the flowers. "Hey now, I told you not to bring anything."

"Sorry. Actually, no, not sorry. I saw these and thought of you."

"You just happened to be wandering through the only florist shop in town. Browsing?"

"Yes. You never know when you might need flowers on a moment's notice. Pays to see what's out there."

Cade stretched out her hand, offering the bouquet. "They're my favorite," Emily said. "Lucky guess." She feigned shock. "Unless you've been spying on me or reading my diary."

Cade clutched her chest. "How dare you question my honor. The woman at the shop recommended them."

"That would be Nancy. They're perfect." Emily took her hand. "Get in here." She led the way back to the kitchen. While she opened a cabinet to retrieve a vase, she watched Cade out of the corner of her eye, walking around the room, checking out the dinner preparations.

"I see you already have flowers. Big, beautiful flowers."

Emily heard the question in Cade's voice and dispelled it quickly. "Clara brought those over. Guess she didn't want the house to look like I'm never here."

"That's okay, Next time, I'll bring something not as common, like maybe a Venus flytrap."

"Don't be silly." Emily poured water in the vase and arranged Cade's bouquet. "I like these better."

"Thanks." She sniffed the air. "Dinner smells delicious by the way."

"I may as well go ahead and tell you that Clara is responsible for dinner too. She brought the food anyway." Emily poured them both a glass of wine and handed one to Cade. "I'm pretty sure she pilfered it from my parents' house. Their chef is out of this world."

"You didn't have to confess, you know." Cade sipped the wine and tilted her glass in a kind of toast. "This is nice. But returning to the subject of your scandalous ways, I probably wouldn't have noticed until our fourth or fifth date that you weren't cooking your own meals."

"Fourth or fifth date, huh?"

"Yep. Although I'm beginning to wonder if you want to be seen in public with me. First you take me to a secret coffee house, then dinner twice, but only at your house. Makes a girl wonder."

Emily considered her answer. The truth was she wanted Cade all to herself, but she wasn't quite sure she wanted to admit that, not right now and not so soon, so she settled on a version of the truth. "Well, on our first date, I introduced you to Becca, and she's my best friend and pretty much the town gossip. On our second and now third date, I invited you here, the historic Sinclair house—maybe you noticed the plaque on the porch? Everyone in town knows this house, and everyone in town notices when there's a strange car in the driveway. I could take out an ad in the paper and it would get less notice.

"The truth is, I don't always get a lot of peace when I go out to dinner. People like to stop and tell me their problems. Everything from the barking dog next door to how the corner store could use better lighting. I imagine after the hearing this afternoon, that's likely to be even more true." She set her wine glass down and walked across the kitchen, stopping when she was only inches from Cade. "We can go out another time." She reached out and ran her hand from Cade's shoulder to her hand and curled her fingers into Cade's palm. "Right now, I'd like to get to know you, and we don't need an audience for that."

Cade raised Emily's hand to her lips and kissed her palm, sending shivers of anticipation through her. All thoughts of dinner and getting to know you talk receded to the back of her mind. Emily stepped closer. "Kiss me."

Cade's smile was super sexy. She used her free hand to feather Emily's hair away from her face before she leaned in and brushed her lips against Emily's in a teasing gesture of foreplay. "Like this?"

Emily groaned at the close, but not quite close enough contact. "More."

Cade ran the tip of her tongue along Emily's lower lip, tracing her way past her parted lips, and this time, she was the one who groaned. Emily ran her hands along Cade's hips and pulled her closer, rocking gently against her pelvis. The kiss was slow at first and gentle, then fast and hard, until kissing wasn't enough and the growing ache between her legs screamed for release. She leaned her head back and panted, "Follow me."

Emily grabbed Cade's hand and led her out of the kitchen, up the stairs, and down the hall, silently cursing the large house and the time she was wasting because her bedroom was so damn far away.

❖

Cade paused in the threshold of Emily's bedroom. She hadn't anticipated they would begin their evening here, but now she couldn't imagine doing anything else. Emily's soft lips, her commanding touch—she was helpless to resist. Besides, sex meant no talking, no uncomfortable questions about the past and future.

"What are you thinking, right now?"

Cade looked down. Emily's arms circled her waist and her eyes were dark with desire. "Thinking is overrated."

"Good," Emily said with a slow sexy smile. "I was starting to wonder if you were deciding between me and lasagna."

"Easy choice." Cade kissed her, losing herself in the heady haze of arousal. When they came up for air, she said, "Not to dis your lasagna, but I can't imagine it tastes better than this."

Emily placed a hand on Cade's chest and began toying with the buttons on her shirt. "Before we walk through this door, I want to tell you something."

"Sounds serious."

"A little." Emily ducked her head. "It's just…"

Cade looked over her shoulder into the bedroom. The light was off, but the moonlight through the window illuminated a beautiful four-poster bed. When she looked back into Emily's eyes she saw hopeful anticipation, and suddenly, she knew what was up. "Let me guess. You don't bring women up here on a regular basis."

"Hardly."

"Never?"

"That makes me sound like a prude."

Cade looked down at her partially unbuttoned shirt and grasped Emily's hands. "I don't think you're in danger of winning that title," she said with a smile. She held Emily's hands to her lips and kissed each knuckle, careful to keep her touch light and playful. "We can go back downstairs and eat dinner if that's what you want."

She pulled back slightly, while still holding on, and waited for Emily's reaction. She was hungry for Emily, but it wouldn't be right unless they were both hungry for the same thing.

When Emily pulled her hands away, Cade sighed and took a few slow deep breaths to rein in her libido, but she'd barely managed to catch her breath before Emily's hands were back on her chest, finishing what she'd started. Her entire body hummed as Emily pushed her shirt open and bent down to deliver featherlight kisses along her chest. She ran her hands through Emily's soft hair, drawing her face up to meet hers. Emily's eyes were glistening with arousal, black with need. She had her answer and she didn't waste any time. She tugged Emily's sweater over her head, and gasped at the sight of her beautiful breasts encased in a lacy black brassiere. "You're so beautiful," she murmured as she kissed her way around the lace. She reached around and unfastened the bra, and pushed the straps off Emily's shoulders. "Is this okay?"

Emily groaned and arched into her embrace. "Way better than okay," she murmured.

Cade smiled as she slid her tongue across one of Emily's nipples, enjoying the way she pushed into the touch. She licked and nipped at her breast until Emily's nipple was a hard point, aching with arousal. She lifted her head and looked into Emily's eyes, still dark with want. "Bed?"

"Yes."

Cade took her hand and led her across the room. The tall queen, four-poster bed was like something out of a magazine, perfectly made up with lots of decorative pillows and matching everything. Cade thought about her own bed at home with its tangled sheets and haphazardly placed pillows. She wondered what Emily would think if she saw her room.

"Is something wrong?"

Cade looked at Emily's face, her expression tentative. "No, not at all."

"I promise I don't always make my bed," Emily said. "I'm not that person, I swear. In fact, I didn't even sleep up here last night. I was downstairs prepping for the hearing, and I fell asleep on the couch."

Cade placed a finger on her lips. "It's okay. I have to admit I do think you might be more of a neat freak than I am, but as long as you don't mind if I wreck this little magazine layout you have going on here, it's all good."

Emily reached up and locked her hands around Cade's neck, pulling her close until their lips were almost touching. She whispered, "Wreck away."

Cade didn't hesitate. She pushed aside the fancy pillows and gently lowered Emily to the bed. With her auburn hair fanned out over the crisp white duvet, Emily was absolutely breathtaking. Cade bent over and ran her tongue along the waistband of Emily's skirt, while her fingers unfastened the button on the side. Emily lifted her hips, and Cade tugged the skirt off and tossed it on the floor, sending her panties to join it.

Emily turned her head and looked at her cast-off clothing. "I'm kinda liking your anti-neatfreakness."

Cade leaned over her and nipped her way from Emily's navel to her neck. "Tell me what else you like," she whispered into her ear.

Emily reached up and began unfastening the rest of the buttons on Cade's shirt. "I'd like you to lose these clothes, and I'd like to feel your skin on mine. Let's start with that and see where it goes from there."

Cade stood up, kicked off her boots, and shucked out of her jeans and underwear. She climbed onto the bed and stretched out next to Emily who wasted no time letting her hands travel from her waist down along her thigh. "That feels so good."

"There's more where that came from, but you have to lose the shirt," Emily said with a teasing tone.

Eager for more, Cade started to pull off her shirt when she remembered the ugly scar on her right side where Fontana's bullet had ripped through her flesh. She reached over and tugged the shirt off her left shoulder, and then shifted so she was lying on her right side, and finished the job by reaching behind her back, hoping Emily didn't notice her contorted machinations. "Better?"

"Much." Emily pulled Cade closer, into a deep kiss. Cade was an amazing kisser, and as she imagined her talented tongue touching the rest of her body, Emily felt a rush of wetness between her legs. The kissing was amazing, but she wanted—no needed—more. "Touch me. Please."

Cade slid a hand between her legs and ran a single finger through her slick, wet folds. Emily bucked at the touch, and then gasped when she felt Cade's mouth close around her breast. "That feels amazing. Please don't stop."

Cade answered by adding another finger to the teasing between her legs. She lifted her head. "Tell me what you want."

"Anything. Everything. I want to feel you inside me." She barely got the words out before Cade entered her, gently at first, and then again with more fingers, more force until she established a steady rhythm. Emily turned her head back and forth, unable to be still, but not wanting to disturb the perfect moment. "So good…" Cade's lips were back at her breasts, her tongue licking fast, keeping a steady pressure with her fingers down below. She could feel the swell of orgasm coursing through her body, begging for release, but she wanted something more, and she reached to claim her desire.

As consumed as she was with drawing pleasure from Emily's body, Cade barely felt the touch at first—a light, feathering trace of a touch along her side, agonizingly slow, but deliciously sure. Her own rhythm lost a beat as Emily's fingers traveled further down, with increasing pressure, teasing and tormenting their way along her inner thigh. "You're killing me," she whispered against Emily's breast, punctuating the remark with a flip of her tongue.

She looked up to see Emily's eyes locked on hers. "Come with me," Emily said. Cade's response was reduced to a groan as Emily smoothed the palm of her hand over her breast and massaged her nipple in tandem with the teasing touch between her legs. She was wet and hard and ready, and she would've said yes to anything.

Chapter Fifteen

Emily opened her eyes to a dark room and rolled over to look at the clock. Nine—a.m., p.m.? She raised up on one arm and looked next to her. Cade was lying on her side, her arm stretched across her stomach, looking adorable with her ruffled hair and sleepy eyes. "Have you been lying there watching me sleep?"

"Maybe," Cade said, her voice crackling with sleep. "Is that a bad thing?"

"No." She nudged her way into the crook of Cade's arm. "I'll tell you what's a bad thing though." She felt Cade's body tense, and she spoke quickly to dispel any notion Cade might have that she thought what they'd just done had been a mistake. "Someone who invites you over for dinner, but doesn't actually feed you."

Cade held her closer. "I'm amazingly satisfied for a hungry person."

"Shall I go downstairs and fix us a plate?"

"I'll come with you."

Emily traced Cade's naked chest with her fingers and shook her head. "I'm not sure I'm ready for you to put your clothes back on."

"Won't the neighbors talk if they see a strange car in your driveway late at night?"

Emily was torn. The neighbors would talk, but talk was just that, talk. If she was going to keep seeing Cade, was she going to be satisfied with early dinners and no sleepovers when it was clear they'd zoomed past that point tonight?

She looked at Cade's body, only partially covered by the sheet, and a surge of heat flooded her body as she remembered every touch they'd shared. She made up her mind. She might not be ready for an overnight, but she wasn't ready for this night to end.

As if sensing her dilemma, Cade pulled her close. "Tell you what, let's compromise," she said. "We'll get dressed, go downstairs, and eat dinner. Then we'll kiss good night, make plans for another date, and repeat this all over again sometime this week."

Cade was right. Hell, it was Monday night and the rest of the week was going to be insane, especially since she'd been crazy enough to agree to Brody Nichols's ludicrous request for a super speedy trial. "Okay, it's a deal, but only because if I don't eat soon I won't have the energy to do this again." Emily gestured at the tangled sheets and piles of tossed-off clothing on the floor. "This was quite the aerobic exercise." She reached over and switched on her bedside lamp, blinking as the bright light filled the room.

"Come on." Cade stood up and held out her hand. Emily looked up at her naked body, admiring her svelte physique that less than an hour earlier had quivered under her hands. As her eyes adjusted to the light, she had a much clearer view of Cade and her view confirmed what she'd felt earlier, but hadn't been able to see. Ignoring Cade's outstretched hand, she reached up and traced a finger around the edge of a nickel-sized scar along Cade's abdomen. "That looks awful. What happened?"

Cade looked down at her finger and flinched. Her expression telegraphed surprise and then fear and her flushed skin blanched.

"I'm sorry," Emily said. "Could I be more insensitive? It's just, it looks like—"

"Hunting accident," Cade interrupted her with a nervous laugh. "I guess I forgot to mention I'm accident prone." She grabbed her shirt from the pile of clothes on the floor and had it on and buttoned in record time. "But I won't be alive much longer if we don't eat."

Emily watched while Cade pulled on her jeans, debating about whether she should push the point. Cade clearly didn't want to discuss her injury, but Emily couldn't help but feel the intimacy they'd shared should have given her the right to ask. *You're being presumptive. She'll share if she wants to and how she got her scar doesn't affect you one way or the other.*

She pushed the detail aside to be examined later and focused on the right now, eager to recapture the incredible closeness they'd experienced moments before. She swung her legs out of bed and pulled on a robe. "Well, keeping you alive is definitely in my best interest."

"Is that all you're going to wear?"

Emily smiled. She loved the way the black silk robe draped against her skin. It stopped mid-thigh, so it wasn't exactly practical for cold weather, but practicality paled in comparison to the reaction it evoked from Cade. She reached over and placed a finger under Cade's chin, pulling her glance back up to eye level. "You keep looking at me like that and you're going to starve to death."

Cade laughed. "Yeah, but what a way to go."

Emily pointed at the door. "Downstairs now. If you still feel the same way after dinner, we can reevaluate the situation." She could hardly believe her own words, but her resolve was slipping. What was the point now anyway? It was way too late to take things slowly. The sex might have been fast and furious, but the cuddling and the banter signaled she was quickly becoming attached to Cade.

You hardly know her. She's hiding something. Emily let the refrain play for a few seconds before she pushed the doubts away. The reservations were real, but she was drawn to this woman, both mentally and physically, and she wasn't ready to pick apart the attraction.

Tomorrow. Tomorrow she'd sort out what was real and what wasn't, but tonight she refused to let her natural instinct for rooting out the truth ruin this perfect evening.

A few minutes later, they dove into the still warm lasagna.

"This is heavenly," Cade said between bites. "I'm thinking of breaking into your parents' house and raiding their refrigerator on a regular basis." She mocked an alarmed expression. "Guess I shouldn't have admitted that to the top prosecutor in town."

Emily laughed. "Don't worry. I have a feeling I might be a bit too busy over the next couple of months to prosecute a food burglar."

"That's right, the murder case. Did you know the victim? I didn't, but a lot of people I work with did."

"I recognize his picture, but I don't know if we ever met. I've met so many people over the past year, I started to lose track."

"Right, the election. I can see where, even in a small county, it would be impossible to get to know everyone."

"Don't get me wrong. I know a lot of people in Lawson. Remember, I grew up in a political family, and my dad started on the local level. A lot of my childhood was spent holding an American flag and pretending to enjoy all the Democratic rallies we attended every election season. I hated it at the time, but I guess it's in my blood." She took a sip of wine. "It helped me as a prosecutor to know all these people. Made it more real when the time came to talk to juries about the need to protect the community."

"Speaking of protection, have you tried many murder cases?"

"A few, but they're pretty rare here."

"Do you really think the Miller case will go to trial in a month?"

"Absolutely," Emily said. "Well, I guess the defendant could ask for a continuance, but he'd have to have a pretty damn good reason after Brody invoked the speedy trial request today."

"But thirty days is speedier than usual, right? I mean, do you honestly think anyone could realistically prepare for a murder case in thirty days?"

Emily heard the challenge in Cade's voice, but she wasn't exactly sure what she was challenging. "Well, I know I'll be ready."

"Really? You're going to try it yourself?"

"You sound surprised," Emily said, aware of the edge in her tone and trying to shake it. Cade's questions were simple and the kind she should anticipate from the local press, so why did she feel defensive?

"Isn't it a little unusual for the state's, I mean, district attorney, to personally handle a case at trial?"

"Not necessarily. One of my campaign promises was to be more hands-on than my predecessor. Besides, it's not like I don't know what I'm doing. I spent the last twelve years in the courtroom, and up until a few months ago, I was one of the top prosecutors in my office."

Cade held up a hand. "Hey, I'm not questioning your ability. I'm sure you're a skilled litigator. The defendant's lawyer seemed a bit out of his element. Guess I'm thinking it's a little David and Goliath anyway, and rushing off to trial in the next month seems to throw things completely out of balance."

"Did you just call me Goliath?" She didn't try to hide her growing agitation.

"Maybe it wasn't the best analogy, but you have to admit it seems a bit unfair."

"Actually no, I don't have to admit any such thing." Emily set her fork down, her appetite vanished. "It's not my job to make sure the defendant has the best representation possible. It's my job to make sure the laws are enforced for the protection of the citizens of this county."

"Did the defendant choose his lawyer or was the guy appointed?"

Emily took a swig from her wine glass. This conversation was spiraling out of control, but she couldn't seem to stop feeling defensive. "What does it matter to you? Last I checked you were just a librarian, not a lawyer. You thinking about leaving your quiet gig to go to law school so you can start defending murderers?"

Cade's expression shifted from curious to stricken, and despite her own aggravation, Emily wished she could reel the words back in. She set down her glass and stepped closer to Cade. "That was harsh. I'm sorry."

Cade backed away. "I think I should go."

Emily searched her eyes for any sign this situation was salvageable, but Cade's steely expression signaled she had erected a wall around the subject. "I'm really sorry. I didn't mean to hurt your feelings, but I promise you I know what I'm doing. I get it. From the outside looking in, things might seem unfair, but trust me, this is the way it's done."

"Was that supposed to be a less condescending way of saying what you said before?" Cade's asked, her sharp tone incredulous. "It's one of two things. You either think I don't know what I'm talking about or you don't care if I do."

Why was Cade suddenly the defensive one? "What do you want me to say? This is my job and I've been doing it for a while now. So well, in fact, the citizens of this county elected me to run the place." Emily could hear her voice rising, but she couldn't seem to stop this train wreck before it got out of hand. "Forgive me if I don't feel like I have to explain every decision to someone who's never had to stand in front of a jury and convince them to deprive someone of their freedom." Her words skidded to a stop as Cade's face furrowed into a firm scowl. She waited for some kind of response, but all she got was a shaking head and stony silence.

They stared at each other for what felt like forever before Cade said good night and started walking out of the room. Emily looked at her back. Was this really happening? Less than an hour ago, they'd been lying naked in her bed tangled in each other's arms, basking in the afterglow of amazing sex. How had their relationship disintegrated so quickly?

Because we don't have a relationship. Emily gave a silent curse for jumping into bed with Cade when she barely knew her. It was completely out of character, but she'd done it anyway. The pressure of the past year, the toll it had taken on her social life—she'd let her lonesome libido make the decisions tonight. This was no way to find a future wife. If they had a better foundation, maybe the argument they'd had this evening wouldn't have escalated.

She had a choice. Write the entire episode off or try to reconcile their differences. No matter what anyone ever said about her, she wasn't a quitter. She jogged across the kitchen after Cade. "Wait. Please."

Cade stopped but didn't turn around. Not the scenario Emily would have preferred to make her apology, but it would have to do. "Let's talk about this. Tonight was amazing, and I'm not ready to write it off over one silly argument. Please stay."

She silently counted the seconds she spent waiting for Cade's response. One, two, three…she made it to five before Cade was in motion again, but she wasn't headed back. She was headed for the door.

❖

Cade pulled into her driveway, shut off the engine, and leaned her head against the steering wheel. The night had started with such promise. A beautiful woman, a quiet romantic dinner. Before she arrived at Emily's house it hadn't even crossed her mind they would have sex tonight. Well, that wasn't entirely true. She had allowed a few fleeting fantasies, but for the fantasy to turn to reality? Totally not on her radar.

Emily had taken the lead, and she'd willingly followed because what fool wouldn't want to sleep with a woman as beautiful, smart, and passionate as Emily? But now she knew she'd made a huge mistake, and it had started the moment Emily noticed her scar, and reached its pinnacle during their argument over the Miller case. Getting close meant risking exposure. Women like Emily weren't satisfied with vague or glib answers in response to personal questions, and they didn't take well to having their integrity questioned.

She beat her palms against the steering wheel. Whatever had been blossoming between her and Emily was over. She didn't have to like it, but it was for the best. Relationships necessarily came with truth-telling, and her entire life was a lie.

A bright light caught her eye and she looked across the street to see Mavis Percy framed in the front window of her house. *Great. Way to draw attention to yourself.* She waved in Mavis's direction before pulling into the garage. She fumbled as she entered the house, having forgotten to leave a light on. When she finally flipped the switch, she kicked off her boots and tossed her jacket over a chair in a display of apathy. She was never going to have anyone besides Kennedy over, so what was the point of her obsessive need to keep things in order? There was no order to her life other than the need to keep up pretenses at all costs.

The kitchen was as clean and bright as when she'd left it earlier in the day. She pulled a glass from the cabinet and poured two fingers of the whisky she'd purchased when she'd picked up the bottle of wine she'd taken to Emily's on their first real date. At the time, she'd imagined they'd share the expensive single malt, maybe on their fourth or fifth date, maybe even here, at her place, but as she looked around the room, she realized her plan had been doomed to failure.

Where Emily's house was rich with history, hers revealed only scant traces of the person she was. No pictures, no knick-knacks. No mugs in the cabinet purchased on tourist junkets or souvenirs of any kind. Her dishes and furnishings were Pier One plain, nothing about anything in this house told her story because she didn't have a story, which meant she would never have a real life.

Chapter Sixteen

Emily stood up to stretch her legs and nearly tripped over a box. Two weeks after Miller's indictment, she'd taken up residence in the war room they'd created for trial prep. Her administrative work had fallen way behind, and she couldn't remember the last time she'd gotten a good night's sleep. She could not be more ready to have things at the office return to normal.

In her early days as a prosecutor, she'd tried dozens of cases on the fly, but they'd all been misdemeanor matters like DWI and criminal trespass. None of those cases had involved DNA evidence or the lifetime consequence of a murder conviction. She'd considered filing a motion to continue the case. Miller's right to a speedy trial meant the trial needed to take place within six months, not the thirty days Brody had requested, but she was reluctant to back down now that she'd agreed to the trial date currently on the calendar. Pride was definitely a factor in her decision, but she figured the rush to trial would ultimately work to Miller's disadvantage since she was a whole lot more experienced than her opponent.

Besides, being so completely caught up in litigation mode meant she didn't have time to think about anything else. She'd managed to beg off family obligations, town hall meetings, and most importantly, she'd managed to avoid processing what had happened between her and Cade Kelly.

Cade. Every time she came to mind, Emily's thoughts were a mixed-up mess of images of Cade, the sensual lover and Cade, the woman who'd challenged her about this case. Emily had made peace with the fact she'd overreacted to Cade's challenges, but since Cade had brushed off her apologies, both that night and in the text she'd sent the next day, it was clear Cade wasn't interested in her anymore.

She'd talked it over with Becca, who'd been no help at all, suggesting a grand gesture as the way to win Cade over, but only three dates into their relationship, Emily couldn't justify a grand gesture. Besides, when it came to Cade Kelly, she had more questions than answers, and since Cade had shut off communications, it didn't look like any of her questions were going to be answered anytime soon. Best to move on. When this case was over, she'd put herself back out there and see if she could find a better match, and hopefully, someone who captivated her interest like Cade had.

In the meantime, this case was her date, and it was as demanding as it was attractive. She'd used the cachet of her last name with the state forensic lab to hurry along the DNA results of the blood on the knife found at Kevin Miller's apartment. The favor had been worth spending since it was a ninety-nine percentile match to the victim. The evidence might all be circumstantial, but the circumstances were all pointing to Miller as the killer. Cade's probing questions about the case still echoed in her head, but she dismissed them every time they threatened to derail her. It wasn't her fault the court had appointed an inexperienced attorney to Miller's case, and she could hardly be blamed if his attorney had insisted on a quick trial. She'd be fair in every respect and let the chips fall where they may.

Seth poked his head in the door. "You ready to meet with the lab analyst? He's waiting outside."

She looked up from her paperwork, his entrance reminding her of another issue she needed to address. "Sorry, I guess I lost track of time." She handed him a folder. "Make sure Brody gets a copy of the lab report today, and make sure he has access to anything else he needs."

One of her campaign promises had been to change the way discovery was handled by the DA's office. Her predecessor had complied with the letter of the law, but never the spirit when it came to sharing information, despite new legislation that required extensive pre-trial disclosures. "I want you to personally ensure there are no missing pages in any of the discovery, and nothing is black-lined. Full disclosure."

"Will do." Seth took the folder she offered and thumbed through the pages. "This case is a slam dunk."

"Take that back, right now! I mean it."

He raised both hands. "Sorry, we haven't tried a case in a while, and I forgot how superstitious you get."

"Don't make fun of me. It's not cool to tempt fate. The case is winnable, and with a lot of hard work and prep, we will win it, but it's never a slam dunk until it's done. Clear?"

"Got it, boss." He stood and tucked the file under his arm. "I'll make sure Brody gets this today. In other news, Vivian is coming by for lunch. Something about pictures of potential wedding venues. Would you like to join us? Please say yes. You can distract her when my eyes start to glaze over."

"I'm going to pretend you didn't just imply that because I'm a woman, I'd be more interested in wedding planning than you are." She bit her bottom lip. She could think of a dozen reasons why she didn't want to join them for lunch. Watching two sickeningly happy people plan a wedding when she didn't seem to be able to get a foothold in any kind of relationship was high on the list. "Seriously, I can't make it. I've got to meet with the county commissioners this afternoon. I've already put it off twice, and I need some time to review the budget before the meeting. Rain check?"

"Fine, but don't think you can show up for the cake tasting if you haven't put in the hard work on the boring part of the planning."

"I completely understand. Count me in for next time," she said, holding out hope that next time would be far, far away.

Seth pointed at the boxes on the floor. "Why don't you let me assign someone to sort all of that into notebooks for trial? Would save us tons of time."

Emily knew that's what most attorneys in her position would do, but she'd developed a winning record by hands-on involvement in her cases. Just because she was in charge, she wasn't going to delegate trial prep to one of the dozen other assistant district attorneys in the office. "You won't know your case unless you build it yourself," she told him, anticipating his eye roll since she'd said the same thing every time they'd tried a case together. Seth had started out working at a large firm in Dallas and had gotten used to having a bevy of secretaries and paralegals at his disposal. He'd eventually adjusted to the slower pace of Lawson County with its do-it-yourself level of practice, but it hadn't been easy.

"Okay. I'll even do my own files when you've decided which witnesses you're going to toss my way."

"About that..." Emily paused as she considered the best way to tell him what was on her mind. She'd been up most of the night thinking about the trial. She's assumed Seth would be the perfect person to try the case with her since they'd come up through the office as trial partners, but lately he was always rushing off at Vivian's beck and call. She didn't begrudge him being involved in planning his own wedding, but she was working around the clock on this case, and she needed someone equally engaged.

"What's up?"

She plunged right in. "I'm a little worried you're distracted."

"What?" Seth's face reflected genuine surprise.

"I get it, I do. If I were planning a wedding, it would probably be the most important thing on my mind," she lied, "but for the next month, I need you completely committed to this case, and that might mean no running off to taste cake and try on tuxes in the middle of the day."

Seth sank back against the wall as if she'd punched him in the gut, and she instantly wished she could have a do-over. "I'm sorry. I realize that sounded harsh." Harsh—the same word she'd used to describe the way she'd reacted to Cade's comments on their final night together. *I'm on a roll.* She cast about for something to say in the face of Seth's silence. "I'm happy for you, I really am. We can figure this out."

"Yeah, okay." Seth pushed away from the wall. "I'll meet you in the conference room." He started to walk out of the office. "And about lunch, don't worry, I'll make it fast."

He exited the room so quickly Emily didn't have a chance to get another word in. She sighed. Was it this case or was she just destined to push people away lately?

❖

Cade sat in front of the computer in the research office, but the words on the screen were a big blur. It had been almost two weeks since her at first perfect and then calamitous last date with Emily, and she still couldn't shake her depression. Nothing about her life was what she'd planned: her career, her relationships, her anything. She was living a lie, and it made her feel powerless.

She didn't care about the work on her computer screen, dammit. She hadn't gone to school for seven years so she could do other people's research. She'd had a career with substance. The cases she had prosecuted protected the community, and she'd made a difference in people's lives, not just their livelihoods. Now, all she did was sit around all day, combing through reference materials with Emily's words echoing through her head. *Just a librarian*. The words hurt, but she couldn't deny the truth. She was just a librarian with no badge, no power, no ability to affect real change, and now that she'd broken things off with Emily, she'd shut out the one person with whom she'd had a real connection since she'd assumed her new identity.

"There you are."

Cade looked up to see Monica standing next to her desk. Great, another person she'd been hiding out from. As much as she could use a friend right now, she'd decided walling herself off was the only way to cope. "Hey."

Undeterred by the unenthusiastic response, Monica pulled up a chair. "You know, we have computers upstairs. I recall seeing one in your office. Care to tell me why you're hiding out down here?"

Cade gestured at the screen. "I'm not hiding out. Holing up maybe."

"Fair enough, but I'm beginning to take it personally. I left you two messages yesterday about the tennis tournament at the club, and I'm not buying that you don't have time to play."

Cade had wanted to ignore Monica's messages, but since they worked together, she'd settled for a little white lie, thankful at how easy it was to dissemble in a text versus in person. Now that she was face-to-face with her, she didn't have a clue what to say, so she settled on, "I had fun the one time, but my heart's really not into it. I'd only hold you back."

Her words were vague, but they were also true. Her heart wasn't into anything right now, and the prospect of running into Emily at the club was a nonstarter. She prayed Monica would drop the subject.

Not a chance. "I call bullshit," Monica said. "I'm talking to you not as your boss, but as someone who'd be a friend if you'd bother to let anyone in. Half the folks who work here are under the impression you think you're too good for them since you barely speak, and you don't make any attempt to be part of the group. I think it's something else, and I've got some ideas, but I'll keep those to myself. I do know this," she said, shaking a finger in Cade's face, "if you close yourself off like this, you're never going to be happy."

Cade flinched at the proclamation, but she couldn't deny the truth. Monica was right, but the problem was Cade didn't think she could ever be happy, and she saw no way out of it. Yet, something Monica had said sparked her to ask, "What are your ideas?"

"What?"

"You said you have some ideas, but you'd keep those to yourself. What are they?"

Monica shook her head. "I'm no gossip."

"Is it really gossip if you're talking to the person the gossip's about?" Cade smiled as she took a moment to digest the crazy of her own thoughts. "You know what I mean."

"I do, but this doesn't involve just you, and I think you know that. All I'll say is this. If you're scared to go out in public because of who you might run into, you're going to have a hard time making it around here. You might have to move to a bigger city."

Cade digested the revelation that Monica knew she and Emily were on the outs, and bit back the impulse to say she would move in a heartbeat if she had the option. From the outside looking in, she had it good here. A low stress job, a nice house in a quiet neighborhood, enough money to provide for whatever she needed, but she missed the things she'd lost, like her condo in the city and the identity defined by her career. She knew she should be happy she was alive and protected. All her basic needs were met except one, and it didn't matter where she lived, she'd never have love because it required honesty, a currency she could never spend. "I'm sorry, I just can't."

Monica shook her head and started to walk away but turned back. "Tell you what. I'm having a couple of close friends over for dinner on Friday night—" Cade started to speak, but Monica held up her hand. "I don't want to hear your excuses. Bring a bottle of wine and show up at my place at seven. You can pretend to have fun, if you want, but it'll make me feel better to know you're not sitting at home sulking. I'll text you the address."

Cade heard the gentle, caring tone behind Monica's command, but the idea of spending the evening with well-meaning strangers was more than she could bear. To keep the peace, she said, "I'll do my best."

Apparently satisfied her work was done, Monica left, and Cade looked back at her computer screen feeling a tiny bit better than she had before Monica had bullied her into submission. She dug into the project in front of her, relishing the opportunity to set aside thoughts of Emily and all the other things she couldn't have.

A couple of hours later, she wandered into the student union to grab some lunch. She was standing in line for a burger and fries, when she heard someone directly behind her say, "Are you really going to put that poison in your body?" When she turned around, she recognized the twenty-something blogger she'd met the day of Kevin Miller's bond hearing.

Cade looked over her shoulder, certain the kid wasn't talking to her.

"Yes, I mean you," blogger girl said. "I expect the other students not to know better, or even to care, but you're a teacher."

"You should probably get your facts straight. I'm just a librarian in need of French fries."

"There's absolutely nothing on that menu that won't leave you with clogged arteries and indigestion."

"Yep." *Maybe if I ignore her she'll go away.* Cade turned back to face the front of the line and willed the short order line to move faster or blogger girl to lose interest.

No such luck. The girl stepped up next to her and said, "You were at Kevin Miller's hearing."

Cade stared at the girl while she tried to shift gears. "Excuse me?"

"You know, the murder case. Kevin Miller? He's going on trial in a couple of weeks. I can't get anyone involved with the case to talk to me about it. Emily Sinclair said she'd meet with me, but she hasn't returned my calls, and Miller's attorney said he doesn't talk to bloggers. I think it's because I'm a girl, which is crazy, but he's pretty young so he should understand how important blogs are in the news world. Whatcha think?"

Holy hell, this girl was a pistol. Cade pondered how badly she wanted the greasy lunch she was about to order. There were three people ahead of her in line, and she didn't think she could take this kid's rapid-fire interrogation much longer. "Don't have a clue."

"But you know Sinclair, don't you? I mean you were there. We met. Remember? I'm Asher, Asher Risley, *The Risley Report*."

Cade remembered the meeting, but she'd been too preoccupied at the time with talking to Emily to remember this girl's name. She looked down at Asher's outstretched hand. She didn't want to engage with her, but impulse made her grasp her outstretched hand, and she was surprised at the firm handshake. "Nice to meet you, Asher," she said, because it was the polite thing to say.

"You can call me Ash if you want. A lot of people do. What's your name?"

"Cade Kelly."

"That's a cool name. Are you Irish?"

Cade started to say no, but decided instead it was the perfect time to test out one of the many little white lies that accompanied her identity. "Definitely have Irish blood in the family. How about you? Asher's a pretty unusual name." She didn't say "for a girl," but she was thinking it.

"Yeah, my parents were convinced they were having a boy, but when I popped out, they were already in love with the name, so they stuck with it. Don't think I haven't endured plenty of eye rolls, especially out here in the sticks."

"What made you want to go to college in the sticks?" Cade couldn't resist hearing the rest of the story.

Asher shrugged. "It's a good school, especially for journalism. And I got a juicy scholarship."

"Makes sense. Do you like it here?"

Asher cocked her head. "You're good."

"Come again?"

"At changing the subject. Suddenly, we're talking about me, and you've never answered any of my questions. Pretty smooth."

Cade found the impertinence refreshing and she had to laugh. "I wouldn't say I'm smooth. If you're looking for a scoop, I'm not your gal. I don't know anything about the Miller case, and Ms. Sinclair and I are only acquaintances."

She struggled not to wince with the last words. Acquaintance. The word didn't even come close to describing what Emily was to her, but she couldn't think of any other way to encapsulate what they'd become. An undeniable attraction, followed by riveting conversation, laughs, and mind-blowing sex would normally equate to at least part-time lover status, but add in the implosion and the fact she wasn't at all who Emily thought she was, and no label seemed to fit. Fraud was the closest, but admitting fraud cast a cloud over everything they'd shared.

Her gaze returned to Asher who was staring intently. "Why are you in this line if you think the food is poison?"

"Girl's gotta do what a girl's gotta do."

"So you'd eat a burger if it meant you'd get a scoop?"

"I'd pretend to."

Cade laughed again. She didn't want to, but she liked this kid. "Tell you what, I can't talk to Ms. Sinclair for you, but I work in the library and have access to LexisNexis and a ton of other helpful sites. If I can help you with research for the case, background information, that kind of thing, let me know."

"Really? You'd do that for me?"

"Sure, but under one condition."

"What's that?"

Cade wasn't entirely sure whether she was interested in hearing about the case, or if her question was a ploy to get information about what Emily was up to, but she ignored the voice in her head telling her not to get involved. She plunged in. "Tell me what you know so far."

"Hey." The kid behind the counter adjusted his white cook hat and leaned toward them. "Are you two going to stand there all day?"

Cade looked up to see the line in front of them had disappeared. "Sorry about that." She grinned at Asher as she asked him, "You have any salads back there?"

A few minutes later, she joined Asher, who'd abandoned her at the burger stand to make a trip to the salad bar. They were at the same table where she'd had lunch with Kennedy last month, the day of the criminal justice panel—the day she counted as her first date with Emily. Kennedy didn't approve of her seeing Emily, and she would probably have a serious issue with her getting involved with the Miller case, even in this most tangential way. She took a bite of her burger and decided she didn't give a damn what Kennedy thought.

"So, what do you want to know?" Asher asked.

Cade watched her shovel a forkful of greens topped with sprouts into her mouth. "Do you really eat all that rabbit food without any dressing?"

"The stuff they have here is loaded with sugar."

"Not following."

"Uh, no." Asher put her fork down. "Are we here to talk about my eating habits or the case? Tell me what you want to know."

"Everything."

"Everything?"

"Am I not enunciating my words? Yes, everything. I only know what I've seen in the papers. A man was robbed, shot, and stabbed. I know he worked here, in the administration. I know the defendant is in jail on a high bond, and his trial is set for a few weeks from now."

"Two weeks to be exact."

Had it really been two weeks since she'd seen Emily? Were they still going forward with the crazy fast trial date? "Unbelievable."

"What?"

Cade shook her head. "Nothing. Seems fast is all."

"That's what I thought, but Sheriff Nash said it's no big deal. He said Miller's attorney is just getting it over with fast since it's a total loser of a case."

"Sounds like something he would say."

"I know, right? He's kind of a jerk." Asher set her fork down. "Okay, well, you know a little, but not much. Here's what I've put together so far."

Cade listened as Asher relayed the details of the case, and she was surprised at all the specifics she'd managed to avoid. While she kept a close eye on the news for any mention of Leo Fontana, since she'd broken things off with Emily, she had made it a practice to switch the channel or stop reading whenever the Miller case was mentioned. Now, after hearing a few choice details, her curiosity was fully engaged.

"This guy, the eyewitness—"

"Ralph Thatcher," Asher said.

"Right, Thatcher. He didn't actually see the murder take place?"

"That's right. He lives next door to Mr. Wade. He drove up in time to see Kevin Miller going through Mr. Wade's pockets. He shouted 'What's going on?' and Miller took off."

Cade nodded for her to go on, but she mentally logged a few additional questions to ask later.

"So, then Thatcher calls the sheriff's office, and they send out a crew of deputies."

"Crime scene analysis?"

"Eventually, but first it was a couple of deputies on patrol."

"How do you know all this?"

"Hello, FOIA," Asher said with a duh-isn't-it-obvious tone. "I got a copy of the report from the sheriff's office." She leaned forward and whispered, "Plus, I listen to the police scanner every night." She pointed at her phone. "On an app. I don't think the sheriff realizes there is such a thing, so please don't tell him. Knowing him, he would figure out a way to block transmissions."

"Who me?" Cade finished her fries and looked at her watch. She needed to get back to the library, but she was actually enjoying herself for the first time in a couple of weeks and was reluctant to go. Asher's natural curiosity and attention to detail reminded her of herself as a young prosecutor, hungry to stand out among her peers. She decided another few minutes wouldn't hurt. "Okay, so back to the case. Wade was shot. Just once or what?"

"Just once in the center of his chest, but that wasn't what killed him."

"Come again?"

"He might have recovered from the gunshot wound, especially since Thatcher heard it and called the cops so quickly, but he didn't have a chance with a slit throat. Guy got his jugular, and he bled out in less than five minutes. Apparently, he lost like—"

Cade gripped the sides of the table, and the rest of Asher's words faded. The blood rushed from her face, and her entire body grew cold and still. She must've heard Asher wrong. Her imagination was playing tricks on her.

"You okay?" Asher asked. "You look kinda pale."

"Tell me again what you said about his throat." Cade could barely get the command out, but she had to know more. Asher recited the details of the wounds Wade had suffered with the same tone she might use to read a grocery list. To her, these specifics were pieces of a puzzle, but to Cade, her worst fear had come to life. She listened carefully to every word, praying her growing anxiety didn't cause her to black out before she could figure out her next step. She had to get out of here. Away from this job, this town, this county, this state, and she had to do it fast.

Chapter Seventeen

Emily sank into the chair and watched Becca prep the perfect pour-over. "I can't tell you how much I've been dying to get over here."

"You know you're welcome anytime. I figured you've been busy with work. Lord knows nothing else decent has been occupying your time."

A week ago, Becca had called to let her know the local gossip mill was reporting the nice-looking librarian hadn't been coming around the DA's house anymore. Not for the first time, Emily wished she could have all the benefits of small town living without the drag of knowing everything she did was fodder for public consumption. She'd told Becca the whole story, starting with how she'd finally gotten laid, but doing so had apparently been a big mistake since Cade went running the same night, and she hadn't heard from her since.

"Work is decent and it fills all my time," Emily said. "That other thing is for the best."

"'That other thing' was the best thing that had happened to you in a while. Good-looking, smart, funny. You sure did perk up when you were around her, and you didn't seem to be letting work get in your way when she was available."

"Then it's a good thing she's not, because I don't have time. The trial is in two weeks."

"How do you know she's not available?"

"I don't, but it doesn't matter."

"Call her."

"Not going to happen."

"Why not?"

"Besides the fact I'm so freaking busy I can't see straight?" Emily took a breath. Becca was her best friend, and she owed her honesty. Her flip answer didn't begin to touch the surface of what was really motivating her to wall off her feelings for Cade. She'd exposed parts of herself to someone she barely knew—that was the problem. "I don't know a damn thing about her."

"Bullshit."

"Seriously, Becca, I know surface things, but there were several times when we were talking, that I knew she was holding something back."

"Even in bed?"

"No." Within seconds of her denial, a memory flashed through her mind. The scar along Cade's side. She knew a bullet hole when she saw one, and it was clear Cade had been on the wrong end of a gun at some point in her life. *Hunting accident, my ass.*

If she didn't have a litany of other examples where Cade ducked questions or offered vague answers, then she might be able to write off her nagging inner voice warning her to proceed with caution. But it didn't matter anyway. Cade had walked away and she wasn't coming back. Emily felt bad about the way things had ended, but she supposed it was inevitable. Her life was transparent and she couldn't afford, professionally or personally, to risk a relationship with someone who had so many secrets.

She took the cup of coffee Becca handed to her. "Look, it's complicated. Can this be one of those times where you trust me when I say it's over and agree not to hassle me about it?"

Becca smiled. "I wasn't aware we had those times, but I suppose I could give you a pass just this once." She paused to take a sip of coffee. "On one condition."

Emily would do just about anything to get Becca to back off the subject of Cade Kelly. "Let's hear it."

"When this trial is over, you'll finally agree to go out on the town with me, and by town, I mean some place where you don't already know everyone. Dallas, Fort Worth, your pick." She held up a hand as if to stave off any protest. "Meeting someone from out of town who doesn't already know your life story, might do you good."

Cade had fit Becca's description, and look how things had turned out. Besides, someone who lived a couple hundred miles away would never be anything more than a fling, since Emily had built her future around a life in Bodark. She started to list all the reasons Becca's idea wouldn't work, but when she saw the look of concern in her eyes, she decided to agree for now and fight the point later. Maybe by then she would have forgotten all about Cade Kelly.

❖

Cade heard the sound of a car, and she looked out the window in time to see Kennedy's Jeep round the corner and pull to a stop out front. In a bizarre mirror image, she saw Mavis Percy's face peering out her curtains. When Kennedy jumped down from her vehicle, Cade could swear Mavis was tracking her movements. Great.

She listened at the door, and when she heard the heavy footfalls of Kennedy's boots hit the porch, she cracked the door just enough to see her face. "Took you long enough," she said, opening the door wider to allow Kennedy in before slamming it shut and throwing all the locks.

"I got here as fast as I could."

It had been two hours since Cade had placed the call to tell Kennedy that Leo Fontana's signature was all over the Sam Wade crime scene. Since then, memories of the day she'd been shot had flooded her brain. Neat bullet holes centered in the chest of the agents and her witness. Biermann's gaping throat. And blood. Gushing, spattered blood.

She'd made the call to Kennedy on one of the burner phones she kept in the duffel bag stowed under her bed. She didn't have much else in the bag: some cash, a couple of changes of clothes, but she'd figured it wasn't a bad idea to have some resources ready in case she ever needed to bug out. What she'd learned from Asher had nearly sent her running, but the delay in Kennedy's arrival had given her time to think. She'd spent half of it pacing and the other half running searches on the Internet about the Miller case. How had she missed a detail this critical?

Because you were so busy trying to get in the DA's bed, you let your guard down. She couldn't deny the voice in her mind, but it wasn't the whole story. The truth was she'd shut herself off from the rest of the world, and in doing so she'd become more vulnerable. Her online searches revealed the DA's office had released the full details regarding the method of Wade's death the day the grand jury reported out. The same day she'd shown up at the courthouse for Miller's bond hearing. The same day she'd slept with Emily.

She hadn't read a paper or watched the news that day because all she could think about was Emily. The only breaking news she'd cared about was how Emily's naked body felt wrapped around hers. And now she had nothing. No Emily and no safe place.

"Why don't we sit down, and you can tell me everything." Kennedy stood in the foyer, her expression a mixture of concern and curiosity.

"Yeah, okay. Let's get away from these windows."

Kennedy glanced at the window. "I had someone drive by a few times. I don't think anyone's watching you. Not right now anyway."

"Maybe no murderers, but the woman across the street is on her usual window patrol." Cade led the way to the kitchen. "Come on. I could use a drink."

She pulled two glasses from the cabinet and held up the bottle of whisky. To her surprise, Kennedy nodded. She poured them a couple of fingers each and handed a glass to Kennedy.

"This is good stuff."

"Drink up. If I have to move, I'm packing light."

Kennedy took another sip. "I made some calls after we talked. Someone's sending me a copy of Sam Wade's autopsy report, but it sounds like they have this Kevin Miller dead to rights. He was found standing over the body, and they found a knife with blood on it in his apartment."

"I've been thinking about that. Maybe he stumbled over the body and picked up the knife, decided to keep it."

"You really think he didn't do it?"

"I know it sounds crazy, but the bullet to the center of the chest, the slit throat? That's Leo Fontana's signature move. He shot three agents and a key witness outside of the Cook County courthouse and he took the time to slit the witness's throat. He did it to send a message. You really think some transient who robbed for a few bucks would do the same?"

"Where did you hear about the exact manner of death?" Kennedy asked. "All I've seen in the news is that he was shot and stabbed."

"Even that's a little excessive for a simple robbery, don't you think?" Cade realized she was ducking Kennedy's question, but she might as well confess her source. "There's this blogger for the campus news, and she—"

"A blogger? Seriously? She probably made up the whole throat slitting thing to sensationalize her story."

Cade tamped down her anger and forced a measured response. "There are two things wrong with what you just said. One, she hasn't published these facts. She just received the police report as part of a FOIA request. And two, if she had made them up, don't you think it's a little weird that her fiction happens to match the modus operandi of a guy who has a lot of motivation to come after me?"

Kennedy drummed her fingers on the table, her face fixed into a scowl. Several minutes passed and Cade waited out the silence, certain she'd finally convinced Kennedy the prospect of immediate danger was real.

"Okay, here's what we do," Kennedy said. "We're going to get you to a safe house until I can find out more." She pulled out her phone. "Grab a bag and I'll make some calls. Make sure you have everything you need to start over in case we can't come back."

Cade had already started to walk toward her bedroom at the words "grab a bag," but Kennedy's last words stopped her cold. "Wait a minute."

Kennedy looked up from her phone. "What?"

"What do you mean, 'in case we can't come back'?" Cade was certain she already knew, but she wanted to hear Kennedy say it.

"If you've been made, we'll have to start over. New name, new location, the works. It makes sense to be ready, just in case."

Cade's head reeled as she processed Kennedy's words and the possibilities facing her. Another home abandoned, another job left. What would Monica think if she never showed up for work again? Granted her job at the library didn't provide the same gratification as her law career had, but walking out on obligations had never been her style. Now it seemed to be all she was capable of. Her first thought when Asher told her about the way Wade had died was to run, flee this place that Fontana had obviously found, but somewhere deep in the back of her mind, she'd been holding on to hope Kennedy would offer some solution that didn't involve completely uprooting her life again.

She glanced toward the bedroom. Her makeshift go-bag was stuffed under the bed. All she had to do was add a few pieces of clothing and she'd be ready to follow Kennedy to safety. There was absolutely nothing else in this house, nothing she'd accumulated since she'd started her new life that she cared about taking with her. Sadness washed over her. She had no outward symbols of worth, no pictures, no mementos. She could disappear right now, and no one's life would be any different, but hers would remain empty, unfulfilled.

Would Emily even notice if she disappeared? Would she miss her? In the first few days since they'd last seen each other, Emily had reached out, but Cade had ignored her attempts, thinking it was best to make a clean break. Now, faced with the prospect of never seeing Emily again, even in a chance meeting, regret consumed her. She should've returned Emily's calls or texts, apologized for the confrontation, and attempted to explain why a relationship between them wouldn't work. If she had it to do all over again, she'd handle the parting differently, perhaps even leaving the door open for more if her circumstances ever changed.

But her circumstances were changing, only for the worse. She glanced at Kennedy. Her eyes were narrowed and the quick nod she gave signaled urgency. Cade was supposed to follow, without question, leave her new life behind, and place herself in the hands of the government once again.

Her gunshot wound might have healed, but Fontana had robbed her of everything else. On the heels of this moment of clarity another crystal clear thought rushed in. *Only if I let him.*

Chapter Eighteen

Emily looked up from her desk, and Janice was standing in the doorframe with a steaming cup of coffee in her hand. "Hey, what's up?"

"I thought you could use this." Janice strode toward her and held out the mug. "Would you like me to order in some food?" She gestured at the stacks of paper on Emily's desk. "Looks like you might be at this for a while."

Emily accepted the mug and took a long swallow of the dark blend. "Hmmm, this is the good stuff."

"Becca sent it over." Janice crossed her arms like a stern schoolteacher. "Now, about food. What would you like?"

"I'm not hungry."

"That's fine, but I'm not leaving your office until you give me a food order."

Emily took another drink of coffee and pushed aside a stack of files to make room for the mug on her desk. After yesterday's conversation with Seth, she'd spent the day working alone, putting together her trial notebook and witness files. Seth was in the building, but he hadn't stopped by once, and it was her fault for the way she'd handled their conversation about his extracurricular activities. She didn't regret broaching the subject, but she wished she'd handled it differently. When he was focused, Seth was an excellent litigator, and she was lucky to have him on her side. What she wished she'd done was assume he would be well-prepped for trial instead of assuming the worst, but jumping to conclusions seemed to be a skill she'd honed to a sharp edge of late.

While she let him cool off, she'd turned her attention to the fast upcoming trial. Today, she was meeting with Brody Nichols. Ostensibly, the meeting was for her to make sure her office had fully complied with the new Michael Morton Act discovery rules, but she had a secondary purpose—to assess whether Miller might be persuaded to take a deal. Light overtures regarding pleading to a lesser included offense had largely been ignored, but Emily was convinced it was because she hadn't had the opportunity to sit down with Brody and walk him through the case, point-by-point, stare him in the eyes, and tell him straight up that his client was going to be found guilty, and he'd be serving the rest of his life in prison.

Seth was still stewing because she'd told him she wanted to take this meeting alone, but she had to if she wanted her plan to work. Based on what she'd seen so far, Brody was like a trapped animal. If he felt cornered, he would run rather than come back swinging. She needed him to feel comfortable enough with her, but uncomfortable enough with the evidence to talk his client into taking a deal.

She looked again, but Janice hadn't left. Fine, maybe food was exactly what she needed, and breaking bread with her adversary would be a perfect way to ease him into her offer. "Order a couple of sandwiches from the Purple Leaf. Roast beef and some of that crazy good pasta salad."

Janice smiled. "Want me to add some of those chocolate chip cookies you like?"

"Yes. I mean no." The cookies were for parties, not negotiations, although now that Janice had mentioned them, they were all she could think about. "No cookies, just the other stuff. Do you think you can get it here in time for the meeting?"

"You really have no idea how skilled I am, do you?" Janice whirled out of the room before Emily could reply.

Thirty minutes later, Janice returned with the food and Brody Nichols. She set the lunch up on Emily's credenza and excused herself from the room.

"I hope you don't mind," Emily said, pointing at the sandwiches. "I haven't eaten, and I thought it would be nice if we took a few minutes to get to know each other. I had a lot of respect for your father."

Brody cracked a smile, but it didn't reach his eyes. "Most people did. He cast a big shadow."

"I know what that's like." Emily infused as much empathy as she could into her words, hoping this might be the connection she was seeking.

Brody cocked his head. "I guess you would. How is Senator Sinclair?"

"The usual. Bigger than life. Proud of his daughter, but probably secretly wishing she was in the family business."

Brody nodded. The next few minutes were filled with a semi-comfortable silence as they dug into lunch. Emily polished off half a roast beef sandwich in a few quick bites, surprised at how hungry she'd gotten. She hadn't had a decent meal in the last two weeks, subsisting on snacks, frozen dinners, and protein bars. She'd begged off Sunday brunches with the family, partly because she was busy, but mostly because she didn't want to run into Cade at the club, and she could do without her mother's offers to set her up on a date.

Maybe after the trial she'd consider venturing out into the dating pool again, but it wouldn't be with some Junior League setup. She wanted someone who wasn't connected to the country club set, the powerful elite. She wanted someone down-to-earth, someone who could make her laugh and someone who didn't care about pretense. She wanted Cade.

"I assume you invited me here to make your best offer."

She looked up into Brody's inquiring gaze. God, she had to stop drifting off into fantasyland. She put her half-eaten sandwich down and folded her hands on the desk. "I did. I assume you've had time to review all of the evidence?"

"I have."

"Then I don't need to tell you we have a solid case. I know you haven't tried many criminal cases." She held up a hand as he started to speak. "Don't get me wrong, I'm not picking on your lack of experience, but you probably haven't had an opportunity to see some of the witnesses in action." She paused for a moment to give Brody an opportunity to relax back into his chair. "Juries love Sheriff Nash. I know he can be a bit blustery, and I personally find it off-putting, but when he testifies, he has the entire jury in the palm of his hand.

"Dr. Narey is another great witness. He doesn't try to impress juries with a bunch of big words and complicated medical terms. He's going to lay out the case step by step. He'll tell the jury how the blood on Miller's knife was a DNA match for the victim, and he'll do it in terms even a preschooler could understand."

"I assume you haven't found the gun?"

Emily cleared her throat. "Not yet." The missing gun was a thorn in the side of the case. Nash insisted his deputies had scoured the creek area where Miller had run to after the witness scared him from the scene, but so far they hadn't located the weapon. She planned to convince the jury that the knife was the real murder weapon, so the missing gun shouldn't matter. But it mattered to her. Based on the bullet forensics, the gun was a forty-five caliber Desert Warrior. Where had Kevin Miller gotten such an expensive gun? Where had he ditched it? Something about it felt off to her, but she didn't know what to do about it, and they had enough evidence to go forward without it. She offered a compromise. "If you'd like to ask for a continuance to give us more time to find it, I won't object."

"Not likely." Brody leaned back in his chair. "I know you think I'm in over my head, but even you started somewhere."

"I may have started my career in criminal law with a misdemeanor or two, but definitely not a murder case."

"Fair enough. But here's the deal. I have a client who's stuck in jail with absolutely no possibility of being able to bond out. He wants to go to trial right away, and I work for him. The last thing I'm going to do is give you more time to gather evidence against him."

"I have enough evidence now for a conviction."

"You might."

Emily stared across the table. She knew a bluff when she saw it, and she remembered bluffing her way through some cases when she was new to the criminal bar. She was torn between wanting to help Brody save face and getting the life sentence she knew she could get at trial. The very best thing for all involved was to avoid a trial. Wade's family would be spared the indignity of a public spectacle, and the citizens of Lawson County would be spared the expense and publicity of a murder trial. She looked down at her notes and made a split-second decision not to engage in the usual back and forth of plea negotiating by shaving ten years off the offer she'd initially been prepared to make. "Thirty years."

To his credit, Brody's only discernible reaction was a slight blink of his eyes. Emily hoped it was because he'd been expecting her to offer more time.

A few beats passed and he said, "Thirty years is a long time."

"Yes, but it's not life," she replied. "Your guy is what, forty-five? He takes thirty and he'll be eligible for parole in fifteen. If he gets out then, he'll have time to make a new life."

"And if the jury finds him not guilty, he'll walk out of jail in a couple of weeks, a free man."

Emily drummed her fingers on the desk but didn't reply. There wasn't much use trying to talk Brody out of his fantasy. She supposed he had to believe a not guilty verdict was a possible outcome or why even try? She waited, thinking he would counter, but knowing she'd already played her best hand.

A moment later, he stood up, shook her hand, and thanked her for the meeting. He was gone before she could ask him if there was any amount of time his client would consider taking. *Well, that was a colossal waste of time*. Emily stabbed her fork into the last of the pasta salad from the Purple Leaf and contemplated what had just happened. She couldn't put a finger on why, but she had the strangest feeling she'd lost the upper hand. That seemed to be happening a lot lately.

Cade slid into a seat at the Purple Leaf Cafe and glanced around. The predictable purple walls featured a bunch of fun typography and original paintings by art students at Jordan College, but what caught her attention was the heavenly aroma of fresh roasted coffee and the scent of chocolate.

She'd barely assessed her bearings when bells jingled to announce someone new had walked into the shop, and she saw Asher headed toward her. Out of the corner of her eye, she watched as the tall, bulky man at the table closest to the door shifted in his seat. Asher gave the guy a hard look before she made her way over to Cade's table.

"Hey, I was hoping you'd call," Asher said as she plopped into the seat opposite Cade's. "Did you change your mind and talk to Sinclair for me?"

"Slow down, blogger girl," Cade said. She pointed at the bakery case. "You want something, or are baked goods not on your list of approved food groups?"

"If you're buying, I'll have a triple espresso and a slice of the turtle cake. Ask them to sprinkle a few extra pecans on top. Please."

Cade looked at the skinny kid and laughed. "Let me guess, your only form of exercise is lifting a coffee cup to your lips several times a day?"

Asher grinned. "Pretty much."

Cade slid a twenty across the table. "I'll buy, but you order. Bring me a regular cup of coffee."

Asher stood and stuffed the bill in her pocket. Before she made her way to the counter, she leaned over and whispered in Cade's ear. "Pretty sure the guy at the table by the door has the hots for you. He keeps looking over here. Either that or you owe him money." She barely had the last word out of her mouth before she shuffled off to the counter and placed their order.

Cade shook her head but purposely didn't glance at the guy Asher had pointed out. Eric Bosco had appeared on her doorstep last night in response to a call from Kennedy. Cade had braced for the big guy to haul her off against her will, but it turned out Bosco's presence was a compromise, and Kennedy made it clear if Cade refused to leave, she would have to have a bodyguard until they could sort things out.

Maybe she should have left last night. It would have been easy to pack a couple of bags and ride off to the next clandestine locale. All the explaining would have been left to Kennedy, and she would've had a clean slate in a new life, again.

She'd gone as far as packing her bags, but when the time came to lock up the house and jump-start her new identity, she simply couldn't do it. What if Fontana chased her to the next place? If, as she feared, he'd found her here, who was to say she'd be safe anywhere? She was in a much better position to evade him if she wasn't on the run. If she moved to another town, she'd eventually be lulled into a false sense of security, and one moment of inattention could be her last. No, she'd stay here and lure Fontana out of hiding so he could be taken down like the animal he was.

Kennedy had come unglued when she announced her decision, insisting she was being irrational, but Cade stood her ground, threatening to go public if Kennedy didn't go along.

"I can only guarantee your protection if you do what I say."

"That sounds an awful lot like imprisonment, not protection."

"Call it what you will, but no witness in the program has ever been harmed—"

"If they follow the rules. I know, I know." She explained her position. "I've followed all of your rules, but it looks like Fontana has figured out where I am. Did you know Sam Wade worked in the personnel department at Jordan? Who's to say he didn't give Fontana information about me before he got his throat slit?"

"No one at the college knows who you really are."

"You can't be certain of that." Cade sighed. "I'm staying here. If you want to pull my protection, go ahead, but then you can explain to Jodie Waverly why you left her key witness twisting in the wind." She stared hard at Kennedy to convey the full force of her will. She wasn't entirely sure she wasn't making a huge mistake, but she couldn't deny the surge of power that came with deciding her own destiny.

Now, seated at this cafe, about to enlist the help of a twenty-year-old blogger, she couldn't help but question the wisdom of her decision. She looked across the room. Asher was flirting with the cashier. One word to Eric and Cade could be out of here, whisked away to someplace far away. She glanced at the door. She could almost see the outline of the courthouse across the square. Was Emily in her office? Did her thoughts ever roam to the brief, but consuming time they'd shared, or was she solely focused on the murder trial set less than two weeks away?

"Black, right?"

She'd missed her window. She could still leave, but if she'd really wanted to, she'd be gone already. She reached for the coffee Asher held. "Sure, thanks."

Asher handed her the coffee and set a tray on the table. The slice of cake was bigger than her head, but Asher tucked into it like she'd conquered it before. Cade pointed at the plate. "Next time you talk to me about poisoning my body, I'll remind you of this."

"Chocolate is medicinal," Asher said as she took another bite. "So, are you going to tell me why you called this meeting?"

Cade took a sip of coffee and used the pause to gather strength. She'd stayed up all night formulating her plan, but now that she was ready to say it out loud, she was certain she'd sound crazy. What the hell? "I want you to tell me everything else you know about the Miller case, and then I want us to go see Brody Nichols."

Asher cocked her head. "Last time I started talking about the case, you got all pale and crazy-eyed."

Cade was ready with an explanation. "Must've been the hamburger. Red meat and murder don't mix well."

"Right."

"Truth. Now, will you tell me what you know?"

"Sure, but first you tell me why you're so interested."

Cade had prepared an answer for this question too. Something vague about research, current events, and library stuff, but when she opened her mouth to answer, instead of the fiction she'd invented for a cover, the truth came tumbling out. "Because Kevin Miller didn't kill Sam Wade, and I want to make sure the person who did doesn't get away with it."

Chapter Nineteen

Emily strode into the war room and dumped her files on the table. "Looks like we're going to trial."

"He should've taken the deal," Seth said. "Forty is a gift compared to what a jury will give."

"Thirty."

"Excuse me?"

"I took pity and offered thirty. I thought he'd at least consider it."

Seth's response was a low whistle. "You're way nicer than me. He'll have to take it to his client."

"I'm sure he will, but don't hold your breath." Emily paced the room, her mind spinning with all the things they still needed to do to get ready for trial. The long list set off a rush of adrenaline that made the thought of spending the rest of the afternoon cooped up in the office inconceivable. "Do you have any witness prep scheduled for the rest of the day?"

"No, why, what do you have in mind?"

"Let's go visit the scene. See if Lance is free so he can come with us," she said, referring to the lead DA investigator. "I don't want any of the sheriff's deputies there. I want to see it fresh, without a play-by-play from Nash's guys."

Seth nodded. "Good idea." He looked at his watch. "Can you give me about thirty minutes? I need to stop by Elena's office. The father of the vehicular homicide victim, Ethan Jansen, is coming by today, and I promised I'd stop by to let him know we're committed to the case and all that. You might want to avoid her office if you don't want to get caught up."

"Thanks. I'll get involved if you need me to, but I'd like to stay focused on this case for now. I'll meet you in the parking lot in thirty." Emily picked up the nearest file and skimmed a few lines, but she forgot what she read faster than she could read it. Determined to clear her head, she opted for a walk around the square while she waited for Seth.

The weather was perfect for a stroll, the only drawback was how many other people were taking advantage of the warm, sunny day. After a half dozen hellos and good afternoons exchanged with random townspeople, followed by idle conversation about the upcoming murder trial, she wished she'd waited for Seth at the courthouse. She'd almost decided to hide out in her car when she spotted the sign for the Purple Leaf Cafe and immediately thought of the cookies she'd been craving since she'd told Janice to leave them off the lunch order. No reason to deny her cravings now. Determined to satisfy one of her desires, she opened the door and ran into someone standing in the doorway. Before she could catch her breath, strong arms circled her in a protective hold, and she looked up into Cade Kelly's searching eyes.

"Are you okay?" Cade asked.

She wasn't. Not now anyway. If she'd known her cookie craving would lead to a chance meeting with Cade, she would've walked on by. But now that they were face-to-face, she floundered, torn by the concern she saw in Cade's eyes. She settled on something she hoped was true. "I will be."

"I'm sorry."

Cade's voice was soft and low and heavy with portent, and Emily was certain the apology extended beyond their mishap in the doorway. Cade's hands, still resting on her waist, only reinforced her belief, but before she could respond, Cade pulled back and her arms dropped to her sides. She stepped to the side of the door and Emily followed, but the spell was broken.

Emily wanted the connection back. "I'm sorry too."

"I should've called, it's just..."

"It's okay." Emily wanted desperately to know the reason Cade hadn't called, but she didn't want to push. Not here, not now. All she wanted in this moment was to suspend time so the surge of heat from Cade's touch would linger. "I've been busy."

"I imagine so."

Cade's voice was sad. Was she the cause? Or was the source of her sadness one of the other secrets Cade had chosen not to share with her? Would she ever know?

Two weeks had passed without a word, and Emily had written off their brief interlude as a bump in the road on her path to a permanent relationship. But standing here, facing Cade, she knew without a doubt what they'd shared was much more than a detour.

If only Cade felt the same way. She'd held out hope, but Cade had walked out on her and continued to shut her out—her actions made it clear what they'd shared was casual sex and nothing more. She should turn around and walk out the door because there was nothing for her here. But she couldn't bring herself to make the break.

"Are you free right now?" Cade asked.

For a brief moment, Emily let everything else slip away: the trial, the fact Seth was probably already outside waiting in the car, and the caution she'd wrapped around her heart. She wanted to say yes. She wanted to join Cade at a table in the quaint cafe. She wanted to hold hands, and spend the rest of the afternoon sharing decadent cookies and conversation about topics having nothing to do with murder and politics. Becca's words about Cade echoed in her head. *Good-looking, smart, funny. You sure did perk up when you were around her, and you didn't seem to be letting work get in your way when she was available.*

And then Emily heard someone else ask the question she'd been about to.

"Cade, are you ready?"

Emily turned toward the sound of the voice and saw the twenty-something girl from Jordan College who'd been dogging her for an interview. Asher Risley. Her head swung back to Cade, and she saw her grimace, like she'd been caught doing something she shouldn't. Caught doing what? The words tumbled from Emily's lips before she could stop them. "Looks like you're the one who isn't free."

She knew she sounded petty and hostile, but she couldn't help it. She'd let down her guard again. No amount of heat and desire could make up for the fact Cade didn't want what she wanted. "I have to go." Emily forced her voice to sound more resolved than she felt.

Cade's hand on her arm was gentle, but insistent. She looked into Cade's eyes, but she couldn't get a read on what Cade wanted; she only knew it wasn't her.

"Please don't go," Cade said.

Out of the corner of her eye, she saw Asher back away. Emily had no idea what she'd stepped into the middle of, but it didn't matter. Nothing had changed between them. Her deep and persistent attraction to Cade wasn't enough to overcome the chasm of secrets that divided them. "It's not going to work."

"We've barely even tried." Cade's eyes dropped. "I have things I need to tell you."

"It might be too late."

"It's never too late."

"I wish I believed that." Emily glanced at the door. Second thoughts threatened to derail her, but she resisted the pull. "I really do have to go."

"I'll call you later."

Emily shook her head and stepped to the door. She pushed through to the outside and gulped in the cool air. She wanted to stay, but she needed to go. She wanted Cade to call, but she needed her to stay away if she had any hope of focusing on her work. When this trial was over, maybe…

She knew exactly how she wanted to finish the thought, but she wasn't ready to hope.

❖

Cade watched Emily walk across the street and get into a blue sedan. She recognized the driver as the prosecutor who'd assisted Emily with Kevin Miller's bond hearing, and she told herself work was the only reason Emily had walked away.

"Everything okay?" Asher asked.

"Yes," Cade lied. Seeing Emily again was a mixed up mess of arousal and pain, and the brief encounter had been too quick, too shallow. She had so much she wanted to tell her, but what was the point if she couldn't tell her everything? "You ready to go?"

"Sure," Asher said, "But I've got a question first."

"Shoot."

"Sinclair's the one trying this case, right?"

Cade nodded, certain she knew where Asher was headed.

"Then why can't you just tell her your theory?"

Cade had spent the last half hour giving Asher a rough sketch of her ideas about the Miller case, including a vague reference to other murders with similar MOs, but she had no desire to get into why she didn't think Emily would be receptive to her insights. Describing the way Emily had already derided her questions about the case would get into other more personal topics, like their brief, now nonexistent relationship. It would be better for everyone if she shared her information with Miller's attorney and let him do the heavy lifting. She settled on a simple answer to Asher's question, hoping she wouldn't persist. "It's complicated."

It took a minute, but Asher's eyes grew wide, and she nodded her head vigorously. "Oh, okay. I get it. I was totally getting a vibe between the two of you."

Damn observant kid. "Are we going or not?" Cade asked in a stern tone, hoping to shut down any further conversation about Emily.

Asher answered by leading her down the street, in the opposite direction of the courthouse. Cade saw Eric, her bodyguard, cross the street, and then discreetly double back to follow. She hoped Asher wouldn't notice him, but her worry was wasted since they didn't go far. Brody Nichols's office was a two-story Victorian, located a block away on a side street off the main square. Cade followed Asher up the steps to the expansive porch, but she stopped near the rail.

Asher looked over her shoulder. "Change your mind?"

Cade held up a hand. "Give me a sec." Truth was she hadn't thought this through. If she marched into Nichols's office and told him she knew who the real killer was, he was going to want proof. All she had to offer was a strong hunch based on her own personal story, a tale she wasn't ready to disclose, especially not to a total stranger. Cade knew in her gut Leo Fontana had killed Sam Wade, but hunches only mattered to the people that had them. Nichols would want to see some evidence, and he'd be more likely to accept it as credible if he respected the source. She'd have to figure out a way to earn his trust, but she didn't have much time to do it.

She tapped into her past. She'd done this before dozens of times. Every time she'd gone to trial, she'd stood in front a jury of complete strangers and asked them to trust the evidence she was about to present, to accept it as truth, and return after their deliberations with a guilty verdict. She'd earned their respect by cutting through the bullshit, and she'd earned their trust by telling them a story using the evidence as highlights and filling in the rest with the most credible theories she could postulate.

"I've got this," she told Asher. "Whatever happens in there, follow my lead. Okay?" She waited until Asher nodded. "Let's go."

The office wasn't at all what she expected. Brody Nichols was young, only a year out of law school, but this place was dripping in money. While Asher gave their names to the elderly woman who sat at the front desk, Cade looked around, admiring the massive mahogany desks, built-in bookcases, and beautiful antique rugs—all symbols of success. Since yesterday, she'd searched for everything she could find on the Internet about Brody Nichols. She'd learned he was the grandson of a local district judge who'd retired from the bench years ago and was now retired from private practice. Local county records showed Brody owned this building, but more likely than not, he had inherited these offices from his prominent grandfather. He'd probably also inherited the secretary who looked to be in her eighties.

The thought reminded her of the woman who'd answered the door when she'd shown up at Emily's house for the first time, Clara. Must be a small town thing—coming into your own, but still saddled with the trappings of your family. Had Emily paid a price for having an influential US senator as a father or had her family's clout been what propelled her to success?

That wasn't fair. Based on her research, Emily had paid her dues. She'd started as an entry-level misdemeanor prosecutor and worked her way up to a felony trial litigator. She had a stellar record, and many members of the local bar had worked hard on her campaign. It probably hadn't hurt that she was a Sinclair, but it didn't appear she had traded on her name to garner her win.

The real question here was how had Brody Nichols, a rookie, been appointed to handle a murder case? Cade was certain his family name had factored into his appointment since he hadn't been in practice long enough to acquire the kind of experience he'd need to attract a client charged with murder.

"Mr. Nichols will see you now."

The ancient secretary led them down a long hallway. Cade looked around as they walked, but she didn't spot anyone else working, and the empty desks looked like they'd been empty for a while. When they reached the end of the hall, the woman rapped on the heavy wood and pressed her ear against the door. After a moment, she said "you can go on in," and she stepped out of the way.

Cade opened the door and waved Asher in, and then followed close behind. Brody was sitting behind an enormous desk completely covered with a haphazard spread of papers. He looked up and gestured for them to sit in the chairs across from the desk. "Lois said you had some discovery to drop off from the DA's office. Do you need me to sign for it personally?"

Cade shot Asher a look, and she was met with a shrug. Silently cursing her cohort for lying to get them in the door, she fumbled to find a plausible way to get to the heart of why they'd shown up uninvited. "Actually, I think she may have misunderstood," Cade said. "My name is Cade Kelly. I work at the library at Jordan College and this is Asher Risley. She's a journalist with the campus newspaper."

Brody stared across the desk, his expression morphing from vaguely interested to pretty pissed off. He picked up the phone on his desk, but before he could punch the buttons to summon Lois to escort them out, Cade intervened.

"Give us fifteen minutes of your time. I promise it'll be worth it."

Brody looked between them, and Cade could only imagine what was going through his head. A librarian and a blogger show up at a lawyer's office. It sounded like the beginning of a bad joke, but there was nothing funny about the story she was about to tell.

After several seconds of silent surveillance, Brody put the phone down and leaned back in his chair. "Fifteen minutes."

Asher opened her mouth to speak, but Cade beat her to it. "I've been doing research on murder cases for a paper I'm working on. It's for my post-graduate work, and because I work at the library, I have access to a lot of online research databases. Asher here has been working as my intern and helping with the research. She also writes a blog for the campus news, so naturally when Sam Wade was killed, she started looking into the case, not just because Sam was a respected member of the administration, but also because his death frightened a lot of people on campus. It was so sudden and shocking, you know?"

She paused and looked at Asher, who nodded for her to go on. Certain she was rambling, she launched in again, for fear Brody would cut her off in the middle of her muddled tale and toss them out of his office.

"My interest in researching these type of cases came from my uncle. He's an attorney back East. He's retired now, but during his career he worked on lots of criminal cases, and I always found them fascinating. Anyway, I was asking him something about my paper, and I happened to mention this case and the circumstances of Sam's death. I mean, how many would-be robbers take the time to shoot their victims and then slit their throats? Seemed really odd to me." She paused for a second, and Brody nodded his agreement.

"So my uncle, he says, 'You know, Cade, I recall reading about a couple of cases around here with that same MO, but they were gangland style killings, meant to send a message.'"

She took a breath and assessed her audience. Asher was on the edge of her seat, scribbling notes in a small spiral flip top notebook, and Brody was staring holes through her. She couldn't tell if he was interested in what she was saying or contemplating the easiest way to throw them out.

"What's your uncle's name?"

Cade swallowed hard, her throat thick with angst. She'd hoped to skate through by being as vague as possible, but apparently, Brody wanted a few actual facts before he'd hear her out completely. "John Kelly. He's retired now, but he practiced in Saint Louis."

Lies, but chances were good there was some attorney with the name John Kelly in Saint Louis, although she doubted Brody would ever check. His questions were likely more about evaluating her overall trustworthiness rather than verifying specific facts. "Anyway, I did some additional research and found a few articles referencing this type of killing. Apparently, there's a particular mob enforcer who's known for this method, and he's wanted by the FBI."

She reached in her jacket, pulled out a folded up printout from LexisNexis, and held it out to him. Her hand in mid-air, she watched his face, willing him to take the paper. He stared at it, then flicked a glance at Asher and back to her. With a heavy sigh, he reached for the printout, unfolded the paper, and smoothed it out on his desk.

"So, what am I looking at here?"

"Reasonable doubt."

His head jerked up. "What?"

Cade silently cursed. She needed to dial back the legal jargon. She wasn't here as a lawyer. All she needed to do was point him in the right direction and let him do the rest. She shrugged. "I'm not sure what it all means, but if there's someone else who uses this particular method of killing people, then maybe you could use that somehow, you know, to maybe create doubt about whether your client is guilty." She shrugged again in an "I don't know how all this works, but I'm just trying to help" kind of way. To deflect attention from herself, she pointed to Asher. "Asher here is planning to write an article calling into question your client's arrest and pointing to these other killings as something the sheriff's department should have researched."

Cade shot a look at Asher who did a pretty damn good job of keeping her composure in view of the fact they hadn't discussed writing any such article.

Asher tapped her pen on her pad, and said, "Yep. I'm planning a whole series of blogs about the trial starting with what she said."

Brody steepled his fingers and stared at the printout Cade had given him. "There's just one problem."

Cade knew what he was going to say, but she resisted the urge to demonstrate she'd anticipated his question. She flashed him her best questioning expression. "What is it?"

"Even if we assume the same person was responsible for Sam Wade's death as these other murders, how do we explain why this person singled out Wade? Are you trying to tell me Sam Wade was connected to the mob?"

He was right. The leap of logic was a big one, and she had no idea how he could overcome it without the information only she and a few federal agents possessed. Not for the first time in the last few days, the urge to blurt out her entire story was strong. She examined her options. If Leo Fontana really wanted to kill her, why hadn't he done so yet? If he was the one who'd killed Sam Wade, he'd certainly gotten close enough. Had he gone underground after Wade's murder?

Not likely. She pictured him standing on the street outside of the courthouse in Chicago, firing his weapon and not caring who saw him. He'd only ducked into hiding at the risk of being caught. But here, someone else had been tagged for his crimes.

Maybe that was it. Another murder in a nearby town would cast doubt on Kevin Miller's guilt, and law enforcement would likely start to connect the two crimes. Fontana was probably biding his time so he could take her out without the scrutiny of an entire town already hyper-focused on the big trial about to take place. In the meantime, she didn't know how to answer Brody's question.

"We don't know yet, but we're willing to help you find out," Asher said. She reached over and gave Cade a light shoulder punch. "Right, Cade?"

"Yes," Cade answered, her mind whirring. "In addition to Asher's investigative reporting, I can offer my research services at no charge, as long as I can use this case as part of my project. Who knows? We might be able to find some answers, but if nothing else, I can promise you we'll look harder than the sheriff's department did." She watched Brody's face, hoping the pride of youth wouldn't keep him from accepting her offer of help.

After a long pause, Brody said, "I do have a few things I could use help on. Judge Burson allocated some funds for an investigator, but the only guy I could get to work for court appointed rates doesn't seem inspired to do the work. I'm pretty sure he's shoved my assignments to the bottom of his stack." The minute he finished talking, he pointed at Asher. "That's not for public consumption, got it?"

Asher raised her hand to her mouth and mimicked locking her lips and throwing away the key.

Watching her, Cade came up with an idea. "You know, you could use some press. Everything I've read so far has your client tried and convicted, already. Maybe..." She let her mind race while she considered the pros and cons of what she was about to propose.

Asher and Brody both stared her down until finally Asher said, "Spit it out already."

"Okay, here's what I'm thinking." She pointed at Brody. "You'll give Asher exclusive access, and she can do a series of blogs with more of a personal interest angle than straight-up reporting. She can write about how you're the underdog, going up against the system, and all the cards are stacked against you. You'll have an opportunity to float your theories about what really happened and a chance to plant seeds of doubt in the community."

"I don't mean to be a jerk," Brody said, "But the students at Jordan College aren't likely to be serving on this jury. Over half of them aren't even residents of Lawson County."

Asher jumped in. "But *The Risley Report*'s on the Internet. I'll optimize it so anyone doing a search for information about the case will see it at the top of their feed. If we can saturate the search engines, there's a good chance the local news outlets will pick it up, and it may even get some regional coverage."

Cade suppressed a grin at Asher's enthusiasm, hoping her zeal would convince Brody to accept their offer. She didn't have to wait long for his answer.

"Okay, let's do this," he said. "When can you start?"

Chapter Twenty

Emily stared out the car window, her eyes sweeping over every detail of the exterior of the single-story white bungalow that had been Sam Wade's home. The town of Rymer was the same size as Bodark, but not as quaint. The houses along this street in particular were fairly plain, although they appeared to be well cared for. Lawns were mowed, leaves raked, but absent were the extra details like garden beds and ornamental trees. In front of Wade's home, a long, wide driveway led to a small front porch enclosed by a wood railing lined with potted plants in various stages of demise. As they drew closer, she heard Seth engage the turn signal, and she placed a hand on his arm. "Let's park on the street."

"Right," he said. "Good plan." He pulled to the curb and shut off the engine. "Lance said he'd be about ten minutes behind us. Do you want to wait for him?"

"Why don't you wait here for him while I take a look around?" She didn't wait for his response before she climbed out of the car. She stood at the curb and surveyed the neighborhood. Ralph Thatcher, the witness who'd arrived home to find the person he identified as Kevin Miller standing over Sam's body, lived in the house to the left of Wade's, but his driveway was located on the far side of his home.

Emily mentally cued up the narrative from the police report. Thatcher told the sheriff's deputies that as he drove past Wade's house the night of the murder, he noticed a man in Wade's driveway, hunched beside Wade's Ford Explorer. It was dusk at the time, and his first thought was the figure was Wade, looking for something on the ground. He rolled down his window and called out, which apparently startled the man, who stood up straight and faced him head on. Within about two seconds, Thatcher could tell the man staring at him wasn't Wade at all, but a bum from the run-down apartment complex less than a quarter mile away. He'd encountered the same man in the neighborhood, knocking on doors, looking for odd jobs as recently as the week before Wade's death.

Thatcher having seen Miller before was a lucky break because the front porch light wasn't on at Wade's house the night of the murder, which would have made it difficult for Thatcher to see enough detail to give the sheriff's office much in the way of a description if he hadn't already known what Miller looked like.

Unlike the night of the murder, the driveway was now empty. No Ford Explorer, no Sam Wade, and barely even a trace of a bloodstain on the concrete drive. Still, Emily needed to stand where Wade had stood when he climbed down from his SUV. She needed to close her eyes and imagine the last few minutes of Wade's life as horrific as it may be. Doing so would allow her to channel the details of the senseless act of violence into a riveting opening at trial. Fully focused on her task, she took a step toward the driveway, but the rumble of a car engine stopped her progress.

Lance Tobin, the chief investigator for her office, pulled over and parked his giant pickup directly behind Seth's car. He unfolded his tall, lanky body out of the door slowly and methodically and walked over to where Emily was standing. "We looking for anything in particular?" he asked.

"The usual—trying to get a feel for the scene." Emily motioned to Seth who was walking toward them. "You want to give us a rundown?"

"Sounds good," Lance said. "Follow me." He led them to the porch and pointed at a single light fixture by the door. "According to Deputy Bowman, this light was out that night."

Emily nodded at the mention of the first officer on the scene. "I saw that in his report. Do we know if the bulb had burned out or was it just not turned on?"

Lance's response was a puzzled look, and Emily said, "What?"

"The light was out because there was no bulb in it."

Seth flipped through the pages of the report he'd brought along. "Odd, the report doesn't mention that."

Lance frowned. "Bowman told me himself. I guess I'd assumed he told you too."

Emily stared at the light fixture, bugged by the circumstance, but not quite able to put her finger on why. "Lance, I need you to talk to Thatcher and some of the other neighbors again. I want to know if Wade's light was normally on."

"Will do." Lance fished a battered notebook out of his pocket and scribbled a few lines. "What else?"

"Ask them again about the gunshot. I can't believe no one heard anything." The ME's best guess was Wade had been shot close to the time Thatcher happened upon Miller standing over him. At least three close neighbors had been home at the time, but everyone the sheriff's deputies spoke to denied having heard a thing. Either their walls were all super soundproofed, or people in Rymer were way less interested in their neighbor's business than the citizens of Bodark.

Lance nodded. "I'll go door-to-door when we're done here, maybe catch some folks coming home from work."

"Thanks," Emily said. "I'd like to go inside. You have the key?"

Lance produced a key ring from his pocket, unlocked the door, and held it open. He knew her well enough not to point out that the inside of Wade's home wasn't technically part of the crime scene. She crossed the threshold and took a moment to breathe in the faint scent of vanilla tobacco. Wade had been a pipe smoker. His sister, Wendy, had talked about his pipe collection when Emily interviewed her last week. She'd gone on and on about how they'd found pipes in almost every drawer of the house as if Sam couldn't bear the thought of being stuck in a room without one. Emily had let her ramble on about the pipes for a good twenty minutes, certain it was a necessary part of her grieving process.

Now, standing in Wade's home, she cataloged the tale as one of the stories she would tell to the jury so they could understand that a real person with real human interest had been abruptly taken away from his family, his friends, and his community.

"Anything interesting in here?" Seth asked. He'd followed her in and was standing right behind her.

"The family left everything the way it was for now. They have an estate sale company coming in next week to start pricing everything, but they probably won't have the sale until after the trial." Emily picked up a photo of Wade and his sister and two brothers. "None of them live around here, and they decided it would be easier to travel back just once for the trial and then to take care of the estate."

"What's this?"

Emily looked at the shiny square object on the shelf Seth had pointed to. "I don't know. Lance, any ideas?"

Lance picked up the square and examined it. "Looks like a signal mirror, the kind they used in the army. This one's really old, like World War II era. There are a few other things like this in his den."

"Wendy mentioned their grandfather fought in the war," Emily said. "Lance, do you mind getting a picture of this and the other things you mentioned?" Her mind started formulating her opening statement. She'd paint a picture of Sam Wade for the jury, a quiet man who'd worked a long week at the local college. He'd driven home, planning to spend a quiet evening in his home, surrounded by his collection of pipes, family photos, and the souvenirs of his grandfather's service to his country.

It was a start, but her preparation was thrown by a nagging feeling something was off. While Lance snapped pictures, she led Seth back outside. "This light thing is bothering me."

"What's the big deal?"

"Let's see what the neighbors say, but if Wade's light was usually on, the bulb being gone could be an issue."

"I'm not following. Maybe the bulb burned out and he removed it."

"Without replacing it? How many times do you remove a burned out bulb without putting in a new one? If a bulb burns out at my house, I leave the damn thing in until I have a new one."

"Fair enough, but I still don't see your point."

"What if someone unscrewed the light bulb so they could hide out and surprise Wade when he got home?"

Seth shook his head. "I don't make Miller for thinking that one through. He's more the smash and grab kind of guy."

"Exactly."

Seth stared at her for a moment. "What a minute, you're not thinking it could have been someone else that killed Wade, are you?"

Emily shook her head. "No, but you have to admit it makes you think. I do know this, Bowman's report should have said the bulb was missing, and either he needs to issue an amended report or we need to tell Brody."

"You're kidding, right? That's splitting hairs. The report says the light was out, so Brody's on notice. What difference does it make if it was a burned out bulb versus a missing one?"

"Probably nothing, but I'm not going to risk appellate issues because we complied with the letter, but not the spirit of the law. Give him the light bulb information and, if he tries to make something out of it, we'll deal with it then."

Seth's tone made it clear he wasn't happy about her decision, but she didn't care. She would do this right or not at all. The memory of her argument with Cade about the case surfaced, and Emily's first thought was that if Cade did call, she could tell Cade she wasn't a prosecutorial jerk after all. She shook her head. No, if Cade called, the last thing she wanted to talk about was this case.

After three hours of staring at police reports and the evidence in the case, Cade told Brody she'd be back the next day, and she left his stuffy office. Asher had left an hour earlier so she could make her deadline for tomorrow's edition of *The Risley Report*. Her first story was going to be about how quickly the sheriff's department had rushed to zero in on a suspect, even though they had yet to find the gun involved. She'd follow that up with a piece about the inherent unreliability of eyewitness testimony. Cade had pointed her in the direction of some research on the subject.

Cade stepped down from the porch and looked around. She didn't see Eric, her US Marshal babysitter, but she suspected he was nearby. She considered her next action in light of whether she wanted him to witness what she was about to do. Deciding to hell with it, she pulled out her phone and sent Emily a text. *Are you free? Can we talk? In person.*

She looked at the time on her phone. Almost seven thirty. With the trial only a couple of weeks away, Emily was probably still working. No doubt, if this were her case to prosecute she'd be working around the clock until the trial was over.

But if it were her case, would she be pursuing the charges? Cade liked to think she wouldn't, that she would have opposed the quick trial date to allow more time to develop the evidence and force the cops to explore all angles, but it was easy to say that from her position on the outside. Emily was an elected official, and as much as she probably didn't want to admit it, politics necessarily played into her decisions. The local news outlets were applauding the swift move toward justice as well as Emily's decision to try the case herself, and Cade could hardly blame her for getting caught up in the momentum of what could be the headline case of her career.

Her phone buzzed to signal an incoming text. *Yes to both. Where are you?*

Cade typed: *Outside the courthouse*. She hit send, and then quickly added: *Not stalking you. I promise*, hoping a little levity would take the edge off.

Meet you there in five.

Cade shoved her phone in her pocket and paced to kill time. Twenty steps to the end of the block and twenty steps back. She resisted the temptation to check her watch, and repeated the process several times, varying the length of her stride to keep from thinking about what she planned to say when Emily showed up. On her fourth turn to head back to the courthouse, she stopped cold.

Emily was standing at the bottom of the steps. She was wearing the same coat she'd had on the night they'd first met, in this very spot. The weather was cool, like it had been that night, and Emily was as beautiful as she remembered, but everything else had changed. Cade took a deep breath and walked toward her, ready to tackle the obstacles between them.

As Cade drew closer, Emily called out, "If I'd known you like to hang around courthouses so much, I would have offered you a tour early on."

Cade smiled, happy they were starting this conversation with some of the easy banter she'd enjoyed between them. "Maybe I'll take you up on that one day."

Emily stepped closer, a tentative smile playing along the edge of her mouth. "I'm glad you reached out."

"Me too."

"Walk with me?"

Cade nodded, and Emily locked their arms and led her down the street, in the opposite direction from Brody's office. Cade wanted to ask where they were going, but she didn't want to break the spell with details. Not yet. For now it was enough they were arm-in-arm, sharing a quiet moment alone.

At the end of the block, Emily pointed at an arbor marking the entrance to a small park. Cade followed her inside, taking in the quaint gaslights and iron benches with ornate scrollwork on the backs. She wondered how she'd missed this romantic spot in downtown Bodark.

They'd barely settled onto a bench before Emily said, "I've missed you." Her voice was low, her tone serious.

"I've missed you too."

"I'd about given up." Emily's voice cracked as she delivered the short declaration.

Cade searched her eyes and saw a flash of hurt. She hated to think she was responsible for causing Emily any pain, and all she could think about was clearing the air between them. "I need to talk to you, but…" Cade paused, her explanation stalled in the face of Emily's hopeful expression.

"But?"

"It has to do with the Miller case." Cade blurted out the words and watched Emily's body stiffen at the mention of the case.

"Considering how our last conversation on this topic ended," Emily said, "maybe we should talk about something else."

"I understand, I really do, but it's important."

Emily shook her head. "But it's not. Trust me, I have an entire public to check my work, from the press to the county commissioners to the defense bar." She reached for Cade's hands, locking their fingers. "I'm truly sorry for the things I said to you. I was defensive when I should have just said talking about work was the last thing I wanted to do after we'd spent the evening making love." She pulled Cade's hands to her mouth and grazed them with her lips.

The light and simple touch sent charges through Cade's core, but Emily's next words threatened to push her over the edge.

"And talking about work is the last thing I want to do right now."

There was no mistaking the strong promise behind Emily's declaration or the burning passion in her gaze, and Cade couldn't agree more. She didn't want to talk about the case, about her true identity, or the very real possibility a ruthless killer was on her trail. The only thing she wanted was to take Emily home, rip her clothes off, and spend the rest of the night worshiping her body. The desire was strong and it surged through her veins, warming her from the inside out. All she had to do was keep her mouth shut and she could have what she wanted.

For now. But tomorrow, when the sun came up, nothing would have changed. She'd still be Cade Kelly, posing as a librarian, hiding from a killer, and working with Emily's opponent to help the man Emily had charged with murder.

Carefully, gently, Cade pulled away and fisted her hands against her side to keep from taking what she knew she couldn't have. Not yet.

Emily's eyes clouded with disappointment. "What is it?"

"I want you."

"I hear a very loud but, again." Emily's smile looked forced. "Please don't tell me you called me out here so you could walk out on me again."

If Emily wouldn't hear her out, that was exactly what she had to do, to preserve her own dignity and to respect whatever chance they might have to find something real and meaningful between them. Cade stood and paced to try to siphon off the adrenaline that was pounding big beats through her heart and her head. She'd made a mistake coming to Emily like this, armed with only words, to try to convince her to point her prosecution elsewhere. She didn't want to risk another argument in their already tenuous relationship. She should have known that face-to-face, she wouldn't be able to risk the rift the truth would cause between them.

It had been so much easier to share what she knew about the case with Brody, not just because he wanted to believe what she had to say, but because to him, she was an objective outsider, but to Emily she appeared disloyal by not taking her side.

Objective outsider. That was the key. She could get the facts to Emily another way, one that didn't involve her directly. She knew exactly how to get it done.

Which left the issue about her identity—the biggest lie between them. She had to tell Emily the truth if she had any hope of a future with her, but this wasn't the time. Not when Fontana was closing in, not when Emily was consumed with the upcoming trial. She needed to let Emily know the real her, and blurting it out by gaslight in the middle of a public park wasn't at all what she had in mind. Desperate for a solution, she came up with a hasty temporary fix.

Cade stepped closer to Emily and grasped her hands again. When their eyes met, it took every ounce of self-control not to fall into her arms, but instead she plunged into her hastily prepared explanation. "I know you've felt distance between us."

Emily started to say something, but Cade placed her finger on her lips. "Wait, let me get this out." She took a breath and started again. "I'm sorry because I want to be close to you. I want nothing to come between us. From the first moment we met, I've been drawn to you, but I have a few things I need to take care of before I can be the person you deserve."

"'Person I deserve'? What does that even mean?" Emily raised her hand and stroked Cade's cheek, a gentle and loving touch. "Cade, baby, you can tell me anything."

The endearment elicited a light moan, and Cade resisted the urge to melt into her touch. "I know. And I will." She leaned in and kissed Emily, soft at first, but then hard and claiming, breaking away only when she was out of breath. "Go and try your case. I'll be waiting when you're done. I'll make everything right then. I promise."

She punctuated her good-bye by stepping back, and the stark cold of familiar loneliness washed over her. She was doing the right thing. Kennedy and her people would catch Fontana, and Cade would leave the program, come out to Emily, and beg for a chance to build a future together. A few weeks wasn't very much time to wait when their entire lives hung in the balance.

❖

It was after dusk by the time Cade arrived home. As she approached her front door, she made a mental note of the lighting outside and remembered what she'd learned from the police reports at Brody's office. She found it difficult to believe Wade's next-door neighbor, Ralph Thatcher, had been able to identify Kevin Miller. According to the report, Thatcher had seen Miller from his car window about fifty feet away at dusk. Granted, Thatcher had seen Miller in the neighborhood before, but that led her to believe he had assumed, rather than actually known it was Miller he'd seen standing over Wade's body.

It was a good theory, but when she'd laid it out for Brody, he told her Miller had already admitted to both him and the police he'd been at the murder scene, only in his version, he'd shown up after the fact. Miller's story was he'd been going door-to-door looking for odd jobs when he saw Wade lying in his driveway next to his SUV. He saw a knife next to Wade's body, and he could tell, based on the extent of Wade's injuries, he wasn't long for this world if he wasn't dead already. What happened next made it clear Miller was a despicable person but not necessarily a murderer.

Hungry and desperate, Miller had plucked the dead man's wallet from his hand. Then, when Thatcher pulled up in his car and yelled out the window, Miller picked up the knife and ran. Later, he took the cash from the wallet and ditched it near the creek at the back of the subdivision, but he hung on to the knife.

Cade checked her mailbox, found it empty, and then she unlocked her front door and stepped inside. At first she didn't notice anything out of order, but when she walked into the living room, she spotted a small stack of mail sitting on the coffee table, and she froze. Had Fontana found her? The possibility paralyzed her until she heard a familiar voice.

"I brought in your mail."

Cade whirled on Kennedy who was standing in the doorway to the kitchen, a bottle of Mexican Coke in one hand. "What the hell?"

"I let myself in. Don't worry. I made sure your nosey neighbor wasn't watching." Kennedy took a drink from the bottle. "We need to talk."

Cade strode past her into the kitchen, purposefully ignoring her comment while she worked to settle her frayed nerves. She opened the fridge and spied another Coke bottle. She grabbed it and held it up in the air. "You moving in?" She didn't wait for an answer before she used the edge of the kitchen counter to pop the cap and took a deep drink. The rush of cold sweet fizz settled her nerves and she took another. When the bottle was half empty, she set it on the counter and wiped her mouth with the back of her hand. "This isn't working for me."

"What's that?"

"You, here, in my house whenever you want to be, and your pal, Hulk Hogan, following me around. I need you and your people to back off."

Kennedy crossed her arms and rocked back on her heels. "Is that so? Would that make it easier for you to go around doing stupid things?"

"I don't know what you're talking about." Cade took another drink to hide the lie. She knew exactly why Kennedy was pissed, but she didn't care.

"Eric told me about your little visit with that blogger, and how the two of you went to see Brody Nichols. I need to know exactly what you told Nichols."

"I told him the truth."

"About what?"

"I told him I didn't think his client killed Sam Wade. I floated a theory about how the method used to kill Wade was overkill for a transient robber, but it was consistent with mob killings. I suggested he might want to research other similar killings, and I volunteered to help him."

Kennedy shook her head. "You have no idea what you're doing."

"I know exactly what I'm doing. Key word *doing*. I've spent the last few months letting everyone else take the lead, but it's time for me to take charge of my own destiny." Cade's confidence rose as she spoke, and she grew more determined with every word. "You can have your pal follow me all over this county, but you can't make me stop trying to find the truth. An innocent man could get convicted if I don't speak up. Of course you could clue in the local cops that they may have the wrong guy." She waited a few beats, but Kennedy's silence told her everything she needed to know. "Like I said, you can't make me stop."

"Would you stop if you thought your girlfriend might be in danger?"

Kennedy's words were like stealth bombs blowing away her bravado, but she wasn't sure which had the bigger impact, danger or girlfriend. "What?"

"You should sit down."

Cade ignored the warning. Whatever Kennedy had to say, she wanted to be poised for action. "Tell me."

"Eric called to tell me you met with Emily Sinclair after you left Nichols's office," Kennedy said. "Am I supposed to believe you didn't already tell her your theory about her case?"

"You can believe what you want, but we didn't talk about the case." Fueled by anxiety at the very idea Emily might be in danger, Cade strode across the room until she was inches from Kennedy. "I swear if you don't tell me what's going on, I'll—"

"Yeah, don't finish that sentence. I kind of like you and I'd hate to have to arrest you for threatening a federal officer." She reached into her pocket and pulled out a jump drive.

"What's that?"

"I'll show you. Where's your computer?"

Cade led her to the guest room, which she'd set up as a combination office/den. She flipped open her laptop, punched the power button, and held out her hand. When the screen came to life, she inserted the drive and clicked it open. It contained two files, named simply Sinclair1 and Sinclair2. "What are these?"

"Martel talked. It took a lot of coaxing, but he gave up the address for Fontana's place outside of Chicago. It doesn't look like he's been there in a while, but we found this drive and a few others hidden in the floorboards. Along with some damning paperwork about the Oliveris' business operations, they contain video files and some photographs." She pointed at the computer screen. "Most of the video clips had to do with Senator Sinclair. Apparently, the Oliveris are very interested in making his acquaintance seeing as how he was recently appointed head of the senate judiciary committee. Seems they have a certain judge in their pocket they would like appointed to a federal bench."

Cade's mind whirred with the information, but she still didn't quite follow. "I don't get it. What does this have to do with Emily?"

Kennedy pulled the laptop toward her and punched a few buttons. "Vincente Oliveri told Fontana to start gathering information about Senator Sinclair. Here's one of the things he found."

She pressed play and moved the screen so they could both see the newsclip. It took Cade a moment to recognize the lobby of the Bodark Inn. The camera panned and she saw red, white, and blue balloons lining the entrance to the ballroom and the sign she recognized from her first night in town: *Sinclair for District Attorney, A New Era*.

She turned to Kennedy. "What is this?"

"Keep watching."

Cade looked back at the screen, but she knew what was coming next. The camera panned and there, standing next to the bellman, shaking her way out of her drenched coat, stood Emily Sinclair. Cade's breath hitched as she remembered the first time she'd seen her. She'd been captivated from the start, and she was captivated now. She watched as the camera tracked Emily who squared her shoulders, took a deep breath, and strode toward the entrance to the ballroom.

And there in the corner of the screen, like an eerie mirror, Cade stood off to the side, eyes glued on Emily's every move. For a brief moment, their eyes met and Emily flashed a brilliant smile, and then she was gone and the screen went black.

"What does this mean?" Cade didn't bother trying to hide the edge in her voice.

"It means Fontana definitely knows where you are. And he's been watching Emily too." Kennedy typed on the laptop keyboard again, opened the second folder, and started slowly scrolling through a handful of still photographs.

Cade gasped. The first picture was a crisp, clear shot of her, standing next to Emily outside the Bodark Inn, the night Emily introduced her to Becca's secret coffee haunt. The next few were her alone—walking into the campus library, getting into her car at the end of her shift, standing in her driveway at home.

Cade pointed at the screen. "How did he find out where I work, where I live?"

Kennedy faced her square on. "We found a copy of the résumé and cover letter we prepared for you on one of these drives. I don't know how he got it, but it looks like it may have come from someone who had access to our files. Rest assured, we are looking into it, and if someone on our end leaked information, they will go down."

Cade didn't feel assured about anything at that point, but before she could digest Kennedy's bombshell, she sucked in a breath at the image on the screen. The last picture Kennedy opened had been taken outside of Emily's house. In the center of the frame, Emily was in the front doorway, and Cade was standing in front of her on the porch.

She knew instantly this picture had been taken the night she and Emily had made love. The night she'd walked out, not knowing if she'd ever see Emily again. Had Fontana been outside the house the entire time? Had he managed to witness what went on between them that night? Cade shuddered, violated by the very idea he might have witnessed their intimate moments or their explosive argument. But more importantly, she'd placed Emily in danger.

"If he knows where I am, why hasn't he…"

"Killed you?"

Cade nodded, strangely appreciative of Kennedy's willingness to cut to the chase.

"Good question. The FBI is working on getting a wiretap order for Vincente's phone, but in the meantime, all we have are records of calls between him and Fontana, and the cell tower pings show Fontana has been in the area on more than one occasion. I can only think he's got something more involved in mind. Something that will give the Oliveris leverage with the senator."

Something that involved Emily. Kennedy didn't have to say the words for Cade to know they were true.

Chapter Twenty-one

The next morning, Emily woke to a loud, rattling sound. Her left hand slapped the air, searching for the alarm clock on her nightstand and coming up empty. Frustrated at her inability to make the noise stop, she partially opened her eyes and gave her surroundings a squinty once-over.

She was in her office, sitting in her chair behind her desk, dressed in the suit she'd worn the day before. She glanced at the door and instantly identified the source of the noise. "I'll be right there," she called out to whoever was desperately trying to enter. Using her framed law school diploma as a mirror, she fluffed her hair and rubbed away the smeared mascara under her eyes. It wasn't great, but it would have to do.

When she unlocked the door, she was relieved to find Becca on the other side, holding a brown paper bag and a steaming cup of coffee. She motioned her into the room and shut the door behind them.

"You look like shit," Becca said.

"Thanks." Emily pointed at the coffee. "Please say that's for me."

"Yes, but it's probably not big enough judging by the fact that you look like you slept here in your clothes."

Emily grabbed the cup of coffee and drank deeply, despite the scalding temperature. When she finally felt fortified, she said, "Apparently, I did sleep here last night, or at least this morning. Last time I looked at the clock it was four a.m. That's all I remember before you started banging down the door."

Becca wagged her finger and pulled two enormous blackberry muffins out of the bag. She handed one over. "Eat. I bet you skipped dinner last night."

"You should be a detective."

"Doesn't take a gumshoe to see you're burying yourself in work to avoid other things."

Emily knew exactly what she was referring to, but she wasn't going to bite. "Uh, murder trial in less than two weeks? I'm pretty sure I'll be spending plenty of nights here before this case is over."

"Whatever. Word is you ducked out of the office last night and met some tall gorgeous stranger in front of the courthouse. When you came back to the office, you were completely distracted and kind of bitchy."

Seth. He'd been working late too and must've seen her leave. She was annoyed at the characterization of her mood upon her return, but she probably had been a little bitchy. And why not? The impromptu meeting with Cade had thrown her completely off balance. One minute they were kissing, and then Cade was making vague references to reasons why they couldn't be together right now. Next thing she knew, Cade was gone and she was left aroused and unsatisfied, with no resolution in sight.

That wasn't completely true. Cade had said they could be together after the trial. She'd thought it was slightly odd at the time, and the more she rolled it over in her mind, the more Cade's reservations rang warning bells. From their initial argument about Brody's speedy trial request to Cade's insistence last night that they discuss the case, this trial was the source of the wedge between them, and she couldn't figure out why.

Emily took a bite of her muffin then practically swallowed the rest whole. She was tired and hungry and dressed in the same suit she'd put on over twenty-four hours before. She was in no shape to figure out the rift between her and Cade, and she had no business expending her energy on anything other than this case. Whatever mysteries Cade was hiding, she'd been absolutely right about one thing—it could wait. She couldn't afford to focus on anything other than this case, and if their intense connection couldn't survive a few weeks of separation, then it wasn't meant to be.

Becca left after they finished their muffins, but not until she made Emily promise she'd come to the Inn for dinner no later than eight o'clock. Emily hoped she would be able to stay awake long enough to keep that promise. She ducked into the bathroom attached to her office and brushed her teeth and doused her face with cold water, before she dove back into her work, hoping to make the most of the caffeine jolt from Becca's brew.

She was about an hour into writing her opening statement when Seth appeared in her doorway. "Mind if I interrupt you?" he asked with a look of trepidation.

Emily smiled. "Not at all. I'm not feeling as bitchy this morning. Only sleepy."

He paused on his way in. "Uh, sorry about that. Becca mentioned you had some other stuff on your mind."

"Becca has a big mouth, and yes, you can tell her I said so." Emily tried, unsuccessfully, to stifle a yawn. "The only thing I have on my mind today is this case. What's up?"

Seth handed her a manila envelope. "We got the amended report from the sheriff's department. One burned out light bulb is now one missing light bulb. You asked me to let you know when it was ready."

Emily opened the envelope and pulled out the single sheet to verify the change had been made. She met Seth's skeptical look. "I know you think this is crazy."

"Maybe a little, but I get it," he said. "Better safe than sorry. Hate to see the guy tie up the case in appeals forever. It would be a big waste of taxpayer money." He pointed at the document. "You want me to have Janice fax it over?"

She should say yes. Janice could make sure the report was delivered, and she could keep plugging away on trial prep in addition to the dozen other administrative tasks demanding her attention. But Brody's office was only a couple of blocks away. If she delivered the report in person, she could stretch her legs, get some fresh air, and clear her head so her afternoon would be much more productive than her morning had been. She picked up the envelope. "Thanks, but I'll take care of it."

"Okay. Guess I'll get back to it." Despite his words, he lingered in front of her desk.

"What else is on your mind?"

"Is everything okay with you?"

"Yes. Have you heard differently?"

"You just seemed pretty stressed out." He smiled. "But then again, you've never had to prep for trial and be the boss of everyone at the same time."

She laughed. "True. Once we get started, I'll forget about everything else. Speaking of which, what happened with Ethan Jansen the other day?"

"He's still on the warpath, but we're trying to work out a deal with the defendant. I'm not sure Jansen's going to be on board with any kind of deal."

"Let me know if I need to get involved. That case doesn't need to go to trial."

Seth assured her he would and left the office. He was right. She was stressed out, and a lot of her anxiety had to do with Cade, a subject completely out of her control. If she didn't compartmentalize her feelings, she was going to be in big trouble professionally. This case, not Cade Kelly, had to be her only focus. Emily grabbed the envelope with the report from the sheriff's office and buzzed Janice to tell her she was heading out to run a quick errand. She'd be back before lunch and ready to give all her attention to the case.

❖

Cade walked into Brody's offices and nodded at the gray-haired secretary she now knew was named Doris Hamilton aka Miss Doris. Miss Doris pointed down the hall, and Cade walked on back until she spotted Asher in one of the formerly empty offices, making herself at home behind an enormous, ornate desk. "Shouldn't you be in class?"

"As if. Like this compares to anything I'd learn in a classroom." Asher brushed aside the folders on the desk and waved Cade toward a seat next to the desk. "The real question is where have you been? I thought you were going to be here first thing this morning."

That had been the plan, but yesterday's news about Fontana had derailed everything. Cade had spent the morning trying to persuade Kennedy not to keep her in lock-down at her house under twenty-four hour guard. She'd finally managed to convince her that holing up at home or disappearing—the only two options Kennedy thought viable—were both likely to raise Fontana's suspicions. Plus, she knew if she didn't show up at Brody's office, Asher would hunt her down.

She and Kennedy had settled on a compromise. She'd called Monica and given her some lame excuse for why she'd be late to work, and Kennedy had reluctantly agreed with her plan to make a brief stop by Brody's office. "I had a couple of pressing things to take care of, but since I spent half the night thinking about the case, I think I'm entitled to be a little late." Cade pulled the chair closer to Asher's desk. "I need a favor."

Asher flipped open her notebook to a fresh page and tapped a pencil against the pad. "Shoot."

Cade reached over and snatched the pencil. What college kid these days wrote with a pencil anyway? "Not for public consumption." She pulled an envelope out of her messenger bag. Asher reached for it, but Cade held it slightly out of reach. "I need you to deliver this to Emily Sinclair." She frowned hard to emphasize her next point. "It's not from me. Got it?"

"Is it a love letter?" Asher's whisper was low and teasing and Cade wanted to smack her, but when she considered how it looked for her to be passing secret notes to Emily, she couldn't really blame Asher for giving her a hard time.

"No." She drew out the word to emphasize the point. "It's an outline of the issues with the case I think she should consider before taking this to a jury."

"So, you're giving your *girlfriend* an edge."

"Asher."

"What? I'm just calling it like I see it. You know, investigative reporter and all."

"I need you to turn off your investigative superpowers for a minute. Sometimes prosecutors are stubborn. They start from a presumption of guilt, which makes it hard for them to see anything that might call their judgment into question." She pointed at the envelope. "I may have already tried to discuss some of these things with her, but it didn't go so well. Heat of the moment and all that."

Asher nodded knowingly.

"So, maybe if the information shows up on plain white typing paper, it might be more palatable. Make sense?"

"She hasn't agreed to give me an interview."

"Drop this off with a note saying you plan to publish all of it in the campus paper and you'll get your interview. Even if none of it changes her mind, she's not going to let it stand without a comment. Trust me."

Asher's eyes narrowed, like she was looking for some other meaning to the exercise. Finally, she reached for the envelope and placed it in her bag. "I won't tell anyone," she said. "Not even Brody."

"Thanks." Cade looked at the papers spread out on the desk, anxious to change the subject. "What are you working on?"

"The piece about eyewitness testimony. There's a ton of research on it, but I'm not entirely sure which are the best sources. I plan to ask Brody a few questions about it when he gets back from court."

Cade reached into the messenger bag she'd brought along, pulled out a sheaf of papers, and handed them to Asher. "I printed out some articles and cases for you. The articles come from reputable sources with peer-reviewed studies. All of these have survived *Daubert* hearings and been held up on appeal."

The papers in her hand hung in mid-air and Asher stared at her with a slack-jawed expression. "What?" Cade asked.

"Two things. One, ever heard of email or do you like killing trees? Two, I have no idea what you just said. Da-bear? Explain, please."

Shit. Legalese was going to do her in. She was about to spin some tale about having worked as an intern for her made-up attorney uncle, but a voice behind her saved the day.

"*Daubert* is a case about the admissibility of expert testimony. The case outlines the test to determine if certain scientific evidence is real science or junk. If it's junk, it can't be offered at trial."

Cade turned around and Brody was standing behind her, a curious gleam in his eyes. She scrambled. "Thanks. I'd read that, but you explained it so much better than I could."

"Oh, I don't know. You seemed like you knew what you were talking about."

Cade shrugged and quickly changed the subject. "I'd like to stick around, but I need to get to work, and I can do some research while

I'm there. Is there anything in particular you'd like me to focus on?" She asked the question only to deflect what had just happened since she already had several topics she planned to work on, starting with the validity of the search warrant.

"I was thinking I'd spend some time today looking at Kevin's statement and some cases on police interrogation," Brody said. "If there's a way to keep his statement from coming in at trial, then we'll be in a better position."

It was like the notes in her bag were calling out to him. Cade wanted to tell him issues like admissibility of evidence, including Miller's statement, was one of the many reasons not to rush into trial, but instead she reached in and pulled out another stack of paper and shoved it his way. "You might want to take a look at these. All Texas Court of Criminal Appeals cases on Fifth Amendment and custodial interrogations." She shifted to avoid his curious gaze and added, "I made a few notes. Don't know if they'll be any help, but feel free to use whatever you want."

Without waiting for a response, she hefted the bag onto her shoulder, called out a "see you later" and started toward the door. She'd barely made it past Miss Doris's desk when she heard a familiar voice.

"Cade?"

Emily was standing across the room her narrowed eyes reflecting surprise, but otherwise looking completely composed in one of the tailored but still feminine suits that highlighted her strength and sex appeal. Cade took a step toward her and noticed beneath the professional veneer the first shade of dark circles under her eyes and the bent posture of too many hours hunched over a desk. She wanted to step close and take Emily in her arms, offer to hold her while she slept, massage the ache from her weary muscles, but this wasn't the time or place.

Cade supposed she should've expected to run into Emily this close to the courthouse, but maybe on the street where she could scurry off after a quick wave hello. Definitely not here, in the office of Emily's adversary. She managed a weak smile. "Hi."

"What are you doing here?" The surprise was gone from Emily's expression. The question was blunt and wary with a touch of anger.

So much for rushing away without having to explain. Cade hadn't prepared for this eventuality and her brain was paralyzed. There was no plausible explanation for her to be here. She should be at work, or absent that, at home, but in no scenario would a relative newcomer to town, who worked at the nearby college, be hanging out at the office of a lawyer getting ready to try a murder case.

Well, that wasn't entirely true. She could be here to consult with a lawyer. Brody didn't limit his practice to criminal defense. Hell, for all Emily knew she could be here to talk to him about a will or some other boring legal matter that had nothing to do with crime. While Cade sorted through the options, Emily's intense gaze bored holes through her, and what she at first took as anger covered a layer of something else. Pain? Hurt? And why not? When they'd last talked, Cade had said she wanted nothing to come between them, that she needed a little time to sort things out. She wasn't about to compound the issue by lying to Emily.

"I came by to tell Brody some thoughts I had about the case." The words were barely out of her mouth before Emily's pained gaze became sharp and harsh.

"Is that so?"

Déjà here-we-go-again washed over Cade, and she struggled to keep from getting defensive. "I'm not sure why the fact I shared some opinions and observations with someone bothers you, and I'm sorry it does."

"I wasn't aware you and Brody Nichols were pals. I would think if you had some thoughts you wanted to share, you'd share them with me."

Emily's indignant tone was like a burr under a saddle, and Cade bucked at the implied accusation. "Excuse me, but I did try to talk to you about this case. Last night? In the park? Ring any bells?"

"So this is what you wanted to tell me? That you're working against me?"

"Against you? This isn't about you. Don't you care whether or not you prosecute the right person?" Anger flooded Cade's senses, and she gave in to the pull of raw emotion. "Your narrow-mindedness is going to result in the real killer going free. Way to protect your community, counselor."

"Everything all right out here?"

Cade spun around to see Brody and Asher standing behind her. Judging by their wide eyes and stunned expressions, they'd heard more than a little of her heated exchange with Emily. Before she could speak, Emily stepped forward.

"Sorry about that," she said, directing her words to Brody as if no one else was in the room. "I tend to get a bit passionate when I'm talking about a case." She handed him an envelope. "I came by to drop this off. Not entirely sure if it qualifies as *Brady* material, but I wanted to make sure you have it in case it comes up at trial." Brody barely had the envelope in his grasp before Emily started backing toward the door. "I'll see myself out."

Cade watched her leave, wishing she wouldn't, but powerless to say the words that might stop her with Brody and Asher looking on.

"Who's Brady?" Asher asked.

Cade listened as Brody explained it was a Supreme Court case requiring prosecutors to turn over evidence in their possession that might be helpful to the defense. His explanation was rudimentary, but sound, yet she found herself wanting to interject that in the past, prosecutors weren't required to turn over this kind of information in advance of trial, but a fairly recent, high profile case had changed the rules. She kept her mouth shut. It was clear Brody knew the law, even if he had little experience applying it to real cases. But everyone had to start somewhere.

Why did she care so much about whether Kevin Miller got a fair shake? She'd never even met the guy, but she'd let her concern about his fate rob her of the opportunity to be with Emily at every turn. Was his freedom worth more than hers?

She interrupted Brody who'd moved on to some other topic. "I have to go," she said, already on her way to the door. Out of the corner of her eye, she saw Asher give her a big smile and a thumbs-up. Damn that kid. She was too smart for her own good, but Cade was unable to resist Asher's low-key cheerleading, Cade returned the smile and dashed out of the office, determined to find Emily. She needed all the luck she could get.

Chapter Twenty-two

Emily couldn't get out of Brody's office fast enough. Not caring who saw, she flew down the steps and around the corner, barely pausing at the intersection before charging across the street. Her office loomed in the distance, representing everything she'd worked for, everything she'd achieved, but right now it felt like an albatross dragging her away from the full future she'd imagined. What good was the job if it stood in the way of the other things she wanted: a comfortable home, a woman to love her, and a family of her own to love her back?

Her purpose for this little walk had backfired, and she wasn't ready to go back to the office and dive back into her trial prep. What she really wanted to do was corner Cade Kelly and force her to tell the truth about what she was up to, but the level of betrayal she felt kept her in check. She wasn't ready to put her feelings at risk, and the old trial attorney adage echoed in her head: don't ask a question if you don't already know the answer. Maybe it was best to let Cade's secrets remain so and move on.

But she didn't want to move on. Move on to what? A Junior Leaguer handpicked by her mother? Becca's declaration that Cade was the best thing that ever happened to her both rang true and set off warning bells. Cade wasn't what she'd imagined when she thought about her carefully planned future—too much mystery, too much conflict. But she couldn't deny the idea of waking up next to Cade every day was a fantasy she'd love to bring to life.

What was holding her back? For one thing, Cade's disloyalty. She'd openly admitted talking to Brody Nichols about the Miller case, which brought to mind all kinds of questions. Why was Cade so intensely focused on this case? What could she possibly add to the mix? Sure, she was smart and capable, but she wasn't a lawyer or a cop or a private investigator. She was like all of the other citizens of Lawson County who buttonholed Emily whenever she went out in public so they could give her unsolicited opinions about the cases pending in her office.

Except you actually listen to those folks, and when Cade tried to talk to you about the case, you picked a fight. The first time, yes, Emily acknowledged, but last night she hadn't fought with Cade. Still, she had to admit, she had sidestepped Cade's attempts to discuss the case in order to avoid conflict.

Well, that hadn't worked since she'd only delayed the inevitable. Now she was steeped in conflict again and all she wanted to do was toss the case files in the trash, go back to Brody's office, and drag Cade away to engage in something that had absolutely nothing to do with Kevin Miller.

Tossing the case wasn't an option, but she could be the bigger person. She could go back, talk to Cade, and tell her how she felt. She squared her shoulders and turned to look back across the street, careful this time to watch for cars. When the road was clear, she started to take a step, but a strong hand on her arm held her back. She swiped at the hand and jumped away. "What the hell?"

"Calm down. I didn't mean to scare you."

Sheriff Nash stood next to her with his hands in the air and an amused smile playing at the corner of his lips. Emily wanted to smack him, but she was already embarrassed at her reaction to his manhandling display. "What do you want, Sheriff?"

"I went by your office, but they didn't have a clue where you were."

His tone was accusing, and she struggled to keep her temper under control. "I was delivering an amended investigative report to opposing counsel. Seems your deputies were playing a little fast and loose with some of the facts from the crime scene."

"I'm sure you had your reasons for delivering that report yourself," he said, a smug undercurrent in his voice. "You may have all day to cater to the murdering bastard's lawyer, but I need to talk to you in my office and it's pretty important."

"About the case?"

"Nope." He rocked back on the heels of his snakeskin boots. "Well, maybe."

Emily didn't try to hide her frustration. "Sheriff, I don't have time for games. Tell me."

He preceded his words with a dark frown. "This information is obviously not for public consumption, but I thought you'd like to know the woman you've been keeping company with—the one who's been spending time over at Nichols's office? She isn't who you think she is."

Emily went cold at the words that confirmed her fears, but she had to know more. She had no desire to follow Nash back to his office, but she didn't want to hear the details here on the street where anyone could witness the effect the news would have on her. "Your office now. I want to know everything."

Cade stood at the end of the street, her head swiveling in all directions, but Emily was nowhere in sight. Damn, she'd waited too long and now Emily was probably already back at her office. Cade debated whether she should look for her there. On one hand, it seemed like a bad idea to show up at her work to discuss something very personal, but on the other hand if she chose not to she wasn't likely to have another opportunity until the trial was over, and despite what she'd told Emily in the park last night, she didn't think she could wait that long. Her mind made up, she started walking toward the courthouse.

"Where are you going?"

Kennedy was standing a few feet away. Her presence was disconcerting since, except for the time Kennedy came by her work, she'd rarely seen her in public. Silly as it was, she felt Kennedy's presence exposed her. "Where did you come from?"

Kennedy stepped closer. "We need to talk."

"So talk."

"Not the kind of conversation you want to have in the middle of town." She pointed across the street to her Jeep. "Let's go for a ride."

Cade shook her head. "Sorry, can't. I'm going to work."

"Sure. As soon as we talk, you can go wherever you want."

Kennedy's face was fixed in a firm scowl, but Cade didn't care. Everything she did was voluntary and it was time her keepers remembered that. "You can't make me go with you."

"Cade, please." Kennedy sighed. "Look, you're right, I can't make you do anything, but this is important. Trust me."

Cade stared at her, trying to get a read on what was up, but she got nothing. She might not like having her life micro-managed, but Kennedy had always acted in her best interest, and she had no reason to assume she wasn't doing so now. "Okay."

A few minutes later, they were in the Jeep, driving toward the outskirts of town. They'd spent the first few minutes of the drive in silence, and Cade was tired of waiting for whatever Kennedy had to say. "You wanted to talk, so talk."

Kennedy kept her face forward. "In a minute."

Frustrated, Cade stared out the window at the now familiar Bodark landmarks. The grain refinery. The signs for Lawson Lake. The maroon water tower emblazoned with the mascot of the local high school, the Bodark Lions. For the first time since she'd arrived here, she realized she would miss this place if she had to move. Not just Emily, although she was definitely what she'd miss the most, but the quaintness of the little town. Becca's secret coffee bar, the Purple Leaf Cafe, Ambrosia, Monica, Asher, Jordan College. The list was long—longer than she'd known. All of these places and these people had become part of who she was, and she couldn't imagine a life without them. The very idea she might never see any of them again sent her mind racing. "Is this your way of spiriting me off to another location where I have to start all over again?"

"What?" Kennedy turned her head. "No. Hang on." She jerked the Jeep to the right and pulled off the road near a sign promising a historical landmark. Cade recognized the place from one of her drives around town. The landmark consisted of a plaque dedicated to the settlers of Bodark surrounded by a trio of picnic tables.

Kennedy drove up next to one of the tables and killed the engine. "I need to stretch my legs." She didn't wait for a response before she jumped down from the Jeep and paced around the picnic area. Cade watched from the vehicle for a moment before deciding if she was going to get any idea about what they were doing out here, she'd have to follow.

"Okay, if you're not moving me to another location, what's with all the cloak-and-dagger?"

Kennedy motioned to one of the tables and they both sat down. "No one's been able to locate Fontana. We had been able to track his general whereabouts by triangulating cell signals, but he must have caught on because he's not using the same number anymore. He could be back in Chicago or he could be right around the corner. We have no way of knowing."

"You brought me out here to tell me you don't know anything? Now I know why people complain about government inefficiency."

"Hey, watch it. I'm not calling the shots here. My job is to keep you safe. The FBI is the one hunting Fontana, and they're in charge of the investigation. All of the decisions from here on out are theirs. Remember that when you hear what I have to say."

Cade tensed at the warning, but she concentrated on keeping a cool head. "And just what do you have to say?"

"It's normal protocol to notify local law enforcement authorities about the transfer of a protected witness into their jurisdiction. It's a courtesy to let the cops know we've moved a criminal into their jurisdiction because most of the witnesses we deal with are criminals."

"Are you saying the sheriff's office has known about me all along?"

"No, I made the decision to override protocol and not inform the sheriff. Because A, you're not a criminal, and B, Bodark is a pretty small town and I thought it was best not to tell anyone for fear the word would get out."

Cade let out a breath in relief. The idea that pompous Sheriff Nash would have any power at all over revealing her true identity made her skin crawl, and she was relieved to hear Kennedy had vetoed telling him. But her relief was short-lived as the words Kennedy had spoken earlier came rushing back. "But wait, you said the FBI is calling the shots now."

"Yes, they are. And this morning they told Sheriff Nash about you. Not only that, they told him your theory that Fontana murdered Sam Wade."

"What?"

"You heard me. Apparently, they finally got the wiretap order, and on Fontana's last check in with the boss, he got an earful about his carelessness and it sounded like it wasn't the first time. I don't know all the details, but the FBI agent-in-charge thinks Vincente was talking about Wade's murder. It's probably only a matter of time before Nash talks to Sinclair about it. In fact, I have a feeling they may be talking about it right now. I saw them run into each other on the street just before you came running out of Nichols's office."

"No." Cade banged her hand on the solid wood of the picnic tabletop and stood up. "Take me back to town." She slapped the table again. "Right now."

"Cade, listen to me. Your best bet now is to stay out of sight. I'm not going to relocate you, but I am going to put you in a hotel for a few days, somewhere out of town. I grabbed the duffel bag from your bedroom…"

Kennedy kept talking, but Cade tuned her out. For all she knew, at this very moment asshat Nash was telling Emily she wasn't who she claimed to be. How would Emily feel when she learned that everything Cade had told her during their brief courtship had been a lie? From a purely professional standpoint, Emily had to understand why Cade couldn't tell her the truth, but nothing about their relationship had been professional. The falsehoods paraded through her mind: her education, her occupation, her family, and the hunting accident. That last one had been the worst since she'd delivered the deceit during the most intimate lovemaking of her entire life.

She knew exactly what she needed to do. She leaned over the table until she was inches from Kennedy's face and emphasized each word. "Take me back to town or I will walk there on my own. If I get there under my own power, everything I do from here on out will be my call, not the FBI's, not Waverly's, not yours. Are we clear?"

Kennedy answered by holding up her keys and pointing to the Jeep. Cade could almost swear she saw a flash of admiration pass over Kennedy's face, but she didn't dwell on it. The only person's approval she wanted was Emily's, and she was going to do everything in her power to make things right between them.

❖

Janice called out as Emily walked by her desk, but she waved her off and shut the door behind her. She'd apologize for being rude later. Right now, she was doing everything she could to hold it together after the bombshell Nash had dropped on her.

She tossed a file onto her desk, slid into her chair, and dropped her head into her hands. Cade Kelly aka Cade Deluca, an assistant state's attorney from Chicago had been shot at point-blank range by Leo Fontana, capo for the Oliveri crime family. Cade had testified about her experience in front of a federal grand jury, and then been whisked away to hide out until the feds found Fontana and brought him to trial.

As if that weren't crazy enough, Cade believed Fontana was the person really responsible for Sam Wade's death, and the FBI had provided Nash with a dossier full of information to back up Cade's assertion, a copy of which was now sitting on her desk. Nash had summarized the facts, but she should read it for herself. She would, but first she had to get past the feeling she'd been duped.

The Cade she knew had been a fiction. Not a librarian, but a lawyer. She hadn't moved here because of a layoff at her former job. She moved here to escape a cold-blooded killer. Emily sorted through all the things Cade had told her, and wondered if there were grains of truth in anything she'd shared.

Professional Emily knew Cade hadn't had a choice in the matter. The lies Cade had told were necessities, made up to protect her life, but on a personal level, Emily couldn't help feeling betrayed because what had happened between them had been intensely intimate. If the feelings between them had been real, why hadn't Cade trusted her enough to share who she really was?

A knock on her door roused her from her round of self-pity. She wanted to tell whomever it was to go away and leave her alone. She wanted to spirit herself out of the office, to her house, where she could hole up and lick her wounds outside the gaze of the prying public. But that wasn't the life she'd chosen. She had a job to do, and after spending a year scouring the county for votes, she owed it to her community to buck up and do what they paid her to do. She placed a hand on the folder Nash had given her and vowed to tackle it as her very next thing. "Come in."

The door opened slowly and Janice poked her head through. Emily waved her in. "Sorry about earlier. I'm having a bad day."

"I occasionally have those," Janice said with a warm smile as she walked into the room. "Just a couple of things. The grand jury on the Jansen case is set next week and Elena asked me to let you know. Defense counsel brought over a packet he'd like to present, and it's on your desk." She pointed to a tabbed black binder. "Do you want me to have Seth look it over?"

Emily shook her head. "No, I'll go through it. What else do you need?"

Janice produced a plain white envelope and held it toward her. "Asher Risley brought this by. She made me promise to put it directly into your hands."

"And you like taking orders from college kids?"

Janice shrugged. "Not really, no, but she seemed so darn serious about it. Like it was a matter of life or death."

Emily took the envelope from Janice. "I'll take a look at it." She set the envelope on the far corner of her desk. "If there's anything on my schedule for the rest of the day, cancel it. I've got a full plate."

"Anything you need me to do?"

"No, I'm good for now. Thanks."

Emily waited until Janice was out of the room, opened the folder Nash had given her, and started skimming the contents. The first few sheets of paper contained bullet point summaries of similar crimes in other jurisdictions, all believed to have been committed by Leo Fontana. She had to admit it seemed like more than coincidence that the signature method employed by a mob enforcer would have been used by a transient looking for a few bucks from a stranger. She scoured the rest of the documents—wiretap transcripts that contained cryptic conversations between mob boss Vincente Oliveri and Fontana. Oliveri was scolding Fontana for not using discretion, but other than that she wasn't sure what to make of it. Nash had told her the feds were fairly confident Cade's theory was correct, but what possible motive could Fontana have had to kill Sam Wade?

She needed coffee if she was going to figure this out, and instinctively, she reached across her desk for her cup from that morning, but stopped when she realized it was probably ice-cold by now. Her gaze fell on the envelope Asher had hand-delivered. *Don't get distracted.* She looked back at the file from Nash, but after a few seconds, curiosity won out. She grabbed the envelope and ripped it open.

A single sheet of paper fell out. Like the information in the file she'd been reading, the piece of paper was covered in bullet points, single-spaced on both sides. She devoured the entire document, finding a careful, calculated presentation of facts that had to have been written by a brilliant legal strategist, designed to convince her there was more than enough reason to doubt Kevin Miller was guilty of Sam Wade's murder. Asher might have delivered this to her, but she knew it had to be Cade's work. Cade, doing everything she could to protect what she thought was an innocent man, even at the risk of her own protection.

Any lingering doubts she might have about the kind of person Cade was receded as she considered the struggle Cade had faced since she'd realized Fontana, the man who wanted her dead, might have been the one who'd killed Wade. The anxiety of knowing he was close by coupled with the fear of not knowing when he might strike against her might have driven a lesser person into hiding, but Cade had used the skills from the life she'd given up to meet the challenge.

She tried to tell me, but I wouldn't listen.

Guilt washed over her, but Emily refused to let it paralyze her. She couldn't do anything about the past, but she could change the future. She pulled out her phone and composed a simple text, hoping it wasn't too late for her to make things right.

CHAPTER TWENTY-THREE

Cade checked her watch again, disappointed to see it was only five minutes later than the last time she'd glanced at it.

"Everything okay with you today?"

Monica's voice was gentle, caring, and Cade felt bad for lying to her about where she'd been all morning and even worse about being completely distracted when she'd finally shown up for work. "I'm sorry. I know I've been worthless today."

Cade had gotten to work around noon, and despite her best efforts to dig in to her work, she couldn't stop thinking about her encounter with Emily at Brody's office. After her little drive in the country with Kennedy, she'd gone directly to Emily's office but didn't get very far. The secretary told her Emily was out and she was tight-lipped when Cade had pressed for details. About an hour later, she'd resigned herself to a long, boring afternoon at work when she'd received a two-line text from Emily: *I know everything. Can we talk?*

She didn't waste any time typing her reply: *Yes. Now?* She hit send before thinking about the ramifications, drawing courage from the knowledge Emily knew the complicated truth and still wanted to talk.

Seven. Where?

Cade stared at the phone for a moment, wavering. If she was going to invite Emily into her life, she needed to go all the way. *My place.* She typed the address before she could change her mind.

I'll be there.

Cade had been counting the minutes ever since.

"You can leave if you have somewhere else you need to be," Monica said.

"You must think I'm a flake."

Monica tilted her head. "No, but I do think you've got something weighing on your mind. I'm happy to listen if you need to talk."

"And I appreciate that, but it's nothing I can share right now. I promise I'll get my act together."

"The offer to leave early still stands."

She wanted to get home just before Emily arrived and no sooner. Extra time would only give her a chance to lose her nerve. "Thanks, but I think I'll stay and try to be of some use here."

"Fair enough." Monica started to walk away, but then turned back. "Hey, I need a fourth for tennis this weekend if you're in."

Even if she was still around, she wasn't ready to commit to something that would cause her to run into Emily until she figured out where things stood between them. She managed a weak smile. "I'll see what I can do."

At six, she grabbed her coat and headed to the parking lot. By now she'd achieved expert status at spotting her tail, and she risked a small wave at Eric who was sitting in an already running sedan parked one row away. Like any well-trained fed, he didn't react, but she spotted him in her rearview mirror as soon as she exited the campus.

The drive home took forever, and she occupied the time practicing what she would say when Emily arrived. Her text said she knew everything, but Cade wasn't quite sure what that meant. Certainly, she knew the highlights of the case in Chicago, the grisly murders, and the reason she was in hiding. But no matter what Kennedy and the FBI told her, Emily couldn't possibly know the things that really mattered. How the memories of that awful day haunted her dreams, both when she was awake and asleep. How incredibly disheartening it had been for her to walk away from the career to which she'd devoted her entire life. How every time she saw Emily with her family—brunch at the club, pictures on the mantel—the pain of never seeing hers again pierced her heart. Did she dare hope by sharing the details with Emily that maybe, just maybe, she would have a chance at recapturing the life she'd lost?

She pulled into her garage, no better equipped to face the unknown, but determined to shoot for a chance to make things work between them. Before she closed the door, she spotted Eric parked on the street, a couple of houses down. There was nothing clandestine about his stakeout, but his overt show of force gave her some comfort. His presence, in addition to the FBI agent stationed out back, was the reason she'd suggested her house for this meeting instead of Emily's more comfortable place.

Cade entered the house through the garage door and looked around, checking to see if anything needed to be cleaned, but her Spartan quarters were well-kept. As her gaze swept the room, she couldn't help but compare the bare bones of her existence to Emily's robust life. Emily had a career she loved, a family who supported her, and friends with whom she could be open and honest.

Cade didn't know if she would ever have those things again. She could leave the protection of the marshals service, but even if Fontana was arrested, the Oliveris might send someone else to take his place. No way would she put Emily's life in danger for her own satisfaction. The revelation told her exactly what she needed to say to Emily tonight.

Resolved, but unhappy, Cade found the liquor bottle she'd purchased several weeks before and set it on the counter with two glasses. She'd always planned to share the expensive whisky with Emily, but as a celebration, not a good-bye. She twisted off the cork top and poured several fingers into each glass, her mind so deep in thought she didn't hear the footsteps behind her until it was too late.

A cold knife against her throat. Hot, panting breath. Her pulse hammered, and sweat trickled down her back. She knew exactly what was happening with the kind of clarity people who have near death experiences always profess. The gravelly voice confirmed her worst fears.

"Nice whisky," Leo Fontana whispered close to her ear, sending chills down her spine. "Too bad you're not going to live to enjoy it."

❖

Emily pulled up to the house and double-checked the text messages on her phone. The front porch lights weren't on, but this was the right address. She glanced around—a sedan on the street, two doors down, probably one of the federal agents assigned to protect Cade, and a nosy neighbor peeking out from behind her drapes.

Emily had been worried about how she was viewed in the public eye, while Cade was under scrutiny of a different kind. Worse really, since her life depended on it. What must it be like to have your entire life turned upside down, your identity vanished, and everything that defined your existence stolen with a single gunshot?

Emily closed her eyes and remembered the scar along Cade's side, a terrible, tangible reminder of the danger Cade had faced and overcome at significant loss. Drawn to Cade's strength, she felt a surge of desire. They would need to talk and clear the air between them, but in this moment, all she really wanted was to hold Cade and keep her safe from anything and anyone that would ever try to hurt her again.

She started toward the door, anxious to see Cade. The afternoon had been a whirlwind spent preparing a packet of information for Brody Nichols based on everything she'd learned from the FBI. She wasn't quite ready to ask the judge to dismiss the case against Kevin Miller, but she'd decided to share what she knew until she could make a final decision. She was about to press the doorbell when her phone buzzed.

Sorry. Running a little late. Key under the mat. Wait for me inside?

Emily hesitated for a moment. The prospect of entering Cade's home when she wasn't there was a little disconcerting, but since the alternative was to loiter on the porch in full view of the curious woman across the street, she decided to go in. She reached down and pulled the key from under the mat and typed her response—*Sure*—but her thumb hovered above the send button.

With all the security measures in place to protect her life, would Cade really leave a key to her house in the most obvious place? And for someone who valued her privacy, it seemed out of character for Cade to tell her to just go on in. Something was off.

She checked her phone again to confirm the text had definitely come from Cade's number. It had. She started to call, but a sense of foreboding stopped her, and she dialed another number instead.

While she waited through the rings, she walked over to the window on the right side of the porch and surreptitiously glanced through the tiny crack between the blind and the frame. Dark. She stopped at the garage door, but it didn't have any windows. Before she could explore any other options, her call was answered.

"Kennedy Stone here."

The voice on the other end of the phone was clear and brisk. Emily paused for a minute feeling a little silly at the prospect of translating gut feelings into a coherent reason for sounding alarms. She kept her voice low. "This is Emily Sinclair. Sheriff Nash gave me your number. I'm the DA for Lawson County. I'm outside Cade Kelly's house," she paused, trying not to stumble over the surname she now knew wasn't real and hoping Inspector Stone wouldn't ask why she was standing outside Cade's home. "She was supposed to meet me here, but she just sent a text saying she's running late, and that I should use a key under the mat to let myself in. Seemed a bit odd to me that she'd leave a key outside, considering..." She let the words trail off, hoping the marshal wouldn't make her spell it all out.

"What time were you supposed to meet her?"

"Seven." Emily glanced at her watch. It was quarter after now. If Cade was running a few minutes late, she should pull up any second.

"Stay on the line. I'll be right back."

The wait was interminable, but Emily hung on, resisting the urge to walk around the perimeter of the house. Finally, Stone came back on the line. "I've tried to reach both of the agents assigned to her detail, but no luck. Maybe Cade stopped somewhere along the way home."

Emily looked down the street at the sedan still parked out front. "Is one of yours in a dark blue Crown Vic? Tinted windows. License plate RSL-7741?"

"Someone's got good observational skills. Yeah, that's one of my guys."

Emily started walking toward the car, tamping down the rising thread of panic spiraling through her insides. "He's parked in front of the neighbor's house. Doesn't sound to me like this particular guy is very good with this whole protection thing."

"His name's Marshal Eric Bosco, and he's one of the best. I'm about fifteen minutes away. Sit tight and I'll be right there."

"Wait a sec. I'm standing right in front of the car. You want to talk to him?"

"Sure, hand him your phone."

Emily knocked on the window, waited, and knocked again. She heard Stone's voice through the phone, asking what was going on, but she ignored her while she looked for answers. The dark night combined with the tinted windows meant she couldn't make out anything inside the car. She reached for the door handle, surprised to see her hand trembling, but when she pulled open the door, her instincts were confirmed.

Eric was slumped in the driver's seat, his entire chest covered with blood. Emily's hands flew to her mouth. Her gut told her to suppress her screams, but she couldn't completely contain her horror. A small cry escaped.

"What is it? What's happening?"

She raised the phone and stared at the screen, frozen with fear.

"Emily, talk to me!"

The sound of her name jarred her into action. "Bosco's unconscious." She took a deep breath and tried to stay calm as she searched for a pulse, but what she found confirmed her fears. "He's dead. He's been shot and his throat's been slit. You need to get here. Right now." Emily took a breath and summoned all her reserve strength. "You and the cavalry. If anything happens to Cade, I will hold you personally responsible." *And I will never forgive myself for pushing her away.*

CHAPTER TWENTY-FOUR

Fontana paced across the kitchen floor, while Cade struggled to stay calm—hard to do considering she was bound to a chair. She dug deep to remember everything she'd learned about him during her investigation of the Oliveri family. One thing stood out—his trademark cool, contained demeanor. The few witnesses who had lived to talk described him as a cold and ruthless killer, and her personal experience bore that out.

But the guy pacing her kitchen floor was anything but calm. Fontana was a hyped-up mess, sweating, jumpy, and his eyes were full of crazy. This guy looked more like an associate on his first job than the capo he was.

"Why don't you tell me what you're after?" she said. "I still have plenty of connections. I can guarantee you'll be safe. We can make a deal to give you whatever you need for the rest of your life."

He laughed, a maniacal sound that sent chills running through her. "Are you talking about witness protection? Of course you are, because you know so much about it." He made a slashing motion through the air with his knife. "Let's talk about how safe the feds have kept you."

Keep cool and keep him talking. "Well, I may not be smart enough to keep a low profile, but you are. How did you find me anyway?"

"Shut up."

"I mean it's pretty clear you want to keep me alive. What's your end game? If you don't want protection, what do you want?"

"I said shut up."

If shutting up would keep her alive, she'd gladly comply, but she'd have a better shot at escape by keeping him rattled, and talking seemed to be doing the trick. "I bet I know what you have in mind."

Fontana merely sneered as he drank down one of the glasses of whisky she'd poured. When it was empty, he slammed it down, and she flinched at the loud crack of the heavy glass against the counter. Suddenly, she was back outside the courthouse in Chicago, walking into the middle of a crime scene, oblivious to the carnage she was about to see. When Fontana's bullet struck her, she thought she'd suffered the worst of it, but the aftermath was a pain that kept on taking. She'd imagined someday she'd have to face Fontana in a courtroom, but she'd never let herself believe he'd show up here to finish the job he'd started.

She looked up and saw him typing on his phone. "Calling for reinforcements?"

"Just letting your girlfriend know she's welcome to join us. It was nice of you to leave a key under the mat for her."

Cade was confused at first, but then she noticed the outline of a phone in his pocket. The phone in his hand was hers and he'd likely taken her keys as well. Damn. She'd never bothered setting up a password on this phone since she didn't keep anything personal on it. Except Emily's number. And the messages they'd exchanged. All short, but precious, since they were the only tangible memories she'd have of their brief relationship when it was all over.

Now he was using the same device that housed her memories as bait to lure Emily in. Every detail of Cade's conversation with Kennedy about what the feds had learned raced through her head. The Oliveris wanted to get to Senator Sinclair. What better way than through his only daughter? Cade realized she was the real bait.

She wanted to grab the phone out of his hand and break his fingers, but her restraints meant her only option was to scream for him to put the phone down. But she didn't. She had to act like it didn't matter what he did. She had to make him believe his text would have no effect in hopes he would abandon the plan and give her a chance to plot some kind of escape. "She's not coming." Cade hoped her tone held more conviction than she felt.

He held up the phone and pointed at the text bubbles. "That's not what this says. She's supposed to be here at seven sharp. I bet she's driving down the street right now."

"We talked. After that text. I called her from work and we argued. She was pissed off when she found out I wasn't who I said I was. She's not coming." She watched his face carefully, certain she saw a trace of doubt in his eyes, but she wasn't sure if he doubted her or himself, so she kept talking. More rambling toward a singular goal. Keep him focused on her, not Emily. Cade didn't hold out any hope she would make it through her second encounter with Leo Fontana alive, but she would do anything in her power to ensure Emily didn't get hurt.

❖

After she disconnected the call with Kennedy, Emily stood on the sidewalk outside Eric's car, her mind whirring through a thousand possibilities. Leo Fontana had killed Eric. She was certain about that, and if he'd murdered one federal agent in cold blood on the street in a quiet neighborhood, the other agent assigned to Cade had probably met a similar fate.

Which left the question of where Fontana was now and what he had done with Cade. She looked down at her phone, scanning the lines of text that had initially triggered her to go on full alert.

Key under the mat. Wait for me inside?

Inside. Cade was in the house, and Fontana was there too, trying to lure her to enter. She'd listened to the FBI briefing that morning, but she'd given short shrift to their theory about Fontana targeting her as some sort of plan to get to her father. Maybe she was too cynical after years of growing up in the spotlight, but being a Sinclair meant sometimes you had to deal with the ravings of the lunatic fringe. If she took every threat seriously, she'd never leave home. She looked back at Cade's house. If Fontana was expecting her to show up inside, what would happen when she didn't?

Kennedy had said to stay put and secure the crime scene until backup arrived, but she hadn't heard a single siren yet. If they were approaching with caution, they were being way too damn slow about it. She heard a door open and glanced over her shoulder, instantly recognizing the neighbor from across the street bustling toward her. The woman's hair was in rollers, and she was wearing a pink chenille robe over a frumpy yellow housedress, but the most remarkable thing about her was the Smith & Wesson 500 revolver weighing down her arm.

"What the hell's going on?" the woman asked in an exaggerated whisper. "I was in the shower and I heard something that sounded like firecrackers. I—" She stopped and gave Emily a hard stare. "Hey, you look familiar."

Emily couldn't look away from the gun. If the woman fired it, the kick would send her flying backward, halfway down the street. But more importantly, the gun inspired an idea. She flipped open the leather case on her cell phone and flashed her ID. It wasn't the same as her badge, which was in her purse in the car, but she hoped it would buy her some sort of deference. "I'm Emily Sinclair, the district attorney. What's your name?"

The woman frowned and squinted as she considered the question and then she finally answered. "Mavis Percy. Something's going on out here, and I'm going to get to the bottom of it."

If getting to the bottom of it involved Mavis firing her beast of a gun, Emily didn't want to know. "Did you see anything?"

"Just this car parked where it shouldn't be. I just got out of the bath and looked out to see if it was still here when I saw you poking around."

"You're right," Emily said. "Something is going on and federal officers are on the way. I need to check something out, so I'm going to—" she searched for the right word, one to make this one-woman neighborhood watch feel important enough to do whatever she commanded, "deputize you to secure this crime scene."

"Where are you going?"

Emily held a finger over her lips and shook her head. "Can't say. Can I trust you to make sure no one touches this car until the feds get here?"

Mavis nodded, her expression solemn. As satisfied as she could be that no one would get past Deputy Percy, Emily sent a quick text to Kennedy along with a photo of Mavis to alert the incoming cavalry not to shoot the woman guarding the scene. Her next stop was her car where she reached into the compartment between the front seats and grabbed her own Smith & Wesson. The snub nose .38 was no match for the hefty revolver Mavis was toting, but it would be much easier to hide and she trusted it to do the job, whatever it turned out to be.

She tucked the loaded gun in her coat pocket and felt the key she'd pulled from under the doormat. Walking through the front door where she'd be expected wasn't an option, but maybe the key worked for the rear door as well, assuming there was one. Casting one last look at Eric's car and the street devoid of responding law enforcement, Emily ducked around the corner of the house to explore her options. She'd barely made it halfway to the back when her search paid off. What she saw nearly shook her resolve to carry on.

Through a window surrounded by a tiny arbor laced with long dead wisteria vine, Emily had a clear view of the kitchen. The room itself was plain and boring. White walls, white counters, not a knickknack in sight, but smack in the middle of the room, Cade was bound to a chair, and Fontana was taunting her with a knife that was a twin to the one the sheriff had found at Kevin Miller's apartment.

She hunched low at the windowsill and took in every detail of the room. Where was the gun? The gun was part of his signature. If she was going to carry out any kind of plan, however half-ass, she needed to know where things stood.

As if on cue, Fontana started pacing. Ducking her head lower, Emily held her breath, praying he wouldn't detect her presence, but scared to look away and miss whatever was about to happen next. Seconds later, he pivoted away from the window and walked back toward Cade. There it was, the gun, stuck in the band of his pants, just like in the movies. Except this was no movie and unlike the big screen, there were no assurances the bad guy would get what he had coming.

She couldn't see any sign of a back door in the kitchen. If there was one, it had to be in some other room in the house. Willing Cade safe until she could get to her, Emily dashed toward the rear of the house and unlatched the low picket fence surrounding the small backyard. A few steps in, she found the back door blocked by the body of another federal agent covered in blood from a gaping wound on his neck and a gunshot wound to the chest. Standing over him, she started to rethink her plan to bust into the house. She'd been taught to shoot from childhood, but this agent on the ground and the one in the car out front were trained in protection, yet both of them had succumbed to Fontana's blistering attack. Who was she to think she would fare better?

She checked her phone again, but there were no updates from Kennedy. She sent a quick text. *Where are you!?*

Almost there. Five minutes.

Five minutes with a knife near Cade's throat was too long. Emily stuffed the phone back in her pocket. She knew what she had to do. She'd never witnessed a hostage situation, but she'd seen plenty on TV. In five minutes an army of cops would show up on the street, locking it down, and some FBI hostage negotiator would try to talk Fontana into giving up Cade and coming out with his hands in the air. Meanwhile snipers would be looking for a clear shot while the SWAT team plotted a way to overtake the house. Maybe Cade would live, maybe she wouldn't. Emily wasn't convinced the feds would care either way as long as they got their man.

But she cared. More than she'd ever thought possible. The very idea Cade was in danger filled her with rage. Rage at the lost opportunities because they'd seemed at cross-purposes even though they really hadn't been. Rage that she'd never have the opportunity to tell Cade she was the best thing to happen to her. Ever.

Emily looked at her phone one last time, but there were no more messages. No miracles. If she wanted to control the outcome of this situation, she had to take control. She might not have the same training as the agents assigned to protect Cade, but she did have one thing they didn't. She had the element of surprise, and she was going to use it to save the woman she loved.

Cade had no idea how much time had passed. From where she was seated, she couldn't see the clock on the stove, and the darkness outside the kitchen window told her nothing since the sun had gone down well before she'd arrived home. Fontana, cursing the sound of her voice, had finally resorted to stuffing a dishcloth in her mouth and securing it with duct tape. Unable to talk, she'd been left with only her anxious thoughts as Fontana's growing impatience manifested into full-blown frenzy.

Every sound made her flinch from the cycling hum of the refrigerator to the dull roar when the furnace kicked on. *Please don't be Emily, please don't be Emily.* She prayed her mental chant would work, but feared it wouldn't. Any moment now, the creak of the front door might signal the end was near. Once Fontana had Emily, once he got what he wanted from her, he'd have no use for either of them, and then he'd do what he did best.

A vision of Fontana's knife against Emily's smooth, slender neck sent waves of panic through Cade's body, but the panic quickly morphed into resolve. She had to find a way to disarm Fontana before Emily arrived. She tugged at the tape binding her arms and legs, but there was no give. She scanned the room, but the block of steak knives on the counter mocked her feeble attempts to escape. Her gaze settled on one of the glasses she'd set on the table earlier. She was close enough to the table that if she used all her energy to bump the chair into it, the glass might fall to the floor, breaking into plenty of sharp shards she could use to cut through her ties.

Except she wouldn't be able to reach them. And Fontana was standing right here. Undaunted, she decided it was her only shot. All she had to do was figure out a way to distract him, make him leave the room, and she'd sort out the rest.

Cade grunted to get his attention, and when Fontana looked her way, she jutted her head forward, over and over, narrowing her eyes into what she hoped was a something important is happening expression. She threw her shoulders into the act, and the urgent movement rocked the chair back and forth. Finally, he strode across the kitchen, leaned down toward her face, and yanked away her gag.

"What the hell are you doing?"

Cade fought the urge to spit in his face. "I heard the front door open," she said, praying he was hopped up enough to check rather than wait and see. His eyes widened, and he tilted his head, like he was listening. Silence.

"You're lying," he said.

"I heard it. I swear. Someone came in the front door." Cade barely had the words out when she did hear something. The unmistakable click of a gun being cocked and a familiar voice.

"Actually, I came in the back, but I guess that doesn't really matter now."

Fontana swung around and reached for his gun.

Cade bobbed her head, trying to see past him. When she spotted Emily standing in the doorway to the kitchen, her feet planted and her hands holding a small revolver pointed directly at Fontana, she'd never looked as beautiful. She started to call out, but stopped when the cold prick of Fontana's knife pressed against her neck.

Emily shook her head, her eyes trained on Fontana. "Don't even try it."

"Well, if it isn't little Miss State's Attorney?"

"I understand you're from out of town, but down here it's *district attorney*."

"Is that so, Miss District Attorney?" Fontana laughed, the same mad, mirthless sound that had made Cade shiver earlier. "I guess it really doesn't matter what they call you," he said, "if you're no longer around."

"You're right," Emily said. "Titles don't mean much, but they do carry a certain amount of power. Whatever you want to call me, I can assure you there are things I can do for you—a phone call is all it takes." She let one hand drop, reached into her jacket, and pulled out her phone, holding it toward him. "My father's on speed dial. Would you like to call him or should I?"

The knife against her neck limited her sightline, but Cade sensed Fontana's energy spike and saw the black metal barrel of his gun twitching at his side. If he reached for the phone, he'd have to either put down the gun or the knife, and then maybe—

A siren, loud and close, interrupted her attempt at strategy. Out of the corner of her eye, she saw Fontana raise his weapon.

Emily dropped the phone and grasped her gun with both hands. They exchanged a brief look, and Cade saw a snip of regret cross Emily's face before the sting of the blade and the sharp crack of gunfire blocked out everything else.

Chapter Twenty-five

Everything happened at once. When Fontana raised his gun, Emily squeezed the trigger of her .38 and fired until he started to fall, taking Cade with him. Emily had barely registered the clatter of his gun on the hard tile, the dull thud of his body, and the harsh scrape of the chair legs losing purchase when new sounds filled the space—loud shouts and heavy footfalls.

She ignored the noise. Cade, still strapped to her chair was in a heap with Fontana. She had to get to her. Nothing else mattered. Emily lunged forward, leading with her gun, but strong arms held her back.

"Ms. Sinclair, wait."

"Let me go!" Emily writhed, struggling to get loose. Cade. She had to get to Cade.

"Emily, stop!"

She knew that voice. Kennedy Stone. She turned her head. The marshal's face was a mixture of command and concern.

"Let me go," Emily said. "Please."

Kennedy nodded. "I will, but I need you to give me the gun."

Emily looked down at her hand, clutching her gun like a lifeline. It kind of was, since a moment earlier it had been the only thing keeping her and Cade alive.

"Cade?" She willed Kennedy to hear the urgency in her voice even as she fought to stay calm.

Kennedy gently extracted the gun from her death grip and handed it to one of the horde of cops swarming the scene. She held out her hand. "Come on."

Emily took her hand, holding tight, and followed Kennedy as she parted the dense crowd. Their destination was only a few feet away, but when she saw the scene, she understood why Kennedy had accompanied her. Fontana lay in a pool of blood on the floor, and agents were pulling Cade's chair upright. As she came into view, Emily gasped at the sight of blood running down her neck. She started to run forward, but Kennedy held her back.

"Hang on."

She crushed Kennedy's hand, but her eyes never left Cade, searching for a sign, any sign, to let her know her efforts hadn't been in vain. She glared as the agents dropped Cade's chair to the ground a few feet away from Fontana. When the chair legs struck the floor, Cade's eyes fluttered open and Emily sagged with relief.

"Okay, go."

Emily rushed past Kennedy, daring any of the other federal agents to stop her. While one of the agents cut through the duct tape binding Cade, Emily kneeled between Cade's legs and placed a hand on the side of her neck. "Baby, you're hurt."

Cade touched her neck and stared at the blood on her fingers, turning them back and forth. "I'm, I'm okay." Her voice was weak. "I think maybe he just nicked me when he went down."

Emily took Cade's hand in hers. "You might be in shock." She used her free hand to yank the sleeve of the agent closest to her and used her best boss voice. "We need a paramedic over here. Right now." She didn't wait for a response, instead turning back to Cade. She couldn't stop looking at her, couldn't believe she was alive and safe. The sentiment spilled from her lips. "I was so worried I was going to lose you."

A shadow passed over Cade's face, and she squeezed Emily's hand. "Nice shot, by the way."

"Thanks. Haven't had time to get to the range in a while. Guess I was lucky it was such a close shot." Emily shuddered. "Too close. I couldn't bear the thought of losing you."

There. She'd spoken her worst fear twice. She searched Cade's eyes for something, anything to show she felt the same way, but Cade was looking past her. Emily turned to see what held her attention. Kennedy was standing behind them, and next to her was a tall, lanky woman wearing an FBI jacket. Emily pulled herself up, balancing on Cade's chair, and faced them with a sense of dread.

"Ms. Sinclair," Kennedy said. "We've already notified Sheriff Nash that the FBI will be handling all matters related to the Fontana case." She motioned to the woman standing beside her. "This is Special Agent-in-Charge Nicole Grant. She'll be conducting the investigation into the shooting."

Emily nodded. "I understand. Dead body means lots of paperwork. I'm happy to cooperate." She watched as Grant and Kennedy exchanged puzzled looks. "What am I missing?"

"Ms. Sinclair," Agent Grant said, "Leo Fontana's wounds are serious, but he's not dead."

Emily clutched the back of the chair. As glad as she was in the abstract that she hadn't killed someone, she'd been relieved that Fontana was gone forever, that he would never haunt Cade again. Now her relief had been yanked away, and its absence left her shaken.

"Are you okay?" Kennedy asked.

Emily took a deep breath and waved a hand in the air. "This is a lot…it's a lot to process."

"It is." Grant was the one speaking this time. "As a courtesy, we can do the interview at your offices. We've got a car waiting outside."

"Right now?" Emily fought the tide of rising panic. She wasn't about to leave Cade's side. Not now anyway. Not when they'd just reconnected again.

Grant started to speak, but Kennedy put a hand on her arm, and said, "It's really important they get your statement right now, while it's fresh." She lowered her voice. "And I'm sure you know how important it is for a future prosecution that you and Cade not be together when you give your versions of what happened."

She did know, but it didn't change the fact she couldn't stand the idea of separating so soon. She looked over at Cade who was watching their exchange with a clouded expression she couldn't read. Something was wrong, but she couldn't tell what. Maybe she was blowing it out of proportion. Cade had spent the last God knows how long with a gun to her head and a knife at her throat. She'd nearly died, and not for the first time. *Quit making your insecurity about someone else.*

"Emily?"

Emily stopped her internal monologue and looked at Cade. "Yes?"

"Go with them. I'll be fine."

Was this a good-bye or was her imagination running wild? Deferring to the later, she asked her own question. "Promise?"

"I promise."

Emily still wasn't convinced, but she was boxed in. She'd go with the agents, give her statement, and make a plan. She'd almost lost any chance to have any sort of future with Cade. She wasn't about to let that happen again.

Cade climbed into Kennedy's Jeep and shut the door, thankful for the short reprieve from the commotion pervading every inch of her house.

Her house. She studied the outside of the bungalow as they drove away and recalled the spark of hope she'd had when Kennedy had driven her here the first time. Now that hope was marred by the reality she might never return and she understood for the first time the house had never really been hers. The tableau of the librarian living in a quaint house in a quiet little town was fiction, and the biggest fiction of all was that she could be safe if she just pretended to be someone else. Which left her with some hard choices.

"You sure you don't need to go to the hospital?" Kennedy asked.

Cade touched the bandage on her neck. She hadn't forgotten, but it was the last thing on her mind. "I'm fine. What's going to happen to Emily?" Emily might be the DA, but she'd still shot someone and the FBI, not to mention the local press, was going to have a lot of questions.

Kennedy started the engine. "They'll take her statement and that will be that. Of course, she's guaranteed to get reelected for the rest of her life. Small town DA shoots mob hit man. Talk about making good on campaign promises to deliver justice."

Cade could tell Kennedy was trying to inject some levity, but she wasn't ready to look on the bright side. "And me? What now?"

"I'm going to debrief you, but I imagine Agent Grant will have some questions once she's done talking to Emily."

Cade waved a hand impatiently. "Not now now. I mean, what about the future? Am I supposed to go on pretending to be Cade Kelly, librarian, or do you already have a new identity lined up for me?"

"To be perfectly honest, I don't know what the department is going to recommend, but I think you'll have some choices to make."

"I can't believe he's still alive."

"I think you're looking at this the wrong way."

"How so?"

"If Fontana is dead, the Oliveris have a reason to avenge his death. But now Fontana has exposed the family and he's alive to talk about it. Even if he keeps omertà, it's likely the family will disavow him. The last thing they want to do is get a US Senator riled up by being connected to the man who tried to kill his daughter. Fontana's only hope at this point is to flip on the Oliveris, but even if he doesn't, there's no way they'll come after Emily."

"And me?"

"They might still want your head on a platter."

"You can't keep me safe." Cade leaned back in her seat. Defeat was exhausting, but accepting it was the first step to getting through it. "Fontana stumbled over me completely by accident. No matter what you do, you can't guard against everything."

"You're right, but we can make it harder."

"How long until I have to decide?"

"It'll probably be a few days before you have to make a permanent decision, but we should move you somewhere safe as soon as we finish today."

Cade nodded. She'd expected as much, but she wasn't prepared to rip the fabric of the new life she'd managed to piece together quite so soon. Emily had come to the house to see her. What might have happened if Fontana hadn't been waiting? Would Emily have forgiven her lies, now that she knew Cade had had no choice? Would they have made plans to begin again? Would Emily have accepted the danger that came from being with her?

The answer to the last question was clear. Emily had already demonstrated risk was no deterrent by engaging Fontana in a gunfight.

She'd won today, but even the greatest shots sometimes miss. Cade's gut clenched at the possibility it might have been Emily on the floor bleeding from a bullet instead of Fontana. She might not care about exposing herself, but she wouldn't be able to bear it if anything happened to Emily because of the risk she'd assumed.

Cade stared out the window while she searched for the strength to let the last few words she'd exchanged with Emily back at the house be their final good-bye. A few minutes later, she noticed they were turning into the parking lot of the courthouse. "What are we doing here?"

"We're doing your debrief at the sheriff's office. The closest FBI division office is in Dallas."

Cade looked at the building. From where they were parked, she could see the front steps of the courthouse where she'd met Emily the first time. A chance meeting but a meaningful one. She'd had hope for the first time since she'd moved to Bodark that a full life was possible, but she'd been deceiving herself from the start.

Three hours later, Cade had repeated the story of what happened at her house over a dozen times. She'd seen Sheriff Nash and his deputies come and go, but no sign of Emily. It was for the best. She'd already decided to let Kennedy find her a new place, a new name, a new start. She no longer cared about her own safety, but she'd do whatever it took to protect the people she loved, and as much as she'd tried to resist it, she loved Emily fiercely. Enough to endure the pain of leaving her so Emily could find happiness with someone who loved her without the trappings of a past that could do her harm.

"Where is Cade?" Emily asked for the third time. She'd spent the last few hours sitting in the same conference room she'd been using as the war room in the Miller case, going over every aspect of today's shooting, from the time she'd left her office and drove to Cade's house, to the moment Fontana crashed to the floor in Cade's kitchen. She'd answered every question, multiple times, but no one had answered hers, and her nerves were frayed as a result. The only information the FBI had shared was that Fontana was in surgery and might recover. The news was bittersweet and she'd become distracted wondering about the implications.

Agent Grant stood. "We're done for now. It's possible we may have more questions later, but I can safely say, you don't have anything to worry about. If you—"

The door burst open and her parents rushed into the room. Both of them ran to her, and their barrage of questions was a welcome reprieve.

"Are you okay? What's going on?"

"We just heard and came as fast as we could."

Emily relaxed into her mother's embrace. Normally, she would have asked them to step aside while she handled her own affairs, but nothing was normal about what had happened today, and she was uncharacteristically happy to have them come to her defense.

"I'm okay," she said. She gave them a quick summary of the shooting, glossing over the part about charging into Cade's house on her own. "And I think Agent Grant is done asking me questions, isn't that right?" She stared pointedly at Grant, daring her to tell her father, the senator, otherwise.

"That's correct," Grant said. "I'll leave you alone so you can talk with your family."

She started toward the door, but Emily called out, "Wait."

Grant turned back. "Yes?"

"Cade Kelly? You were going to tell me where she is."

Grant's jaw was set, but she flicked a glance at Emily's father, and then met Emily's eyes. "She's at the sheriff's office. I'm headed there now." She didn't wait for a reply before she left the room.

Emily started toward the door, but her mother grabbed her arm. "Em, let us take you home."

Emily shook her head. "I can't. I have to find Cade."

"Is that the woman who's life you saved?" her mother asked.

Had she? Or had it been the other way around? She'd spent her life working toward one goal after another, but so far work was all she'd ever accomplished. She'd even made looking for a relationship seem like work, until the day Cade had walked into her life. From their first chance encounter, every moment with Cade had been spontaneous and passionate, whether they were sharing a meal or making love. Hell, even their arguments had been zealous. She smiled at the prospect of sharing a lifetime of heated exchanges with Cade.

A vision of Cade's face before they parted flashed in her mind. Cade had been troubled, and it seemed like more than her near brush with death. Emily had sensed Cade was saying good-bye and not just for now. She could hardly blame Cade for wanting to retreat, but could Cade only find sanctuary if she was on the run? Emily's pulse raced at the idea she might never see her again.

She faced both her parents. "She's the woman I love and I need to find her right now." She ran out of the room without waiting for a response, but she heard their footsteps following close behind. They probably thought she was crazy, but she didn't care. All she cared about was finding Cade.

❖

Cade looked up at the knock on the door. She'd been sitting alone in a small room at the sheriff's office for the last few minutes waiting while Kennedy made a few phone calls in the hall outside.

"Are you ready to go?" Kennedy asked.

"I thought the FBI were going to have some questions."

"They are, but I just talked to Grant and convinced her you could use a change of clothes and a hot meal before they dig in. Come on before she changes her mind."

Cade almost said she would rather just get the interrogation over with, but her body said otherwise. Her head pounded and every muscle ached. She wasn't hungry, but she'd probably feel better if she ate something. "Okay."

She followed Kennedy into the lobby, mindful of the stares from the deputies standing around. They'd probably never seen this much excitement. The story of Leo Fontana's capture would likely become a legend around these parts. Sheriff Nash was probably stewing in his office, consumed with jealousy that Emily, not he or one of his own, had taken Fontana down.

Emily. Where was she right now? Despite Kennedy's assurances, Cade worried about the consequences of Emily's involvement in the shooting. *But you're running away. How worried can you be?*

The thought struck her like a brick. She'd made the decision that it was easier this way, ducking out without saying good-bye, but the decision not to see Emily before she left was a purely selfish maneuver. Emily had shot a man to keep her safe. Her bravery was undeniable. Cade had a choice. She could take the coward's way out or she could honor Emily's actions with some bravery of her own. Once she'd listed the options, she knew there was really only one choice.

They were almost to the door where a car waited outside to whisk her away. Cade grabbed Kennedy's arm. "Where is Emily?"

Kennedy shook her off. "I don't know. Seriously, Cade."

"I'm right here."

Cade spun around. Emily was standing a few feet away. Her face was flushed, she was out of breath, and she was breathtakingly beautiful. Cade closed the distance between them. "Are you okay?"

"I'm not sure yet."

Cade reached for her hand. The connection was strong and immediate. "What can I do?" She took a deep breath and dug for the courage this moment required. "I'll do anything."

Emily's eyes searched hers, but Cade didn't shy away—she'd said she'd do anything and she meant it.

"Stay."

"I want to," Cade said.

"But?"

"I don't want to put the woman I love in danger."

Emily's lips slid into a slow, hazy smile. "Don't you know by now, the woman you love loves you back? Danger, be damned."

Cade answered in the bravest way she knew how, by pulling Emily into her arms and saying, loud enough for everyone around them to hear, "I'll stay with you forever, if you'll have me."

Chapter Twenty-six

June

Cade slowly opened her eyes to soft light filtering through the window. It had taken a while for her to get used to sleeping with the blinds open, but there was no substitute for waking up to the natural light, especially when the morning rays illuminated the beautiful woman lying beside her.

Emily was still asleep. No small wonder since they'd been up half the night making love. The covers were rumpled around her body, revealing the gentle curve of her shoulders and the soft slope of her chest. As much as she didn't want to disturb Emily's sleep, Cade couldn't bear not touching her. Trying her best to be quiet, she leaned close and traced a trail of featherlight kisses from the soft skin of Emily's neck to the hint of cleavage.

"Good morning."

Cade almost regretted waking her. Almost. "Good morning. Sorry about that."

Emily rolled over into her arms. "Sorry about kissing me?" Her tone was light and teasing.

"Never." Cade shoved the covers down and pulled Emily closer, desperate to feel skin on skin, but content to savor the slow, gradual build of arousal she'd come to enjoy since she'd moved in several months ago. She teased her tongue from Emily's mouth down to her chest, dipping to circle her nipples, but easing back as soon as she sensed each wave of pleasure begin to crest.

"You're driving me crazy." Emily's breath was ragged with want.

"That's the plan." Cade nipped at her breast. "Every day for the rest of your life." She sucked one of Emily's taut nipples into her mouth and her pulse pounded as Emily arched closer. Seconds later, she groaned as Emily trailed a hand along her inner thigh.

"Someone woke up ready," Emily murmured as she slid her fingers through Cade's silky, wet folds, loving the way Cade's body writhed with every pass.

They'd danced this dance dozens of times since Cade had moved in. Every time was different, but every time was the same, and Emily had learned to count on the consistent surprises of their lovemaking. Morning sex had become one of her new favorite things, and her breath hitched as she recognized the signs Cade was getting ready to come. She slowed her strokes to savor the moment. "I'm getting used to this."

"Taking control?" Cade asked, her voice weak.

"Maybe."

"I'm getting used to letting you."

Emily answered with a deep kiss, using her tongue to explore Cade's hot and ready mouth while she used her fingers to keep a steady rhythm. It wasn't long before the slick caresses left Emily aching for more, and she entered Cade with first one finger, then another, reveling in the way Cade's body thrashed beneath her in response to the increasing pressure. "That's it, baby. I love making you come."

Cade whimpered, her eyes hazy and dark, and Emily knew she was close. She lowered her mouth to Cade's breasts, and as she began licking her way between them, she shuddered at the feel of friction between her own legs. Cade's thigh brushed against her swollen sex with increasing pressure and she settled into the touch, riding the steady build of ecstasy.

"Come. With. Me."

The staccato of Cade's request signaled it was time. Emily quickened the pace, her fingers penetrating steady and hard while she grazed Cade's clit with the pad of her thumb and coaxed Cade's body to stiffen and then quake with the beginnings of a powerful orgasm. Within seconds, Emily felt Cade's hand in her hair, pulling her closer.

Their lips met and at the same instant Cade rubbed her finger against Emily's throbbing clit sending her spiraling with her into waves of euphoria until they were both consumed.

❖

An hour later, Emily walked into the living room wearing a short, silk robe, and Cade sucked in a breath. "I need you to put more clothes on if you expect me to get any studying done."

"Was this morning not enough?" Emily teased her.

Cade shook her head. "Never."

"Not to worry, I'm leaving for the office soon." Emily pointed at the television. "Besides, that, my dear, is not studying."

Cade used the remote to turn the volume down. "I beg to differ." She pointed at Emily's father on the screen. "Senate hearings are an excellent example of the legislative process and constitutional law in play. What do you want to bet there's a question on the bar exam about it?"

Cade slid over to allow Emily room on the couch, and for a few minutes they both remained riveted to the screen. Last month, Senator Sinclair had approached Cade to help him draft comprehensive legislation to toughen up the laws used to combat organized crime. Cade had worked with him on the language, and she'd been impressed with how swiftly the senator had formed a coalition to support the proposals in his bill, including increased penalty ranges and special grants to beef up enforcement agencies dedicated to going after big crime families.

For the past few weeks, she'd spent her days at the senator's local office, doing preliminary research to help him prepare for the hearings, and as a result, she'd gained access to inside details of the federal case into Vincente Oliveri. What she'd learned about the reach of the Oliveri family astounded her, particularly as it applied to her.

Sam Wade, the murder victim who'd worked in personnel at Jordan College had had a pretty bad gambling problem, and his Vegas bookie owed a debt to the Oliveris. Fontana confessed to the feds that once he obtained the information that Cade was working at Jordan College, he'd used the Oliveri connection as leverage to get Wade to provide him with Cade's home address, which hadn't been included in the same file as her career dossier. Apparently, Fontana thought it would be cleaner to get the info from Wade rather than following Cade around under the watchful eye of Bodark citizens.

When he met Wade to get the information, Wade tried to blackmail him, and died because of it. When Miller stumbled onto the crime scene, Fontana figured it was a brilliant stroke of luck that would allow him to evade detection, so he could take his time plotting a way to make the most of his information. His employer, on the other hand, had chastised him repeatedly for his carelessness. Seeking redemption, Fontana had concocted the haphazard scheme to lure Emily into his grasp and use her as leverage to get Senator Sinclair to do Oliveri's bidding. When his plan failed, he knew he was finished with Oliveri, and made the decision to rat him out to save his own hide.

Now the senate hearings were shining a bright light on the entire Oliveri family operation. Cade had been angry at first that Fontana now received the same protection as she did, but she'd come around to the realization that Fontana's cooperation and the attention it drew to the Oliveris made it less likely they'd risk revenge.

"I owe your dad for the last few weeks," Cade said. "Plus, I don't know if anyone else involved in the case would have ever told me about Wade. I still feel bad for him, but now at least I know he wasn't an innocent bystander."

Emily scooted closer. "I'm pretty sure Dad's the one who owes you. You practically wrote the Sinclair bill, and you're not getting any credit for it."

"Don't want any." Cade wrapped an arm around Emily and kissed her on the shoulder. Senator Sinclair had invited her to travel to DC to attend the hearings, but she'd already made other plans that involved staying close to home. "I have everything I want right here. Besides, I'd much rather be watching the hearings sitting next to the senator's half-naked daughter than sitting in a room full of politicians." She pointed at the TV. "They're just getting started, but it's already getting heated." She traced the hem of Emily's robe with her finger, and the voices on TV receded. "Speaking of heated."

Emily swatted her hand. "Don't you dare. I have to be in court in an hour."

"Good thing we live only a few blocks from your office."

"And yours if you're serious about working with Brody after you pass the bar exam."

"I am."

Emily reached up and brushed a strand of hair from her face. "You know that means we're going to wind up being on opposite sides sometimes."

Cade heard the tentative tone in her voice. She didn't blame Emily for being hesitant. She was too. They'd briefly discussed her taking a position at the DA's office, but decided their personal relationship would be better off if their professional one wasn't boss to employee. With Brody, she'd have the opportunity to be a mentor, and as an added bonus, Asher was now working part-time for the firm doing investigative work. After the bar exam and an extended trip to visit her family, including her newly-arrived niece, Cade planned to join Brody and Asher and start her new career as a defense attorney.

The only drawback with her plans was the certainty she'd have to go up against Emily from time to time, but after everything they'd been through, she was confident they'd be able to navigate any obstacles between them. She pulled Emily into her arms and held her tight. "We may be on opposite sides, but we'll always be working toward the same goal."

Emily grinned. "Cade Kelly, you say the smartest things."

Cade smiled at the sound of her name on Emily's lips. She'd decided to keep the new last name since it represented her new life—a life she couldn't imagine being without. "Keep that in mind when you're trying to kick my ass in court."

"I will. Just remember one thing."

"What's that?"

"No matter how many times I win in the courtroom, our love is the biggest win of my life."

Cade's heart swelled. "I couldn't agree more."

THE END

About the Author

Carsen Taite's goal as an author is to spin tales with plot lines as interesting as the cases she encountered in her career as a criminal defense lawyer. She is the award-winning author of over a dozen novels of romantic intrigue, including the Luca Bennett Bounty Hunter series and the Lone Star Law series. Learn more at www.carsentaite.com.

About the Author

Books Available from Bold Strokes Books

18 Months by Samantha Boyette. Alissa Reeves has only had two girlfriends and they've both gone missing. Now it's up to her to find out why. (978-1-62639-804-7)

Arrested Hearts by Holly Stratimore. A reckless cop with a secret death wish and a health nut who is afraid to die might be a perfect combination for love. (978-1-62639-809-2)

Capturing Jessica by Jane Hardee. Hyperrealist sculptor Michael tries desperately to conceal the love she holds for best friend, Jess, unaware Jess's feelings for her are changing. (978-1-62639-836-8)

Counting to Zero by AJ Quinn. NSA agent Emma Thorpe and computer hacker Paxton James must learn to trust each other as they work to stop a threat clock that's rapidly counting down to zero. (978-1-62639-783-5)

Courageous Love by KC Richardson. Two women fight a devastating disease, and their own demons, while trying to fall in love. (978-1-62639-797-2)

Pathogen by Jessica L. Webb. Can Dr. Kate Morrison navigate a deadly virus and the threat of bioterrorism, as well as her new relationship with Sergeant Andy Wyles and her own troubled past? (978-1-62639-833-7)

Rainbow Gap by Lee Lynch. Jaudon Vickers and Berry Garland, polar opposites, dream and love in this tale of lesbian lives set in Central Florida against the tapestry of societal change and the Vietnam War. (978-1-62639-799-6)

Steel and Promise by Alexa Black. Lady Nivrai's cruel desires and modified body make most of the galaxy fear her, but courtesan Cailyn Derys soon discovers the real monsters are the ones without the claws. (978-1-62639-805-4)

Swelter by D. Jackson Leigh. Teal Giovanni's mistake shines an unwanted spotlight on a small Texas ranch where August Reese is secluded until she can testify against a powerful drug kingpin. (978-1-62639-795-8)

Without Justice by Carsen Taite. Cade Kelly and Emily Sinclair must battle each other in the pursuit of justice, but can they fight their undeniable attraction outside the walls of the courtroom? (978-1-62639-560-2)

21 Questions by Mason Dixon. To find love, start by asking the right questions. (978-1-62639-724-8)

A Palette for Love by Charlotte Greene. When newly minted Ph.D. Chloé Devereaux returns to New Orleans, she doesn't expect her new job, and her powerful employer—Amelia Winters—to be so appealing. (978-1-62639-758-3)

By the Dark of Her Eyes by Cameron MacElvee. When Brenna Taylor inherits a decrepit property haunted by tormented ghosts, Alejandra Santana must not only restore Brenna's house and property but also save her soul. (978-1-62639-834-4)

Cash Braddock by Ashley Bartlett. Cash Braddock just wants to hang with her cat, fall in love, and deal drugs. What's the problem with that? (978-1-62639-706-4)

Gravity by Juliann Rich. How can Ellie Engebretsen, Olympic ski jumping hopeful with her eye on the gold, soar through the air when all she feels like doing is falling hard for Kate Moreau, her greatest competitor and the girl of her dreams? (978-1-62639-483-4)

Lone Ranger by VK Powell. Reporter Emma Ferguson stirs up a thirty-year-old mystery that threatens Park Ranger Carter West's family and jeopardizes any hope for a relationship between the two women. (978-1-62639-767-5)

Love on Call by Radclyffe. Ex-Army medic Glenn Archer and recent LA transplant Mariana Mateo fight their mutual desire in the face of past losses as they work together in the Rivers Community Hospital ER. (978-1-62639-843-6)

Never Enough by Robyn Nyx. Can two women put aside their pasts to find love before it's too late? (978-1-62639-629-6)

Two Souls by Kathleen Knowles. Can love blossom in the wake of tragedy? (978-1-62639-641-8)

Camp Rewind by Meghan O'Brien. A summer camp for grown-ups becomes the site of an unlikely romance between a shy, introverted divorcee and one of the Internet's most infamous cultural critics—who attends undercover. (978-1-62639-793-4)

Cross Purposes by Gina L. Dartt. In pursuit of a lost Acadian treasure, three women must not only work out the clues, but also the complicated tangle of emotion and attraction developing between them. (978-1-62639-713-2)

Imperfect Truth by C.A. Popovich. Can an imperfect truth stand in the way of love? (978-1-62639-787-3)

Life in Death by M. Ullrich. Sometimes the devastating end is your only chance for a new beginning. (978-1-62639-773-6)

Love on Liberty by MJ Williamz. Hearts collide when politics clash. (978-1-62639-639-5)

Serious Potential by Maggie Cummings. Pro golfer Tracy Allen plans to forget her ex during a visit to Bay West, a lesbian condo community in NYC, but when she meets Dr. Jennifer Betsy, she gets more than she bargained for. (978-1-62639-633-3)

Taste by Kris Bryant. Accomplished chef Taryn has walked away from her promising career in the city's top restaurant to devote her life to her five-year-old daughter and is content until Ki Blake comes along. (978-1-62639-718-7)

The Second Wave by Jean Copeland. Can star-crossed lovers have a second chance after decades apart, or does the love of a lifetime only happen once? (978-1-62639-830-6)

Valley of Fire by Missouri Vaun. Taken captive in a desert outpost after their small aircraft is hijacked, Ava and her captivating passenger discover things about each other and themselves that will change them both forever. (978-1-62639-496-4)

Basic Training of the Heart by Jaycie Morrison. In 1944, socialite Elizabeth Carlton joins the Women's Army Corps to escape family expectations and love's disappointments. Can Sergeant Gale Rains get her through Basic Training with their hearts intact? (978-1-62639-818-4)

Before by KE Payne. When Tally falls in love with her band's new recruit, she has a tough decision to make. What does she want more—Alex or the band? (978-1-62639-677-7)

Believing in Blue by Maggie Morton. Growing up gay in a small town has been hard, but it can't compare to the next challenge Wren—with her new, sky-blue wings—faces: saving two entire worlds. (978-1-62639-691-3)

Coils by Barbara Ann Wright. A modern young woman follows her aunt into the Greek Underworld and makes a pact with Medusa to win her freedom by killing a hero of legend. (978-1-62639-598-5)

Courting the Countess by Jenny Frame. When relationship-phobic Lady Henrietta Knight starts to care about housekeeper Annie Brannigan and her daughter, can she overcome her fears and promise Annie the forever that she demands? (978-1-62639-785-9)

For Money or Love by Heather Blackmore. Jessica Spaulding must choose between ignoring the truth to keep everything she has, and doing the right thing only to lose it all—including the woman she loves. (978-1-62639-756-9)

Hooked by Jaime Maddox. With the help of sexy Detective Mac Calabrese, Dr. Jessica Benson is working hard to overcome her past, but it may not be enough to stop a murderer. (978-1-62639-689-0)

Lands End by Jackie D. Public relations superstar Amy Kline is dealing with a media nightmare, and the last thing she expects is for restaurateur Lena Michaels to change everything, but she will. (978-1-62639-739-2)

Lysistrata Cove by Dena Hankins. Jack and Eve navigate the maelstrom of their darkest desires and find love by transgressing gender, dominance, submission, and the law on the crystal blue Caribbean Sea. (978-1-62639-821-4)

Twisted Screams by Sheri Lewis Wohl. Reluctant psychic Lorna Dutton doesn't want to forgive, but if she doesn't do just that an innocent woman will die. (978-1-62639-647-0)